VALENTINO:
FILM DETECTIVE

Loren D. Estleman
(Photograph: Deborah Morgan)

VALENTINO:
FILM DETECTIVE

LOREN D. ESTLEMAN

Crippen & Landru Publishers
Norfolk, Virginia
2011

Cover painting by Carol Heyer

Design by Deborah Miller

Crippen & Landru logo by Eric D. Greene

ISBN (signed, numbered clothbound edition): 978-1-932009-95-8

ISBN (trade softcover edition): 978-1-932009-96-5

FIRST EDITION

*Printed in the United States of America
on recycled acid-free paper*

Crippen & Landru Publishers
P. O. Box 9315
Norfolk, VA 23505
USA

Email: info@crippenlandru.com
Web: www.crippenlandru.com

CONTENTS

Preface: Hostage to Hollywood

My first babysitters were Clark Gable, Katharine Hepburn, Boris Karloff, and Rin-Tin-Tin.

Karloff in particular was a smuggled sin. My parents seldom censored their children's entertainment, but *Shock Theater*, where Karloff and Bela Lugosi and Lon Chaney, Jr. and their alter egos Frankenstein, Dracula, and the Wolf Man lived, aired on TV past our bedtime Friday night. My brother and I lived for those occasions when our parents went out, leaving our grandmother to look after us; she could always be depended upon to fall asleep by 11:30, just before that hideous human skull sprang onscreen and the creepy voice of the announcer advised us to lock our doors and close our windows. (Those Universal monsters are still my warm-and-fuzzies. The first time I saw *Frankenstein*, my pet Chihuahua-terrier, Pepi, was curled up in my lap, and I still feel her there whenever Colin Clive throws the switch on that massive inert form stretched out on his surgical table.)

Movies were all over network and local television in those days. They ran in the morning and afternoon, ruthlessly mutilated to sell used cars and storm windows, kept people home Saturday night, and sprawled across most of the day Sunday with fifteen-minute station breaks during which the garrulous hosts answered movie-trivia questions put to them by viewers on the telephone. Johnny Weissmuller wrestled crocodiles on a continuous loop, Shirley Temple danced her cute little dimpled butt off day after day, and James Cagney ran up the body count on the South Side regular as the mail. The original *King Kong* always wrapped up with enough daylight left for me to risk my fool neck swinging from the rafters in the barn out back in pursuit of my own version of Fay Wray.

The TV was black-and-white, but that didn't matter because so were most of the movies. That was in the fifties and early sixties. However, as late as the mid-seventies, CBS ran thirty-year-old films after the Eleven O'clock News in competition with talk shows on the other channels. The program director of a Detroit station even got the bright idea of screening the first half-hour of a movie at eleven, then breaking for thirty minutes of news, weather, and sports before returning to the feature. The experiment lasted about three weeks; I assume the program director didn't.

Cable and satellite ended this Hollywood parade in the 1980s. The movies decamped to the premium channels, and the only way most of us could enjoy a rousing western or gaze upon Hedy Lamarr's flawless face was to pop for an exorbitant package or embrace the nascent concept of home theater.

A word about videocassette records and DVD players.

Yea!

TV Guide once published an article about Howard Hughes and his solution to the dearth of his kind of entertainment on TV at 2:00 A.M., when he finished buying countries and disinfecting his environment and wanted to relax: He bought a local station, stocked it with westerns and aviation films, and called the night man there to tell him when he was ready to watch and what feature to put on. If he became bored with one, Hughes would call the station again to yank it and substitute something else. This was a flagrant violation of FCC regulations—the airwaves belong to the public, after all, or did then, before the authorities cracked down on satellite hackers for theft of services. I personally thought it was neat. I wanted to be Howard Hughes.

Thanks to modern technology, I can be. The generation that has grown up since the first affordable VCR appeared on the market will never know the wonder connected with being able to watch any movie one wants, any time one wants to watch. Even so, I put off making the purchase, waiting for prices to come down, until Ted Turner began colorizing films originally released in black-and-white to reach a younger audience. Fearing that unadulterated *Casablancas* and *Citizen Kanes* would soon be extinct, I bit the bullet, bought the doohickey, locked myself up with it for twenty-four hours while I figured out how to set the clock, and pioneered the home theater before the term existed, designating a room just for watching movies and filling the shelves with all my favorites.

Any collector will sympathize. The urge to amass begins with the delusion that if I don't save all this crap from destruction, no one else will. That's how people manage to suffocate themselves under tons of newspapers they can't bring themselves to part with.

Movies, I love 'em. Old-time horror flicks, musicals, horse operas, prison pictures, classic science fiction, gangster sagas, Garbo weepies, Elvis playing guys named Steve and Rick and Lucky. I like a lot of the new stuff nearly as well as some of the old, but don't ask me to watch Adam Sandler remaking a Gary Cooper landmark or any horror film made since *The Exorcist*; both make me throw up.

My family bonded in front of *Saturday Night at the Movies*, and I got to know my father after he retired on a disability, watching afternoon features with him when I got home from school and staying up late with him to catch bottom-of-the-bill fare on obscure stations the antenna couldn't receive during the day. We developed the habit of reading the closing credits to identify the character actors we saw so often: Barton MacLane, Joe Sawyer, Beryl Mercer, Allen Jenkins, Jo Van Fleet, who worked so steadily, appearing in ten or more pictures a year, you just knew they always showed up on time, on their marks and sober, and probably lent a lot of money to the lead players. I read all the credits to this day, even when they run twenty minutes to include the caterers and limo drivers. My wife shares the practice, and we're frequently the last people in the auditorium, with the cleaning crew fuming, waiting to get at all those wads of gum before they petrify. (We wonder what the negative cutter does now that movies have gone digital.)

What I'm saying, to paraphrase Mae West on the role of Diamond Lil, is I'm Valentino; he's me, and we're each other. Mind, I'm no film detective. That's a specialized skill, and Kevin Brownlow, the genius behind the greatest cinema finds of the last century and this, has it more than anyone else, inspiring the creation of Valentino. But the fellow with the name that fairly drips Hollywood has my compulsive obsession with movies and movie lore. Cut us, we bleed pure popcorn butter. We would rather watch a star at work than be one, and if *The Divine Woman* ever resurfaced and showed on Channel Six on our wedding night, we'd be divorced by morning. Valentino loves his work, and I love mine. Having explored the birth of Hollywood in detail in *Billy Gashade* and *The Rocky Mountain Moving Picture Association* and the murky world of film *noir* at length in *Never Street*, and peppered my books and stories with motion picture references for thirty years, I write off a percentage of my viewing equipment and film library every year with a clear conscience.

Valentino evolved a good deal before his first appearance in "Dark Lady Down." Years earlier, in a raw version of that story called "Death of a Vamp," his name was Lawrence Little, and he was a former child star known first as Baby Larry and Little Larry Little. The story never sold, and neither did a portion of a novel featuring him, *The Frankenstein Imperative*—presented here, in drastically altered form, as "The Frankenstein Footage." One editor complained that the character's name was distracting, especially in sentences that began like, "Little knew . . ." Looking back, I'm happy the series never took off in that incarnation. A child actor from Hollywood's Golden Age would be getting too long in the tooth about now to run around sleuthing after lost films and murderers, and in any case "Vamp," with its storyline centering on a reclusive silent star, bore too close a resemblance to *Sunset Boulevard* for comfort. Also, at ninety-nine and counting, even the youngest players from that period have grown too old to commit a satisfying murder or to bother murdering. Better the victim should be an aging *femme fatale* from the heyday of *noir*.

Good-bye, then, to Lawrence Little and his early career in films. But Valentino still wasn't Valentino, not yet. At one point I considered calling him Hitchcock, but since I hadn't decided to submit his first adventure to *Ellery Queen's Mystery Magazine* (or that it would be accepted there), the prospect of offering it to *Alfred Hitchcock's Mystery Magazine* and the inevitable name confusion it would cause set me to thinking the thing through.

Hollywood would be a very different place without Rudolph Valentino having participated in it. The surname also has an exotic sound—romantic, on the very face of it—and the opportunities for comedy were unlimited. He would be forever distancing himself from the star of *The Sheik* (in the presence of those familiar with screen history) or from the fashion designer (for those whose entertainment education begins and ends with *Access Hollywood*). With a last name like that, there never was a need to give him a first, and giving him a slight physical resemblance to the original Valentino sharpened his character by adding to his travails and removed the need to find new ways to describe him physically. ("You look like him," new acquaintances declare; differing versions of that. Next line.)

The idea was a natural, and after nearly ten years I can't get over the fact that no one else beat me to it. Mystery writers have plundered Hollywood and the cinema of plots for decades, but it never occurred to any of them that an archivist whose job is to circle the globe assembling bits and pieces of celluloid is uniquely suited to solving puzzles connected with murder. Brownlow's own recollections, in *The Parade's Gone By* and his introduction to Abel Gance's shooting script for *Napoleon*, on his twenty-year search for every extant inch of the director's silent masterpiece, culminating in its triumphant second premiere in 1979, reads like a vintage detective story.

The movies and literature—for want of a term less lofty—have been joined at the hip since before D.W. Griffith invented the close-up. Screenwriters have adapted the heart out of all the good books and most of the bad, sometimes ignoring the polite gesture of paying their authors, and writers of books have in turn borrowed heavily from the cinema, employing wide shots and tracking, whether or not they were aware of the debt. I discovered Raymond Chandler through a beat-up 1963 paperback of *The Little Sister* in the nickel bin of a used bookstore, and goggled at his cynical view of Golden Age Hollywood: ". . . a square building . . . with small white leaded bay windows and a Greek porch over the front door and what looked, from across the street, like an antique pewter doorknob. . . . I went for the knocker, but they had thought of that too. It was all in one piece and didn't knock." And: "Wonderful what Hollywood will do to a nobody. It will make a radiant glamour queen out of a drab little wench who ought to be ironing a truck driver's shirts, a he-man hero with shining eyes and brilliant smile reeking of sexual charm out of some overgrown kid who was meant to go to work with a lunchbox. Out of a Texas car hop with the literacy of a character in a comic strip it will make an international courtesan, married six times to six millionaires and so blasé and decadent at the end of it that her idea of a thrill is to seduce a furniture mover in a sweaty undershirt." Lesser lights such as Jackie Collins and Jacqueline Susann built whole careers out of Tinseltown bitchiness, and Stuart Kaminsky, a genuine insider, has delighted legions with private eye Toby Peters, confidant to the likes of Errol Flynn, Mae West, and Groucho Marks; but it was Chandler—with a nod to Nathanel West's shockingly jaundiced *Day of the Locust*—who stripped away the glitter and exposed a grubby factory town, laced with larceny and license.

But this is not a treatise on the history of pictures and penmen. There's enough material there to fill a book ten times as long as this one. Suffice it to say that the relationship is long and intimate.

Enough with the overture. The lights come down, the gauzy crimson curtain slides away from the screen—a honking big one, I hope, not that basement window in the little freight car where Merchant Ivory gets drowned out by the latest excrescence from George Lucas in the theater next door. Sit back, take your shoes off, and don't forget to take advantage of the refreshment opportunities available in the lobby.

Loren D. Estleman

Dark Lady Down

"Valentino?" said the woman.

"Valentino," said Valentino.

"Seriously?"

"Unfortunately."

She chuckled. The famous husky voice had been further roughened by fifty years of cigarettes. "I was told you died the year I was born."

"That would be a mistake. I'm a big fan."

"You needn't flatter me, Mr. Valentino. I've already decided to receive you tomorrow afternoon. Would one o'clock be convenient?"

He said it would be if it was for her, and they broke the connection.

The next day, Valentino put on his best summer-weight suit with a pale blue shirt. He hesitated over whether to wear a necktie, then selected one of the handful he kept for excursions east. He always felt conspicuous wearing one in southern California, but the Old Hollywood had different standards. He wanted to make a good impression.

The house was one of the stately sprawling old Spanish villas pegged to the side of Laurel Canyon. Climbing the long flight of flagstone steps to the front door, Valentino felt a niggling sense of déjà vu. He wondered where he had seen the place before.

Then he remembered: It was the house where Ivy Lane had shot Cornel Wilde in *Switchback*. These were the very steps where Wilde had stumbled and then rolled down, finally landing on his back in the street. His costar had either lent her own home to the production or had become enamored with it during filming and bought it later. It looked less forbidding in color than it had in black and white. She had removed the sinister hedges and planted flowers in boxes under the windows.

Immediately after he rang the bell, the door was opened by a man whose broad bulk filled the opening as thoroughly as a second door. He wore a tan poplin sportcoat over a white knitted shirt, open at the neck to show his smooth tanned throat.

"Are you with the police or the coroner's office?"

The voice was a deep drumroll. Stepping back, the visitor stared up into a pair of nostrils like ship's funnels and said, "Neither. I have an appointment with Miss Lane. The name is Valentino."

The man-mountain rumbled. The noise seemed to indicate amusement. "Yeah. You sure look like him."

Sadly, that was true. His light olive coloring, clean profile, and the glossy black hair that he could only control by brushing it straight back from his forehead were a coincidence that vexed him constantly. As far as he knew, there was no blood relationship between his family and the silent-film star, but all the same he had had to put up with lame jokes all his life. In college he had been known as the Sheik, a nickname he would likely still be struggling under if the new generation's knowledge of the cinema of the past didn't stop at *Star Wars*.

"Please tell Miss Lane I'm here," he said.

"All her appointments are canceled, sorry." The door started to close.

A female voice called from the other side of the poplin sportcoat. "Who is it, Vivien?"

Vivien?

"Someone who says his name is Valentino, and it fits. Come to see Miss Lane. I told him—"

"Yes, I heard that part. Show him in."

The giant hesitated, then moved to one side. Valentino stepped over the threshold and surrendered his hand to a solid grip belonging to a woman nearly as tall as he. She wore large red-framed glasses and a tailored red suit without a blouse that did wondrous things for a figure that didn't seem to need to have much done for it. Her honey-colored hair was caught loosely behind her neck.

"I'm Georgia Tanner, Ivy Lane's attorney. She mentioned your conversation."

"Then I won't have to explain myself," he said.

"Something about one of Ivy's films."

"*Shades of Night*. It was about a plot by American Nazis to assassinate the president. RKO withdrew it from theaters when Roosevelt died and shelved it. I fully believe Miss Lane's print is the only complete one in existence. If it's for sale I'd like to make an offer."

"Ah. You're a collector." She might have said, *You clean toilets*.

"Not personally, although I suffer from most of the symptoms. I'm a film historian, under contract to UCLA. My job is to locate and acquire rare motion pictures so they can be preserved for future generations to see and appreciate."

"It sounds a little like detective work."

"Sometimes it's exactly like it. Some films seem just as determined to stay lost as any fugitive from justice."

"A dick," rumbled big Vivien. "I said it the second I saw him."

Valentino looked at him, and felt a shock of recognition. Now that there was distance between them, he could take in the huge man's mane of thick black hair, graying now, square chin, and eyebrows that collided over his nose. The name hadn't been Vivien. In the early sixties, he was billed on drive-in screens across the country as "Bull" Broderick, one of the later, dumber Tarzans. The foyers and pantries of Greater Los Angeles were littered with more half-forgotten faces than a cutting room floor.

The film detective glanced at his watch. He had a man to see in Thousand Oaks about sixty feet of an undiscovered Chaplin two-reeler at four o'clock. "Could I see Miss Lane now?"

The professional smile left the attorney's face. Watching her, Valentino wasn't sure it had ever been there.

"Miss Lane is dead. She committed suicide late last night or early this morning."

The news came as a physical blow. Valentino had never lived in a world that didn't contain Ivy Lane. She had sounded so lively over the telephone, so much more like herself than the dozens of female impressionists who had done her onstage in years past. "Have the police definitely established suicide?"

"We're waiting for them now," Georgia Tanner said. "She always came down promptly at eleven for brunch. When she was more than a half-hour late, Vivien went up to look in on her. He tried to wake her, but her skin was already cool. He called me. I found an empty prescription bottle on her bedside table. It was Seconal."

"Vivien is the butler?"

"Bodyguard," said the giant.

Valentino looked from him to the attorney. "Why would a seventy-year-old woman need a bodyguard?"

"She didn't. She hadn't since she quit being Hollywood's Bitch Goddess when CinemaScope came in. But she was accustomed to having one around. She played so many villainesses, you see, and some moviegoers had trouble separating screen reality from the genuine article. That was over long before Vivien came. In his two years here he was more of a companion. He was absolutely devoted to her."

He looked again at the big man, and saw that his eyes were pink and swollen. Valentino felt a little more kindly toward him then. They were both fans of Ivy Lane.

"May I see her?"

Ms. Tanner was startled. "Why?"

"I've waited all my life. Of course, I'll understand if you refuse."

She consulted the floor. It was blue and white Mexican tile, the same shining squares William Demarest had dropped his cigar ashes on when he came to investigate Cornel Wilde's murder.

"I don't suppose it would do any harm," she said.

"I go too." Vivien sounded like the ape man of old.

The three walked through large, sun-splashed rooms and up an open swirl of staircase with a brass banister like the railing of an ocean liner. Original paintings for posters advertising Ivy Lane's movies lined the staircase wall: Ivy locked in steamy embraces with Wilde, Dick Powell, John Payne, Robert Mitchum, Alan Ladd. Invariably, a sinister figure lurked in the keylit background, gripping a gun: Peter Lorre, Elijah Cook, Jr., Steve Brodie—a pictorial *Who's Who* of shady supporting players from Central Casting's endless supply of bottom-feeders. The original Dark Lady of the uncertain postwar period, Lane was the stereotypical seductress who lured the ambivalent hero to the wrong side of the law, and eventually his doom. Her gleaming black tresses and predatory purr had furnished an insidious antidote to the blond, perky heroines who had dominated the cinema before Pearl Harbor.

The bedroom, done entirely in cream and black and as big as a warehouse, was scarcely large enough to contain the enormity of death. Fresh flowers bloomed unaware in a vase on a low dresser cluttered with unposed family pictures in silver frames; a pair of fuzzy pink slippers on the floor beside the bed and a pale pink silk dressing gown draped over the footboard awaited their mistress. Here the only item pertaining to her movies was the honorary Oscar presented to her two years before by a grateful Academy, looking lonely on a corner of the vanity table. A framed certificate commemorating her efforts on behalf of the World Hunger Foundation occupied a much more prominent position on the wall just inside the door.

As the trio entered, a man and woman seated next to the sleigh bed looked up at them with bleak eyes. The man was gray-haired, dressed expensively but rather obviously in stacked lapels and a yellow silk handkerchief, and might have been considered large in any company that didn't include the hulking Vivien. The woman was a few years younger and wore plain slacks and a sweater and no makeup. Her hair was cut short.

"Dale Grant, Miss Lane's nephew," said Ms. Tanner. "His wife, Louise. This is Mr. Valentino."

"Valentino will do," said Valentino.

Grant rose and offered a listless hand. "Are you a policeman?"

Valentino shook his head. That made twice in his thirty-three years he'd been mistaken for the law, both times on the same day. "Just a fan. With your permission, I'd like to pay my respects."

"Don't tell me it's on the news already. I wouldn't have thought she was such good copy. It's been so long since she retired."

Miss Tanner said, "Valentino is here by invitation. He made an appointment yesterday."

"That's odd." Grant's brow puckered. "Aunt Ivy was scrupulous about keeping commitments. Even despondent as she must have been—"

The attorney interrupted. "These decisions are often made on the spur of the moment, Dale. She put up a cheerful front, but I don't suppose she ever forgave Hollywood for tossing her on the scrap heap at the age of thirty. There's talk of remaking *Carlotta*, with Madonna, of all people. That was Ivy's signature film. It must have eaten at her, though she wouldn't show it. She seemed in good spirits when I left her last night; but then, she was an actress."

"Perhaps you're right. Be my guest, Valentino. She'll be on exhibit from now until she's buried anyway. Too bad she can't enjoy it. She pretended otherwise, but she enjoyed being the center of attention. If you'll excuse me." He went out. His wife remained in her chair for an undecided moment, then got up and followed him.

"He loved his aunt very much," Georgia Tanner said. "It was a shock for him to come here for brunch and hear the news."

"Is he a bitter man usually?"

"Only with himself. I understand there was a row when he dropped out of medical school and went into business. Things were never the same between aunt and nephew after that. Not that they ever spoke of it when I was around."

Valentino approached the small still figure on the bed. Age had scored and lengthened the face that had seduced half the second string of leading men, and yet the features were girlish in repose. Her hair, tinted yellow now to conceal the gray, was arranged in a demure braid over her left shoulder. She wore a plain flannel nightgown and her slim perfect hands were nearly as pale as the cream-colored spread upon which they rested.

"Did she leave a note?"

The attorney shook her head, watching the inert face. "She wasn't much for writing, notes or letters."

"Was she as vain as Grant said?"

"Not among friends and family, but she liked to put on a show for strangers. She said people who came to see Ivy Lane expected an event, and she wasn't about to disappoint them."

As she spoke, Valentino wandered the room, unobtrusively peeping inside drawers and closets. The inlaid ebony dresser was full of extravagant evening gowns, the racks a riot of rainbow silk and satin negligees. Some still had price tags.

Vivien's steam-shovel paw descended upon Valentino's shoulder.

"Get your jollies looking at dead women's undies?" The bodyguard's voice was a low growl.

Valentino ignored him—so far as one could ignore a garage door with an attitude. "Was Grant her only living relative?" he asked Ms. Tanner.

"Yes. There was a son by her first marriage, but he was killed in Vietnam. Why?"

"Close family members are generally well provided for in wills."

She smiled then. "I think you're starting to take the detecting part of your work too seriously. As much as an adoring fan might prefer to think otherwise, there's nothing to indicate Ivy didn't take her own life."

"Attorneys who execute wills frequently come in for a handsome commission," he said.

Vivien squeezed Valentino's shoulder. The bones shifted. "You paid your respects, Monsieur Beaucaire. Hit the road."

Valentino gritted his teeth against the pain. "What's a bodyguard's devotion worth in probate?"

The reply was a Tarzan yell and constricted ligaments. The film detective felt his blood draining into his feet.

"We'll humor him, Vivien. He's starstruck."

The hand lifted.

Ms. Tanner crossed her arms. "Ivy's third husband went through what was left of her fortune thirty years ago. Aside from this house and property, her Social Security pension was all she had, and most of that went into taxes and upkeep. I charged her a minimal fee to manage her affairs."

"Was Grant here last night?" he asked Vivien.

The bodyguard scowled. "No. This is the first time he and Mrs. Grant have been in all week."

"Does he have a key?"

"Sure. He's her nephew. But nobody comes in or goes out without me knowing."

"Where do you sleep?"

"Other end of the hall."

"Let's go talk to Grant."

"Did I hear my name?"

The three turned as Dale Grant opened the door from the hall. His wife fluttered in behind him.

Valentino said, "One question, Grant. How'd you do it?"

"Do what?" The nephew's big heatlamp-tanned face was flat.

Georgia Tanner unfolded her arms. "Now I'm beginning to side with Vivien. Weren't you listening, Valentino, when I said Miss Lane's estate wasn't worth committing murder to acquire?"

"Wasn't it? A big house on four acres in one of the most exclusive neighborhoods in town? How much was the last offer she refused?"

The attorney's eyes dilated behind her glasses. "A million five. She told the agent she'd see him in hell before she'd let some Arab potentate house his harem in the garden."

"Was Grant present when the offer was made?"

Grant's face darkened. He took a step toward Valentino. The bodyguard held up an index finger as big as a sash weight and he stopped.

"I'll guess your method," the film detective said. "I've made a career out of assembling things from scrap. Last night, after Ms. Tanner left and you were sure your aunt and her watchdog were asleep, you let yourself in, dissolved a lethal dose of Seconal into a solution, and injected it into her bloodstream. You'd know how much to use from your medical school training, and anyone can get hold of a hypodermic. Vivien wouldn't have heard anything from his room because there was no struggle. Being family, you knew where she kept the pills. It wouldn't have taken any time at all to empty the bottle into a sink, wipe off your fingerprints, and place it on her bedside table to make it look like suicide. A million dollars for ten minutes' work is good wages even by Hollywood standards."

Grant turned to Vivien. "This is my house now. Throw this man out."

The big man stayed put. "I don't come with the house."

"Please go on," said Georgia Tanner.

Valentino said, "Grant forgot one thing: Miss Lane's nightgown. You said she liked to put on a show for strangers, and he said himself his aunt liked being the center of attention. She had closets full of beautiful negligees. She would never have taken her own life in plain flannel."

A howl, as of a mortally wounded grizzly, shattered the tension in the room. Vivien reached down, gathered Dale Grant's stacked lapels in his enormous hands, and lifted him off the floor. The nephew gulped air.

"Put him down!"

Three heads swiveled toward Louise Grant. Dale's wife had her purse open in one hand and a hypodermic syringe in the other. She held the needle in an underhand grip like a switchblade. The point glittered. "Put him down or I'll stick this in one of your kidneys," she told Vivien. Her thin, drawn face was feral.

After a moment the bodyguard lowered her husband to the floor and let go. Grant clawed the yellow handkerchief out of his pocket and mopped his face.

"She wouldn't die."

The others said nothing, watching the woman. Her knuckles were white on the barrel of the syringe.

"She was going to outlive us all," she said. "Dale's business was failing. She could have sold the house and bailed him out and had plenty left over, but she wouldn't. I pleaded with her. She said he should have considered the consequences when he dropped out of medical school."

"Louise." Grant twisted his handkerchief between his fists.

"I knew you'd never do it. She made you dance to her tune the same way she manipulated the men in her movies. I was a registered nurse when I married you. Remember how refreshed you felt this morning? You never suspected I put Seconal in your tea last night. I was gone for over an hour with your keys and you slept right through it."

"What are you going to do, Mrs. Grant?" Valentino asked. "There's no place to run."

For a second she appeared lost. Then her eyes grew as cold as the corpse on the bed.

"Yes, there is," she said. "The same place I sent the old hag." And before anyone could move, she stabbed the needle into her left arm and rammed home the plunger.

"That should do it." The lieutenant from L.A. Homicide, blond and freckled in a Michael Jackson suit—narrow lapels and a ribbon tie—flipped shut his notebook. He was no William Demarest. "Your name's Valentino?"

Valentino nodded and braced himself.

"That's Spanish, isn't it?"

He relaxed. "Italian. Several generations back."

"No kidding. I've got an uncle who's Neapolitan. He married into the family."

He wondered if the lieutenant even knew that films had once been silent.

"Will Mrs. Grant live?" Georgia Tanner asked.

"Maybe. The EMS boys said there's a good chance there was just some residue in the needle. If she does it's off to lockup."

He reminded them to come downtown later and make a statement for the record, then left. Valentino and the attorney were standing in the tiled foyer. Dale Grant had accompanied his wife in the ambulance and Vivien was outside making sure the morgue attendants didn't drop the stretcher containing the mortal remains of Ivy Lane. Ms. Tanner said, "You really are a detective. Did you suspect Louise when you accused Dale?"

"If I said I did, would you believe me?"

"I'd give you the benefit of the doubt."

"Anyway, I didn't think Miss Lane would kill herself because they were doing a crummy remake of one of her best pictures. I saw her bedroom. She placed more importance on old family snapshots and her charity work than she did on her acting career. She may have been a little vain, but she was no Norma Desmond."

"Poor Ivy. How she'd have reveled in all this fuss." She opened the front door for him. "She wasn't rich, but she always made good on her debts. How can she repay you for solving her murder?"

Six months later, when California Probate Court was satisfied with the division of the Ivy Lane Estate, a messenger came to Valentino's office carrying a package containing all four reels of *Shades of Night*.

The Frankenstein Footage

Valentino fixed a drink and slumped into the glistening leather armchair he'd bought at Sotheby's. Both Humphrey Bogart and Sidney Greenstreet had sat in it in Sam Spade's apartment in *The Maltese Falcon*, and although it had since been reupholstered, the chair's new owner felt as if he drew strength and spirit from it whenever he sat there. Tonight he was low on both.

The telephone purred on the table beside the chair.

"Valentino?"

The furred, broken voice on the other end aroused his suspicions. Valentino's number was unlisted, yet hardly a week went by that some drunk didn't call and ask to borrow the camel.

"That's right," he said. "Just Valentino. Not Rudolph. No relation, and anyway, he's dead. Who's this?"

"It's Craig."

He groaned. Craig Hunter had been a popular action-movie star before changing tastes and a messy public divorce reduced him to an occasional bit on TV. He and Valentino had been friends, but lately Hunter had become a pest, calling him up at all hours, usually from some bar and invariably finishing with an appeal for a loan.

"Craig, I'm not in the mood. Viacom just outbid me for rights to a silent Buster Keaton comedy two-reeler. I was this close to closing the deal."

"That's not—"

"Don't ask me for money. I'm through subsidizing half the distilleries and bookies in the U.S."

"Gimme a minute, okay? I'm in a bar in Dan Shie—I mean, in San Diego—"

"What did you do, drink up all the stock in L.A.?"

"Valentino, I need help. I'll make it worth your while."

"You know what would be worth my while, Craig? It would be worth my while if you'd stop pestering me for something you can only give yourself. Call A.A."

"Listen. Don't—"

He banged down the receiver. When the telephone purred again he lifted the handset, replaced it, then lifted it again and laid it on the table. Then he went to bed.

His business cards identified Valentino as a "film detective," a romantic indulgence. As a consultant with the film department at UCLA, he was often compelled to jet to some remote region to track down a fragment of some great motion picture long considered lost. At these times he was more Sherlock Holmes than Joe Academic, and it was this part of the work that had drawn him to it. His name, and his unfortunate resemblance to the Great Lover of the silent screen, caused him a good deal of embarrassment, but unlike much of Hollywood he refused to change his name or his appearance for mere convenience. On some rare occasions he benefited: They might lose his card, but they seldom forgot his name.

His office was a shoebox in a building that had once been part of the university's power plant, cluttered with film books and piles of video cassettes, but he had partial use of a secretary named Ruth, iron-haired old dragon that she was. She fixed him with her gray, polished-stone gaze when he walked in a little after eight. "You look like Georgie Jessel the morning after he turned down *The Jazz Singer*," she said.

"I lost the Keaton. To Viacom."

"Oh, that. I knew yesterday they were going to outbid you. I had lunch with one of the secretaries in their video division."

"Thanks for warning me."

"We learn from loss, kiddo. Say, you in trouble with the law? You had two calls this morning from a Sergeant Fish with the police." She squinted at the scratches on her message pad.

"What did he want?"

She shrugged. "Maybe one of his snitches tipped him where to look for Von Stroheim's *Greed*."

"If he calls again, tell him the line forms to the left."

He was at his desk, viewing outtakes from *Easy Rider* on the Movieola, when Ruth buzzed. "That policeman again."

"Which line?"

"He's not on the phone. He's here, and he brought company."

"Shoo them in, Ruthie. Shoo them in."

"No more of that. I knew Bogie; you don't sound a bit like him. And if you ever call me Ruthie again, you'll end up sounding like Linda Darnell."

He rose as two young men entered. The first had short sandy hair and clean-shaven cheeks with a suggestion of baby fat. His eyes were anything but babyish. The other, slightly older, had the bold nose and high flat cheeks of an Indian.

"Sergeant Fish?" Valentino shook the hand of the younger man, who looked as if he was in charge. His grip was moderate.

"Gill. Ernest Gill. This is my partner, John Redfern."

Silently cursing Ruth's bad memory for names, the film detective rescued his fingers from the Indian's corded grasp. "Did I nick Al Pacino's Mercedes in the Safeway parking lot?"

Gill didn't smile. "We're not with the L.A.P.D., Mr. Valentino. We're San Diego Homicide."

San Diego went off in his head like a late-night telephone bell. "Is it Craig Hunter?"

"Have you heard from him?"

"He called me last night from a bar there. He was drunk. If I'd thought he was driving—"

"He wasn't in an accident," Gill said. "His body was found in the men's room of a place called The Grotto at one fifty-five this morning. He was beaten to death."

Beaten to death. Numbly, Valentino cleared piles of bound scripts and publicity stills from a pair of scoop chairs and sank into his own behind the desk. While Gill sat, Redfern wandered the room, looking at the framed movie posters on the walls.

"Phone company says Hunter charged two long-distance calls last night to his home number," Gill said. "One was to his ex-wife in Laurel Canyon. The other was to your place on Sunset."

"He said he needed help."

"What kind of help?" The sergeant had his notebook out.

"I hung up on him before he could tell me. I assumed he was putting the arm on me, as usual. I wasn't up to it."

"He didn't say anything else?"

"He said he'd make it worth my while. He never had before, so I blew him off." Valentino talked through his guilt. "What was it, a mugging gone wrong?"

"It wasn't robbery. He still had his wrist watch and sixty dollars in his wallet."

"Maybe the mugger panicked and ran."

Redfern turned away from a scuffed and faded lobby card for *The Cabinet of Dr. Caligari.* "His arms were broken just below the elbows." His voice was a flat guttural. "It's a local signature. Grundage muscle does it all the time."

"Mike Grundage?"

"You've heard of him?" Sergeant Gill leaned forward.

"It'd be hard not to have. He's appearing before a grand jury investigating organized crime in the motion picture industry. What would Craig have to do with Grundage?"

"We were hoping you could tell us."

"Have you talked to Lorna Hunter? That's his ex-wife."

"We talked to her." Gill stood. "Thanks for your time. We may need a statement later. It's possible you were the last person to talk to Hunter."

The information did exactly nothing for Valentino's conscience.

Once, working for Kevin Brownlow, Valentino had found twenty-six feet of a key sequence from Abel Gance's epic *Napoleon* being used to demonstrate a home projector in a camera store in Lyons. Piecing together the circumstances of Craig Hunter's murder couldn't be much more difficult than assembling the scraps of a seventy-year-old movie.

Lorna Hunter lived in the house the court had awarded her, a pink stucco Spanish modern with a red-tile roof at the end of a street that twisted like a creek. Valentino had his finger on the buzzer when the door opened and he found himself in an embrace that smelled pungently of scent and gin.

"Thanks for coming," Lorna said when they parted. "Craig didn't have many friends left."

"I wish I'd been a better one."

"The better ones were the last to go."

He touched her shoulder and they moved inside. A tall blonde with a clean profile that was even more classical at thirty-one than it had been at twenty, Lorna was slim and fit in a cashmere top, tailored slacks, and sandals on her bare feet. Six years earlier she had startled ABC and a million fans by dropping out of the number-three sitcom in America, announcing her plans to devote all her time to making one man happy. Two years after the divorce, she was still not returning agents' calls.

Valentino accepted a glass of water and sat on the end of the big sofa that dominated the living room. Lorna curled up on the other end with a gin and tonic. He had never seen her drink before; at 9:45 A.M. she appeared to have a head start on the day.

"Did you know Craig was in this kind of trouble?" he asked.

"His gambling worried me. It used to be just recreation, but the last several times I saw him, all he could talk about was poker and the ponies and getting even. Until last Friday."

"What happened last Friday?"

"He came here to use the telephone. He said his call couldn't wait until he got to his apartment in Long Beach. Craig's dream was to start his own acting school. He was drunk, babbling something about having enough money soon to open a chain. I assumed he had a hot tip and was calling his bookie."

"Was he?"

"I don't know. He made the call from his old office with the door closed. He left here more excited than when he came."

Valentino sipped water. "Do you know if Craig owed money to Mike Grundage's loan sharks?"

"That's the assumption I made when the police told me Grundage was involved. He must have been borrowing to pay off his debts. I mean, why else would someone—" She drained her glass quickly.

"Lorna, the sharks don't kill you for not paying up. It's bad business. At most they would have roughed him up and then worked out some sort of payment plan. A dead man is a dead loss."

"What, then?"

"I don't know. May I look in his office?"

She rose, swaying a little. He followed her into a small den containing a desk and chair and a stereo system as complicated as a NASA control panel. Valentino pointed at a battered trunk in the corner. "That doesn't quite match the room."

"Craig brought it with him Friday. He said there wasn't room in his apartment and asked if he could store it here. You can look inside; the police did. It's just some books."

He looked. They were filmographies: *Heroes of the Horrors*, *The Films of Boris Karloff*, *The Films of Bela Lugosi*, *The Man Behind the Cape*, *Dear Boris*—a dozen others, all similar. "Was Craig interested in horror films?"

"He hated them. His first part was a bit in *Bloodbath IV*. He said it was a junk genre and always had been."

Valentino closed the trunk and stood. The console telephone caught his eye. "Has anyone used this phone since Craig?"

"No. I almost never come in here."

He lifted the receiver and punched the Redial button.

A cool feminine voice answered. "Horace Lysander's office."

He hung up and looked at Lorna. "Who represented Craig during your divorce?"

"Cooper and Clive. Craig retained them ever since that phony paternity suit five years ago."

"He never used Horace Lysander?"

"Is that who answered? I never heard of him."

"You would if you watched the news. Lysander is Mike Grundage's legal counsel before the grand jury."

No shady Mob mouthpiece out of Central Casting, Horace Lysander was senior partner in a firm that took up two floors of a sparkling glass tower at Century City. A lacquered-looking receptionist let Valentino wait forty minutes, then waved him into an office nine times the size of his own, with a glass wall looking out on most of Southern California. A large, soft, smiling pink bald man in a beautiful gray suit, Lysander shook his hand and they sat down on either side of a desk the size of the battleship *Potemkin*.

"Are you with the police, Mr. Valentino?" The lawyer looked dubiously at his sweatshirt and brushed jeans.

"No, I'm looking into Craig Hunter's death as a friend."

"Two detectives were here earlier asking about Mr. Grundage, who's in New York on business. I assured them that to my knowledge my client never had any contact with this man Hunter."

"But you did, last Friday. He called you."

Lysander smiled. "I'm an old courtroom attorney, Mr. Valentino. I know when I'm being bluffed."

"So do I. Your office number was on his redial."

"Granted that's true, it proves nothing." But he shrugged. "His business was with Elizabeth Grundage, not Mike."

"His wife?"

"His mother. You're too young to remember Mike's father. Tony Grundage represented certain eastern interests in Hollywood during the so-called Golden Age of the thirties. He arranged the financing for *All Quiet on the Western Front*, *The Wizard of Oz*, *Frankenstein*—"

"*Frankenstein?*" Valentino remembered the books in Craig's office.

"Yes. That was before my time, of course, but I became his attorney in his last years, and represented Elizabeth when his will was probated. She was much younger than Tony. The family has retained me ever since."

"What business could Craig have had with a racketeer's widow?"

"I can't discuss details. He approached her with a transaction. When he found out I'd advised Elizabeth against it, he called me and became abusive, threatening. He was drunk. I hung up on him."

"How much of this have you told the police?"

"None of it. They asked if Mike Grundage knew Hunter and I denied it. They didn't ask if his mother knew him. I suppose I'll have to tell them now that I've told you."

"They'll ask about the transaction."

"That's privileged."

"It's withholding evidence in a homicide."

"Are you a lawyer, Mr. Valentino?"

"No, but I helped restore three Perry Mason movies starring Warren William." He smiled briefly. "One way or another the police will root out the details. You might as well share them with me."

"Not without my client's permission."

"I can wait outside while you call her."

Lysander smiled again, somewhat differently. He had such an inventory that the single word "smile" was insufficient, like "snow" to an Eskimo. "What do you do for a living, Mr. Valentino?"

Valentino told him, as briefly as possible.

"If you ever need a change, this firm can use an investigator." He lifted his telephone receiver.

After ten minutes, the film detective was invited back into Lysander's office. The atmosphere seemed warmer.

"Are you familiar with an old-time director named Robert Florey?" the lawyer asked.

"*The Murders in the Rue Morgue*. Universal, nineteen thirty-two."

"Also *Frankenstein*."

"That was James Whale."

"Not at the start. Florey, who wrote the screenplay, was to direct the picture originally as a vehicle for Universal's hottest property."

"Bela Lugosi," said Valentino. "The star of *Dracula*. He tested for *Frankenstein*, then backed out."

"I forgot you're a historian. Florey shot two reels of Lugosi stumping around in a costume and makeup of his own device. No one was happy with the result. After Lugosi left, the project was taken away from Florey and given to Whale, who assigned the role of Frankenstein's monster to an unemployed truck driver named William Henry Pratt."

"Boris Karloff."

"It looked better on a marquee. The picture made Karloff a star, saved the studio from bankruptcy, and assured Tony Grundage a power base in Hollywood. On his advice, his people provided the seed money for the project. By now the test was forgotten. The footage was considered destroyed."

Valentino said nothing. In spite of his mission, he was beginning to catch that old familiar scent.

"When Grundage agreed to finance the property, all preproduction materials were turned over to him. Motion picture memorabilia didn't command anywhere near the prices it does now. He placed the material in storage and apparently forgot about it. When Elizabeth came to me with Craig Hunter's offer I advised her against accepting until we knew just what those test reels were worth on the open market."

"How much did he offer?"

"Two hundred fifty thousand dollars."

"Craig would have been hard pressed to raise a hundred dollars, let alone a quarter million."

"Nevertheless, that was the amount."

"Where does Mike Grundage fit in?"

"Nowhere. You're the first person I've discussed this with. Mike never brought it up. He may not even know about the film."

"Craig's two broken arms say he knows something."

"Say that in public and our next conversation will be in court." Lysander's expression went from severe to smiling, like water subsiding. "The police mentioned an ex-wife. Are you acting on her behalf?"

"I've known Lorna nearly as long as I knew Craig."

"I understand. Elizabeth Grundage means more to me than just a client."

Valentino watched the freeways clogging up outside the window. "Are you going to make the test footage available?"

"I'm afraid that's a moot point." The lawyer rolled back his chair and stood. "Two nights ago, someone broke into the storage vault and made off with both reels."

Inching his way home amid rush-hour traffic, Valentino weighed what he'd learned on his mental balance scale. He had no doubt that Craig Hunter had stolen the *Frankenstein* test reels. He wondered if that was the original plan, or if Craig had lined up a buyer who would back his princely offer. It was a sound investment; recently an original preproduction poster for the same film had brought $100,000 at Sotheby's. What Valentino needed to know was who was interested, and how Craig had found out about the footage to begin with.

At a video store three blocks from his house, the film detective rented *Frankenstein* and *Dracula*. The kid behind the counter tried to interest him in a low-budget slasher film instead. "You'll wet your pants screaming."

"As attractive as that sounds, I'll stick with these."

At home he called his contact at Sotheby's and asked for the name of the party who had paid so much for the rare *Frankenstein* poster. Reluctant at first, upon being reminded how much of UCLA's acquisition funds Valentino had channeled to the auction house, the contact came up with the name J. Arthur Greenwood.

"The magazine publisher?"

"He's almost as regular a customer as you are."

Later Valentino fixed a simple dinner and ate it in his screening room, where he watched the two horror classics on his front-projection system. Although creaky in places, both were entertaining, and occasionally still frightening. Karloff, he noted, brought a heartbreaking eloquence to Frankenstein's mute monster that was missing from Lugosi's stilted and somewhat hammy performance as the

Undead Count. Valentino concluded that *Frankenstein* had benefited from the vicissitudes of fate.

He rewound the tapes and called Lorna Hunter. She sounded sleepy. He hoped she wasn't still drunk.

"I just wanted to make sure you're okay," he said.

"That's sweet of you. Now that the shock's worn off, I'm actually relieved. I still cared about Craig; it hurt to see him going down and down. At least he can't go down any farther."

"Have you been eating?"

"You mean am I still drinking. It made me sick, so I stopped. I don't know what Craig saw in it."

Relieved, he said, "I've got a lead on the angle he was working. I'm going to follow it up tomorrow."

"Shouldn't you leave that to the police?"

"I will if it looks like anything. Right now it's just one more theory they don't need."

"Be careful, Val. I'm running out of people I care about."

He assured her he would and said goodbye wondering why he hated ending the conversation.

J. Arthur Greenwood said, "I'd kill for those test reels."

Seated in a conversation area in the magazine publisher's office the morning after screening *Frankenstein* and *Dracula*, Valentino noted the collector's madness in his host's eye. Greenwood, who in his sixties continued to dye his thin hair and pencil moustache a glossy black, leaned forward from his leather sofa, gripping the film detective's knee.

The office was decorated to resemble a dungeon, complete with clammy stone-looking wallpaper, a ceiling fixture that might have been the chandelier from the original silent *Phantom of the Opera*, and an authentic iron maiden leaning in one corner, its deadly spikes glittering like needles. It all went perfectly with the image of the man whose flag-ship publication, *Horrorwood*, had communicated his passion for weird and fantastic movies to the entire baby-boom generation.

"I think Craig Hunter *was* killed for them," Valentino said.

Greenwood straightened. "I heard he was killed. There wasn't anything about the test reels on the news."

"Did you know him?"

"Craig and I were poker buddies. Ever since I interviewed him on the set of *Bloodbath IV*, before he hit the big time."

"What do you know about the *Frankenstein* test?"

"Everything. It's part of horror film lore. But I'm the only one who had the interest and the energy to link the reels' existence to Tony Grundage's widow."

"Then you were the one behind Craig's offer to buy them."

"Who else? Craig was into me for a bundle, and friendly poker is still poker. I told him he could work it off by fronting for me with Elizabeth Grundage. Since I bought the *Frankenstein* poster, everyone knows I'll pay any price for rare horror memorabilia. If she found out I was interested, she might try to hold me up for a million. She *was* married to a gangster."

"Did you authorize him to steal the footage if he had to?"

"Of course not! Half the fun of owning something special is showing it off. I couldn't do that if I got it illegally. Is that what he tried to do?"

"He did more than try. Something he said to his ex-wife makes it look like he was planning to double-cross you and sell the reels himself. A thing like that might make you angry enough to kill him when you found out."

The collector's gleam hardened. "Are you accusing me?"

"You said you'd kill for those reels."

"You're in the business. Can you honestly claim you've never said the same thing about a film you really wanted?"

Valentino thought of the Buster Keaton comedy he had lost to Viacom. Aloud he said, "Some collectors say it and mean it."

The magazine publisher slumped. He was barrel-chested but going soft, poised on the edge of obesity. "I'll never forget the first time I saw *House of Frankenstein* in a neighborhood theater. I identified with the monster, who couldn't help being what he was, but was persecuted by ignorant villagers because he was different. I was a fat kid on a city playground; I couldn't defend myself from bullies, but that poor clumsy brute with spikes in his neck could and did. I found justice there in the dark. Outside, I couldn't even smack a wasp. I still can't."

Valentino believed him. "Can you think of anyone who'd want that footage enough to commit murder for it?"

"Dozens. But they couldn't know Craig had it. What about Mike Grundage?"

"The police are working that angle." The film detective stood. "Thanks for your time. I enjoy your magazine."

"I'm afraid you're in the minority. The new generation isn't interested in the old monsters. They want slashers and flesh-eating zombies and writhing entrails onscreen. No moral code, no mythic quality. Now the monsters are in the audience."

Valentino drove back to UCLA to work. He was out of leads.

He parked underground and boarded the elevator to ground level. Two large men crowded in with him. The doors closed, the car started upward. One of the men squashed the emergency stop button. The car halted with a lurch.

A fist struck Valentino low. He emptied his lungs, groped for the safety bar. His legs were swept from under him. As he fell, a knee came up toward his face. That was the last thing he saw for a while. But he could hear.

"Bust his arms?" A wheezy, broken-windpipe voice.

"Boss said no."

The second voice was flat and toneless. Now he smelled stale cigarette breath, felt the heat of a face bent close to his. The owner of the flat voice said, "Forget *Frankenstein*, Rudolph. Or take the stairs."

The car started moving again. It stopped, the doors rumbled. Fresh air came in. Valentino heard the wheezy voice one last time. "Rudolph. That's rich." The doors closed.

He didn't know how long he lay there before someone found him. It was Ruth, his secretary. "You look like Errol Flynn on Sunday morning." She helped him to his feet. "Want to go to the medical center?"

He could see now. His nose was bleeding, but it seemed unbroken. "Just tip me into my car."

He drove through a pounding headache. At home he vomited into the toilet, washed his face, then vomited again. He'd never been knocked out before; all those Alan Ladd movies he'd seen had said nothing about throwing up.

The doorbell had been ringing for some time before he went to answer it, holding a wet washcloth to his forehead. It was Special Delivery. He signed for it and carried the package inside. It was square, slightly smaller than a pizza box and twice as thick. He recognized Craig Hunter's handwriting.

With unsteady hands he tore off the paper and undid the straps that secured a black metal box. There were two aluminum film cans inside. He prised one open, removed the reel, and unwound enough of the film to study it against the light. For old silver-nitrate stock it was in remarkably good condition; the storage vault must have been climate-controlled. After a minute he rewound the reel and returned it to its can.

His heart was hammering. It throbbed in his aching head, fed his brain. He had a pretty good idea who'd killed Craig.

The telephone rang. "Valentino."

"You recuperate fast. I didn't think you'd pick up so soon."

He recognized the voice. "What do you want?"

"Hunter had only one friend left he could trust with what he had. That's why he called you that night. You know what I want."

"If I don't come through, will you tell them to break my arms next time?"

"I've got someone here who wants to talk to you."

There was a pause, then another voice came on. "Val?"

"Lorna?" He gripped the receiver hard enough to crack it.

Lorna Hunter started to say something, but was cut off. The other voice came back. "You've seen enough crime pictures to know how this works. The film for the woman. No police. Midnight tonight. Here's the address."

Valentino fumbled for a pencil, started to write it down, then stopped. He knew the place.

The Hollywood Wax Museum was one of Valentino's favorite haunts, a place to go and revisit the giants of his *Late Show* youth. At night it seemed less friendly. Its Art Deco façade gleamed like a mortuary in the smog-muted starlight.

The lock on the front door was broken. He'd thought to bring along a flashlight; once inside he poked its beam around the corridor beyond the ticket counter. Although he hadn't been told where to go in the building, he walked past the Indiana Jones and *Star Wars* exhibits, past *Easy Rider* and James Dean and *Gone with the Wind* to the Chamber of Horrors.

Here a single overhead fixture burned, casting atmospheric shadows over the grotesque waxen faces of Lon Chaney, the Creature from the Black Lagoon, Peter Lorre, and the Mummy. He paused between Lugosi's Dracula and Karloff's Monster, but that wasn't where the light was. He found it shining over the dungeon set from *The Pit and the Pendulum*.

It was a lot more convincing than J. Arthur Greenwood's office. The stone walls were realistically moldy-looking, and the blood on the razor-sharp axe swinging above the pallet where Vincent Price lay seemed as if it were about to drip. The woman chained upside down by her ankles eight feet above the floor was the only sour note; nylon blouses and lounging slacks were not yet in fashion at time of the Inquisition. It took Valentino a second to realize that this figure was not made of wax. It was Lorna. Her eyes were wild. She whimpered through her gag.

"Melodramatic, I admit. But it seemed appropriate."

As the newcomer spoke, he strolled forward through the shadows at the end of the corridor.

Valentino recognized the voice from the telephone. He said, "No surprises in this script. Greenwood's too gentle, and you're the only other person who knew Craig had the footage. Mike Grundage wouldn't have cared. He's got his own problems."

Horace Lysander stopped under the light. The lawyer's hands were in the pockets of his suit.

"Fortunately the police aren't as logical as you," he said. "They pile on the first good suspect. That's what I counted on."

Something tugged at the package under the film detective's arm. He wheeled to face a man who might have posed for the figure of Frankenstein's monster. "Let's have the merch, Rudolph." He made a small motion with a big automatic.

His toneless speech was familiar to Valentino. He gave the man the box containing the two test reels.

"What's a high-priced attorney need with a quarter-million dollars in old film?" he asked.

"Not a thing. I'm going to destroy it, along with anyone who would jeopardize Elizabeth Grundage's privacy by bringing up her past associations."

"So you hired this goon and his partner to beat Craig Hunter to death and pin it on Mike Grundage. Wouldn't that reflect just as much light on his mother?"

"They haven't met in years. She had higher hopes for him. Mike's a cheap gangster like his old man Tony. Call it payback for all the crimes he'd have been convicted of but for me."

"Why didn't you have my arms broken in the elevator?"

"You needed them to carry the reels. That's Earl, by the way. You weren't properly introduced before. He and Roy used to work for Mike. Mike thinks they still do, but Mike never got them off a murder charge in open court. Isn't that right, Roy?"

"Sure thing, boss."

The wheezy response drew Valentino's attention to the top of the dungeon's false wall. A man nearly as ugly as Earl stood on a step-ladder behind it, gripping the end of the toggle that secured the chain Lorna was hanging from to the ceiling.

"Tell him to get his hand away," Valentino said. "If she falls she'll break her neck."

Lysander smiled. "One less thing to break when they finish you both off and snap your arms below the elbows."

"It won't wash. Why would Grundage have *us* killed?"

"Because the police think he had Hunter killed for stiffing his sharks, and because you both decided to play Dick Tracy. I never reported those missing reels. Neither did you, or you wouldn't have come here alone." His smile broadened. "I'll defend Mike at his trial. Who knows? I might even get him off."

Earl put down the reels and stuck his gun under his coat, flexing his fingers. Valentino hit him with the flashlight.

"Roy!" barked Lysander.

Roy jerked loose the toggle.

While Earl staggered, Valentino lunged. He caught Lorna around the waist with both arms. Out of the corner of his eye he saw Earl fumbling for his gun.

"Police! Lose it!"

Earl swung on the new voice, automatic in hand. A shot rang off the walls of the corridor. He grasped his arm and fell to one knee. Sergeant Ernest Gill kept his smoking revolver trained on Earl while Officer John Redfern sprinted past, covering Roy and Lysander with an automatic as big as Earl's.

Raising his hands, the lawyer glared at Valentino. "I said no police!"

"You've seen too many movies," said the film detective.

In the screening room in his home, Valentino cradled the receiver of his telephone. "That was Elizabeth Grundage. She's agreed to sell the *Frankenstein* test to UCLA for the amount Craig offered, as soon as the prosecutor's through with it."

Lorna, seated on the sofa, sipped from a glass of iced tea.

"As soon as it's been transferred to safety stock. I won't risk something this valuable to a humid police property room." He finished threading the film through the projector. "Ready?"

"Is it going to be scary?"

"If it is, we'll hang on to each other." He turned off the lights and started the movie.

Director's Cut

J ustin Ring sat beside a table on the edge of the Olympic-size pool behind
his house in Beverly Hills, but he wasn't taking the sun. In his terry robe,
sandals with socks, sail-brimmed straw hat, mirrored glasses, and full beard,
he exposed almost no skin as he sipped from a glass he refilled occasionally from
a pitcher of vodka and orange juice under the umbrella. As he weighed nearly
three hundred pounds, none of it muscle, his visitor didn't regret the cover-up.

"I'm Valentino," said the newcomer, stopping before the table with his back
to the sun. "Thanks for taking the time to see me, Mr. Ring."

Ring's watery eyes studied him above the rims of his glasses. "You look a little
like the Great Lover, at that. I suppose you cultivate the resemblance."

"Just the opposite; or I try. My hair's too straight to hold a perm, and I can't
change my Italian ancestry. Mostly it's an embarrassment."

"You're from UCLA, you said." End of chitchat.

"I'm with the Film Preservation Department. We have a nearly complete collection of the pictures you directed. You ought to come take a look sometime."

"I've seen them all."

"So have I, and I daresay more times even than you. There's no getting around
it, sir; I'm a Justin Ring fan, ever since I saw *Fear the Wicked* the first time on
the late show when I was in high school."

"I tried to get out of that contract. In the end I needed the money to finish
Ibsen. That died. *Fear the Wicked* lives, on cable and video and every time some
chucklehead decides to put together a Ring festival. Is it any wonder I retired?"

Valentino had heard the retirement was less than voluntary. He also thought
the Ibsen biopic pretentious and dull. Aloud he said, "Actually, there's one Ring
film I haven't seen, and neither has anyone else in forty years. That's the reason
I called for this appointment."

"My student film."

"No one who appeared in it has come forward, and the only person who saw
it besides you is dead. That was your instructor for the course."

"There were three in the cast. Two died, and here sits the third. I always was
my favorite lead."

"UCLA has cleared a generous offer for a print for our archives. You can
accept it in cash or donate the film and deduct the amount from your taxes."

"No."

"You haven't heard the amount."

Ring topped off his glass. "You know about my tax problems or you wouldn't have suggested a charitable deduction. It couldn't possibly be enough to offset my debt to the IRS. But that's moot. The film doesn't exist. I burned every print and the negative years ago."

"That's a common ploy to close discussion," Valentino said. "The true *auteur* rarely destroys his work, regardless of its merit. It's like killing one of his children."

"Thank God I never had any. They'd have sided with my ex-wives. Sorry you wasted a trip, Mr. Chaney."

"Valentino. Chaney was the horror star."

"Valentino was pretty horrible in *Son of the Sheik*." Ring chuckled. "I'm through with the movie business, or rather it's through with me. The industry has no room for aging legends. I'm preparing to sail my launch around the world. Fifty-foot waves and a typhoon at sea hold no fears for someone who's dealt with studio accountants. Who is it, Ki?"

The white-coated houseboy who had shown Valentino to the pool materialized at his elbow. Ki was far from a boy: After a heavy rainstorm, the cracks and seams in his ancient Asian face might have held enough water for a desert journey. "Mister Cortez." He thrust a cordless telephone at his employer.

Ring snatched it from him as if it were a gun. "Goodbye, Valentino."

The visitor strode toward the house. As he turned into the flagstone walk that led to the street, he saw that the director was just then raising the receiver to his ear.

They didn't talk again. Three months later, Justin Ring's motor launch, the *Billy Bitzer*, lost radio contact with Australia and was believed to have broken up on the Great Barrier Reef. Rescue craft found splinters of wreckage, but no Ring. All the producers who had refused to finance his later films turned out for the memorial services in Hollywood. One wept for the CNN cameras.

All this happened eight years ago. In the meantime, Valentino was promoted to head the Film Preservation Department at UCLA. His reputation as a bloodhound who sniffed out traces of long-lost celluloid treasures gave birth to an indulgence: He had business cards printed identifying him as a "film detective." He kept his small office, however, explaining that he had enough trouble finding items he'd mislaid without broadening his options. Working out of that cramped venue, Valentino had brought to light nineteen motion pictures whose recovery the cinematic world had despaired of, and was in the process of restoring an additional five.

When the man whose visit would catapult him back eight years knocked on his door, the film detective was in fact deeply ensconced in 1920. Twenty-two feet of the silent feature *Sherlock Holmes*—the key scene between John Barrymore's Holmes and Gustav von Seyffertitz's Professor Moriarty—were jumping and stuttering through the Movieola on his desk. The footage, inexpertly spliced and spotted orange with oxidation, was nevertheless the only significant portion that had surfaced since talkies came in.

Muttering resentment at the interruption, Valentino rewound the reel carefully and placed it in the custom-designed, climate-controlled miniature vault he ruefully referred to as his $12,000 Frigidaire. Then he opened the door to a tall, slender specimen of over-the-hill Malibu surf bum: balding in front, with shoulder-length hair tinted and beautifully styled, and a comfortably threadbare silk sportcoat over a Pink Floyd T-shirt and faded Wranglers. He wore sandals on his bony bare feet.

"Valentino? Man, who's your plastic surgeon?" The man's gaze flicked from his face to Rudolph Valentino's on the framed poster for *The Four Horsemen of the Apocalypse* on the wall behind the desk—the historian's one self-deprecating nod to his immortal namesake—just in case the joke wasn't clear.

Valentino smiled tolerantly. His visitor had a brown paper bundle under one arm. He wondered if this was a marijuana delivery sent to the wrong address. "This is the faculty floor," he said. "I think you want the student lounge downstairs."

"Not unless the movie guy's there. I got something for him." He patted the bundle, which might have contained film reels.

"I'm the movie guy, but if that's your answer to *Endless Summer*, I'm not in the business."

"My name's Elmo Kirdy. You knew my uncle, I think. Justin Ring?"

Valentino searched the man's face, but could see no resemblance to the obese, bearded saurian of Ring's later years. Perhaps there was a little, to photographs taken on the set when he was the *enfant terrible* of a different Hollywood. "I wasn't aware he had any blood relatives."

"Neither was he, apparently, for all the attention he paid my mother, his own sister. He didn't even come to her funeral."

Kirdy's bitter tone made Valentino suspect he'd hacked out a *Mommie Dearest* documentary out of old home movies. The town was full of spoiled industry brats looking to cash in on celebrated dead relatives. He decided to get rid of this one. "I tried to acquire your uncle's student film for the university. He turned me down. That was our only meeting."

"Do you still want it?"

He'd started to close the door. Upon a moment's reflection, he held it for Kirdy to enter. He tried to keep his eyes off the package as the visitor looked around the room, cluttered with film cans, videotapes, and books on cinema history. "I thought you were the big muckety-muck." He sounded disappointed.

"The little muckety-mucks don't get offices. Is that the film?"

"Uh-huh. I found it when I was sorting through some of my mother's things. I'm selling the house. I figured out what it was five minutes after I started watching it on the old family projector. He must have left it with her for safekeeping."

"He didn't give it to her?"

"He might have. I couldn't find anything about it in Mom's old letters. He never wrote to either of us. Anyway, it's the same thing. She wound up with it."

"Maybe not the same. Ring died intestate. The Internal Revenue Service seized his assets for back taxes as soon as he was declared legally dead. Unless it can be proven that he no longer owned the film at the time his boat sank, the government might have a prior claim."

Kirdy scratched his sunburned chin. "I guess it would be different if he were alive."

"Death complicates things."

"Some things. Others it simplifies. I suppose a thing like this needs special care."

"Quite a bit. That old silver-nitrate stock has a tendency to self-destruct."

Kirdy placed the package on Valentino's desk. "Why don't you put it in a safe place until the lawyers finish hassling it out? If there's anything left you can make me an offer."

"I'll give you a receipt." Valentino opened a drawer. He hoped Justin Ring's nephew didn't notice how badly his hand was shaking.

"Not necessary." Kirdy opened the door and stepped out into the hallway.

"Wait! You haven't told me where I can get in touch with you."

"I know where you are." He looked back. "Are you going to watch the film?"

"I screen everything that comes through this office."

"It'll hook you. It hooked me, and I don't like movies much. Do you know what it's about?"

"No."

"It's the story of an artist who fakes his own death."

For a long time after Kirdy left, Valentino stood staring at the bundle on his desk. He wondered if he'd been made the victim of a con. Two or three times a year someone tried to sell him information on the whereabouts of von Stroheim's *Greed* or the scrapped footage from *All Quiet on the Western Front,* and he'd developed a sixth sense for phony tips that spoiled his appetite. So he skipped lunch and took the package to the screening room.

The film, which ran just under forty minutes, suffered from most of the problems associated with an amateur effort, but showed definite signs of a genius in the making. Some of the angles and dolly shots were far ahead of their time, and the uneven pacing foreshadowed the notorious Ring assonance. The story, about a Gaugin-type impressionist painter who stages his false suicide by appearing to leap into an active volcano and thus creates a demand for his work, was compelling, given Justin Ring's own supposed death four decades later, Valentino found himself paying more attention to the plot than to the directorial technique. If, however, the film was a forgery, the telltale traces of oxidation were nearly impossible to manufacture without the assistance of time. He concluded the film was genuine.

The blank screen filled with possibilities. Justin Ring's age and difficult reputation had deprived him of his livelihood. A string of bad marriages, a succession of disastrous cinematic ventures, and tax woes had backed him into a corner he had sought to escape from temporarily by sailing around the world. Then, like the *dues ex machine* endings he delighted in working into his films, a sudden storm and the Great Barrier Reef had conspired to free him from all his worldly obligations. If like his fictional painter, he had rigged his disappearance, his stubborn refusal to allow his student project—his blueprint—out of his hands was explained. It was conceivable that he had destroyed every print in his possession while forgetting all about the one he had placed in his sister's safekeeping sometime back.

Valentino rewound the reels and returned them to their cans. These were automatic actions and unshackled his mind to think.

Justin Ring's first film had to be preserved. It was in the best interest of posterity that the work be done by the experts at UCLA. As long as Ring was legally dead, the only way to proceed without fear of repercussions was to notify the Internal Revenue Service, which would likely attach both reels and store them in some uninsulated barn of a government warehouse where they would deteriorate from humidity and neglect.

Tough decision.

Yeah, right.

Back in his office, he placed the reels in the vault and spent an hour pawing through old filmscripts, yellowed memos, and forgotten actors' faces pickled in ancient publicity stills until he found the composition book containing his notes for the time he had visited Ring's house. Twenty minutes more to decipher his fugitive personal shorthand, then he flipped on his intercom.

"Ruth, I need you to find a telephone listing for a fellow named Ki. He was Justin Ring's houseman eight years ago."

"Ki, Kay Eye?" Ruth's vocal cords had been destroyed by cigarettes when Sam Goldwyn was a pup.

"I think so."

"First name or last?"

"I have no idea."

"Well, what city?"

"I don't know."

"What *do* you know?"

"He's Asian. Chinese or Korean, I think. He was old when I met him. I'm not even sure if he's still alive."

"And they call *you* the detective." She clicked off.

With nothing more to be done, he clamped *Sherlock Holmes* back onto the Movieola and resumed his viewing; but his attention wandered and he found himself wondering what Holmes would have done with the Justin Ring thing.

Ruth buzzed him five minutes before quitting time.

"Fortunately," she said, "there's only one domestic placement service the cream of Hollywood trusts with its precious tchotchkes. *Un*fortunately, they destroy their employment records after five years. Fortunately, a Korean-American named Ki Wan, seventy-four, worked opening doors and bottles of Perrier for Barbra Streisand year before last."

"Which house?"

"The Art Deco. What sort of bonus do I get for all this gumshoe labor?"

"A brand new pair of Nikes."

"Keep 'em. I've worn heels for fifty years. Can't walk in anything else." She gave him Ki Wan's telephone number.

The house was a small stucco box with a faded red tile roof, identical to its neighbors in Tarzana's original housing tract. Valentino found the old Korean, who lived alone, the precise opposite of the inscrutable Oriental of story and film: His guttered face became animated when he spoke of his grandchildren, whose pictures crowded the mantel above the false fireplace in the tiny parlor, and he was not satisfied until his guest agreed to drink something, even the humble glass of ice water he eventually brought. Apart from a pronounced rounding of his back and shoulders, Ki appeared not to have aged in eight years.

The veil dropped into place when Valentino mentioned Mr. Cortez.

"Know no such name." Seated in the wicker chair opposite his guest with his gnarled hands on his knees, he resembled an ivory idol in a Fu Manchu film.

"It might take some remembering," Valentino said. "You brought Mr. Ring a telephone near the end of my visit. He was quick to take it when you said the caller was Mr. Cortez."

"Know no such name."

Ki's expression was as final as a closing credit. Valentino sighed and stood. He held out one of his cards. "Please call me if anything comes back. The university will pay for reliable information."

Ki started to take the card. His eyes went to the line reading "Film Detective." His hand recoiled as if from a snake.

"No take." He clamped his knees.

Valentino started to put the card on the low tea table between the chairs.

"No. Leave. Go, please."

The old man's face, "scrutable" once more, was distorted with fear. Valentino returned the card to his wallet, thanked him for his hospitality, and left.

He used the cellular telephone in his car to make an appointment with Sergeant Zuma at Los Angeles City Hall.

Pete Zuma was a handsome Chicano, sleek-haired and careful in his dress, who had turned down a role in a feature motion picture to continue his career with the L.A.P.D. The role had gone to Al Pacino and Puma was content to limit his show business involvement to an occasional consultancy. Valentino had met him at Zoetrope, showing Harvey Keitel how to operate a Belgian semiautomatic pistol. They had several interests in common, including the love of movies, but this was the first time the film detective had ever consulted the police detective on a matter involving Zuma's specialty.

"So he mistook you for a real detective and it frightened him." The sergeant, wearing a custom shirt and seventy-five-dollar tie, leaned back in his desk chair with his hands behind his head. "After you called I punched up Ki's name on the computer. He's clean, so it's not the police he's afraid of."

Valentino admired a framed photograph of a three-year-old Pedro Zuma sitting on the lap of a long-forgotten Mexican movie star in a tight gaucho costume. He'd been star-struck almost as long as Valentino. "What did you get on Cortez?"

"See for yourself." Zuma tore a long sheet off the printer on his credenza and gave it to him.

The sheer length of the arrest record made Valentino whistle. "How long has he been in San Quentin?"

"Never did a day. See that 'N/C' at the end of every entry? Means 'no conviction.' The cops in three countries have been trying to nail Refugio Cortez for fifteen years. He was a small-time Colombian druglord until he managed to elect a president there. The president was assassinated three years later, but by then he'd gone international."

"What would a Colombian druglord be doing calling Justin Ring?"

"He was too big even then to be acting as a Hollywood connection. Maybe he's a fan."

"The way Ring jumped to take the call, you'd have thought he was the head of Paramount. Also Ring wouldn't speak until I was out of earshot."

"You said Ring's boat went down near Australia?"

He nodded. "It's a long way from Colombia."

"Maybe so, but Cortez owns a shipping company there. He also has legitimate investments in New Zealand and the Solomons. A real Horatio Alger story, as told by Al Capone."

"How did Cortez manage to elect a Colombian president?"

"The details vary. One story is he financed a propaganda film that made the candidate look like a combination of George Washington and Mother Theresa, but that's fishy. Pompon-waving in that part of the world is a clumsy affair. It wouldn't take in an ignorant peasant."

"Who was in charge of making the film?"

"I can't bring that up on my terminal. The department's computer barely has room to store criminal records. It's no crime to make a movie, although it ought to be in certain cases."

The film detective thanked him for his help, made a date for lunch later in the week, and left.

Shortly after midnight, a frantic knocking at the front door of Valentino's house woke him from a deep sleep of exhaustion and frustration. He threw on a shirt and trousers and went down in slippers. A young Hispanic in a sweatshirt, with his hair disheveled, stood on the other side of the peephole looking worried. Valentino opened the door on a flood of Spanish. The homeowner, who knew a little Spanish, told him to slow down.

On the second round he caught *accidente* and *esposa*. Haltingly, he asked the man if his wife was injured.

"*Sí, daño.*" The young man's eyes swam with tears.

Valentino told him to remain calm and turned back inside to call as ambulance. Something hard prodded his right kidney.

"Is a gun, *hermano*," the man hissed in his ear. "Come with me or I blow out your spine."

He was hustled into a white stretch limo at the end of the driveway. The man sat next to him with his revolver resting in the crook of his arm, pointed at Valentino. The back the driver's head was a mile away. They rode without conversation to the top of Mulholland, where a helicopter waited with its blades feathering. Valentino was prodded out of the car and into the seat behind the pilot. Next to the pilot sat a white-haired man wearing a headset. The man was monstrously fat—fatter even than Justin Ring—and had on sunglasses, which the film detective thought pretentious so long past dark. The fat man smiled across the back of his seat, tapping his headset. Valentino found another just like it on the seat beside him and put it on. By then they were airborne, swinging in a broad are over the panoply of light that was Los Angeles after sunset.

"Valentino." The voice in his earphones was lightly accented. "Spanish or Italian?"

"Italian, on my father's side." Valentino spoke into his mouthpiece. "I'm going to take a wild guess and say yours is Cortez."

"An unsecured loan from the great conquistador, I'm afraid. I have family back home that needs protecting. I apologize for our deception. I couldn't be sure you would agree to a meeting."

"Your man's a talented actor." He thought he could see the lights of the limousine carrying the young man back down toward the valley.

"I'll tell him you said so. So far the only work he's been able to get is as an extra. Why are you asking all over town about Justin Ring?"

"I've only asked in two places."

"That isn't an answer. Julio."

The pilot leaned over and opened the door. The air rushed in at Valentino. The helicopter went into a steep bank and he had to clutch his seat to keep from sliding out. There were no safety straps of any kind in the backseat. The helicopter banked the other way and the pilot yanked the door shut. Valentino's heart bounded between his ear phones.

"Julio trained in the Persian Gulf," Cortez said. "He can perform maneuvers with a helicopter that the aerodynamists insist are impossible. Your body will be found lying six inches deep in the pavement on. Santa Monica Boulevard. If you wish to avoid becoming one of Hollywood's enduring mysteries, you need only tell me what your interest is in Justin Ring."

"I want to acquire his student film for the UCLA archives."

"Julio."

The door popped open and the helicopter banked again, more steeply Valentino sank his nails into the seat's slick vinyl surface. The bank went on forever. He started to slide.

"The truth, Mr. Valentino."

"It *is* the truth! I swear it!" The wind skirled up inside the legs of his trousers.

"All right, Julio."

The correcting bank slammed the door shut without the pilot's help.

"Justin Ring is dead," said Cortez.

"His nephew suspects otherwise."

"Why?"

When Valentino hesitated, Cortez sighed and looked at Julio.

"No! Please don't. Ring's student film is about a man who rigs his own death and then goes into hiding. It made us both suspicious. For my part, a live Ring would be easier to negotiate with than a tangled estate."

"What is the nephew's name?"

"He doesn't know anything."

"I'm a busy man, Mr. Valentino. I don't have time to show everyone in Southern California the view from my airship. I merely want his name so I can verify what you're saying. Once more, Julio."

"Elmo Kirdy."

The fat man swung his head around fast enough to dislodge his earphones. Then he began to laugh deeply and heartily, as only a man can who was born to a Latin culture. When at last he ran out of laughter: "Please forgive me, Mr. Valentino. As you Americans used to say in your wartime films, this trip was not necessary. Take us back, Julio."

When they were on the ground with the rotors slowing, Cortez removed his headset. "Don't be embarrassed by your fear, my friend. Ki Wan is old and difficult to frighten, but he was swift to call me after you spoke with him this evening."

Valentino, recovering, laid down his own set. "I'm a Hollywood brat, Mr. Cortez. That means I'm a lot more easy to scare than I am to embarrass. May I give you one more piece of information you may already possess? Your expression will tell me if I'm right."

The druglord raised a conciliatory hand.

Valentino spoke briefly. After a moment, Cortez grinned broad and bright. The film detective nodded and opened the door. "By the way," he said, "your Sidney Greenstreet needs work."

He walked all the way back to his house, slept peacefully until the alarm woke him, and went to the office. Elmo Kirdy called just before noon. Valentino told him he was prepared to make him an offer for Justin Ring's student film. Kirdy agreed to a meeting in Valentino's office in one hour.

He arrived on time, wearing brown corduroys with the ribs worn smooth at the knees and a blue sweatshirt reading HANG TEN FOR JESUS. His beautifully styled silver hair was in place and his face was flushed slightly, as if he'd spent all morning at the beach. Valentino stared.

"If there's anything this town has more of than vain movie stars, it's good plastic surgeons," he said. "Yours could run for mayor."

"Hey, man, this is all me. I take care of myself, you know?"

"You can drop the Brian Wilson act, Ring. Your cover's blown."

Kirdy hesitated. Then he grinned, his capped teeth blue-white against his caramel skin. "You *are* a detective," he said. "The surgeon was in Argentina. He couldn't leave because of some work he'd done on certain German emigrés after World War Two. I was his last case before he retired. He wanted to change me completely, but I insisted on maintaining a family resemblance. Maybe I should have tried to pass for a younger cousin instead."

"No, you look young enough to be your own nephew. Ring's sister died childless, by the way. I verified that this morning. Why'd you fake your own death?"

"It was the only way to get out from under. It doesn't matter anymore, now that I'm legally dead. The IRS can't touch me. When this reaches the media, I'll be a hot property: Justin Ring, back from the grave. Maybe I'll be able to swing the financing to continue my career where I left off. I look young enough to slide in under the invisible wire. Trim enough, too."

"Refugio Cortez hired you to shoot a film that would help put his pet candidate in the executive mansion in Colombia. You did such a good job he was happy to help you 'die.' He sent one of his ships to pluck you off your boat near Australia, blew it up, and got you the surgeon and a place to stay while you shed a hundred and fifty pounds so no one would know you."

"My conscience is clear. The rival candidate was backed by a different druglord."

"Cortez almost killed me when I started investigating your death. You should have clued him in."

"I'm sorry about that. I didn't want anyone to get hurt. I just wanted to beat the studio system."

"I'm happy you shot Cortez's film under the pseudonym Elmo Kirdy. It saved my life." Valentino indicated the two film cans stacked on his desk. "What's your price?"

"A press conference announcing my donation of the film. And your presence at the world premiere of my next feature."

"What are you going to call it?"

Justin Ring smiled. "*Lazarus.*"

The Man in the White Hat

A painting the size of a barn door greeted Valentino inside the entrance to the Red Montana and Dixie Day Museum on Ventura. In it, an implausibly young Montana sat astride a rearing white stallion—Tinderbox, of course—smiling broadly and waving his milk-colored Stetson. Across from it hung a more subdued study of Dixie Day, the cowboy hero's wife, younger still and pretty in tailored white buckskins, leading her mare Cocoa. The guard stationed between the paintings found the visitor's name on the guest list and directed him to the reception.

He found the guests shuffling around a floor with a tile mosaic of Montana and Day backed by Old Glory. Scooping a glass of champagne from a passing tray, he wandered along the walls, admiring the framed stills from the couple's many horse operas until someone signaled for attention.

Red Montana in person was not as tall as he appeared on film, and he had put on weight since retirement; his chins spilled over the knot of his silk necktie. His suit, with flared lapels and arrow pockets, was beautifully cut, although it probably hadn't cost much more than his head of silver hair, a tribute to the wigmaker's craft. His voice was reedy with age, but retained an echo of the hearty bray of a circus ringmaster.

"Howdy, friends and neighbors. I ain't tall on speechifyin', so I'll make this short and sweet. As of this moment, the Dixie Day Foundation has raised more than two million dollars for cancer research. Dixie ain't feeling up to joining us, but she asked me special to thank all you folks for opening up your hearts and pocketbooks."

Hands clapped, flashguns went off. The cowboy star issued a mock-stern order not to be bashful about "bellyin' up to the cook wagon," and then the assembly broke into small groups. Valentino joined a line waiting to shake Montana's hand. He found the old man's grip surprisingly firm.

"You're that detective feller."

Valentino clarified. "*Film* detective. Actually, I'm just a historian."

"Meet me in the curator's office in five minutes."

There were exhibition rooms off the corridor, but Valentino didn't look inside any of them. He'd heard Montana had had the original Tinderbox stuffed and mounted and was reluctant to find out that the story wasn't just an urban myth.

It was obvious the curator's office actually belonged to Montana. The walls were covered with autographed pictures of him shaking hands with various presidents, Ernest Hemingway, and Albert Einstein. Montana's famous silver-studded saddle perched on a stand behind a desk supporting a computer console and a fax machine. The old man was seated at the desk, signing his name to one of a stack of eight-by-ten glossies at his elbow. He placed it on the stack and thanked Valentino for coming.

"Thank you for the invitation." He'd wondered why he'd been on the list, since neither he nor the UCLA Film Preservation Department had contributed to the Dixie Day Foundation.

"They tell me you can sniff out a foot of silver-nitrate stock in a pile of horse manure."

"I hope I'll never have to," Valentino said. "But I've found portions of lost classic films in some unlikely places."

"I need someone with detective skills. I'd go to a pro, but I've been in the movie business sixty years. I only trust film people. I hear you can keep a secret."

"It's important if I'm going to stay ahead of Viacom and Ted Turner." He wondered where this was headed.

"I'm counting on that." Montana produced a key ring with a silver horse's head attached, unlocked a drawer, and drew out an eight-by-ten Manila envelope. "You're aware my wife is dying."

Valentino expressed sympathy. All Hollywood knew Dixie Day had inoperable cancer and that the couple had chosen to spend her last months raising money for cancer research. Her popularity as the Sweetheart of the Range was an asset to the cause.

"These were faxed to me here last week." Montana opened the envelope and handed him a sheaf of paper.

It was plain fax stock. The images that had been scanned onto the sheets were smudged and grainy, but Valentino recognized Dixie Day's face from her old movies. She appeared no older than twenty, naked in the arms of an unclothed anonymous male.

"Are you sure they're genuine?"

"I checked that out years ago, the first time I saw them. They're enlargements of frames from a stag film Dixie made before she broke in at RKO. I paid a hundred thousand cash for the negative, and what I was assured was every existing print, and burned them. I thought that was the end of it."

"You can never be sure how many prints were made. Do you think it's the same blackmailer?" He gave back the pictures.

"I have no idea. I put the cash in a paper sack in a locker at LAX, as I was instructed in the letter that came with the sample print. The next day the negative and prints came by special delivery. I never made direct contact with anyone. This time I haven't even received a demand. Just these." He jammed the sheaf back into the envelope, returned it to the drawer, and closed and locked it. "I want you to find out who sent them."

"I wouldn't know where to start."

"Talk to Sam O'Reilly. He's living at the Actors' Home."

"Your old sidekick? I thought he died."

"He pretty much did, as far as the studios were concerned: drank himself right out of paying work. He's always blamed me for not going to bat for him. Drunks are never responsible for the jackrabbit holes they step in. It'd be just like him to try and get back at me by running Dixie's reputation."

"Why me? You've offered to match every dollar the Foundation brings in. That means you can afford to hire a private agency and pay for its discretion."

"I told you, I only trust film people. And I've got incentive. Switch off that light, will you, son?"

Valentino flipped the switch next to the door, plunging the room into darkness. At the same moment, Montana pressed something under the desk. A white screen hummed down from the ceiling and a wall panel opened behind the desk, exposing a projector. Montana pressed something else and the projector came on with a whir.

For the next five minutes, the film detective was entranced by ancient black-and-white images of galloping horses and smoking six-guns, accompanied by a tinny soundtrack full of thundering music and hard-bitten frontier dialogue. When his host turned off the projector, it took him a moment to find the light switch.

"*Six-gun Sonata*," Valentino said, recovering. "The first feature to pair Red Montana and Dixie Day. I heard it was lost."

"I bought it from Republic cheap in nineteen forty and put it in a vault. Later I struck off a new master on safety stock and destroyed the original nitrate print. A collector offered me a quarter-million for it last year. I told him I didn't have it. What do I need with another quarter-million? Now I'm offering it to you, payable on delivery of the blackmailer's name."

"I'm really not that kind of detective."

Montana sat back, resting his hands on his paunch. "*Six-gun Sonata* means nothing to me. If you turn me down, I'll burn it."

"What makes that different from blackmail?"

"I didn't say I was better than this scum. Just richer."

Valentino thought. He was reeling from the double blow of finding, then perhaps losing, a cinematic treasure and learning that this champion of the Code of the West had much in common with the blackguards he'd pursued in feature after feature.

"I'll see O'Reilly," he said. "I can't promise anything."

"There's the difference." Montana took a cigar from the box on the desk and produced a lighter with a diamond horseshoe on it. "I can." The jet of flame signaled the end of the meeting.

"He said *that?*"

Sam "Slap" O'Reilly hadn't changed so much physically that the film detective couldn't recognize him from his comic bits in Red Montana movies. The whiskey welts on his long horsey features were new and his hair was thin, but brushed neatly. His room at the Motion Picture Actors Home was as tidy as the man himself, seated in a deep armchair in loose tan slacks, slippers, and a white shirt buttoned to the neck. There was nothing present to mark his career in movies, only family photographs and a letter in crayon from a great-grandchild, tacked to a bulletin board.

"Montana's a liar," he went on. "It's true my drinking cut short my livelihood, but I never asked anyone to bail me out, least of all him. I haven't touched a drop in thirty years."

"What split you up, if not that?" Valentino asked.

"We never did like each other. Audiences liked me, and that was enough to keep me on contract. But I never really hated him until he stole Dixie from me."

"You and Dixie Day?"

He grinned, spurring memories of his old dimwit persona. "I was quite a man with the ladies off the set, guess you didn't know that. But it was a mistake to introduce Dixie to Montana. We were shooting a three-day oater on loan to RKO. He talked to the director and got her a bit, one line. The audience fell for her. Republic signed her and the next thing you know they're both billed above the title. They got married a year later."

"You must resent them both."

"Not Dixie. You can't blame a girl for taking advantage of a break, and anyway I don't think she felt anything for me. I did for her, though. Montana knew that, and he went after her the way he went after money and glory, and God help whoever got in his way."

"That was almost sixty years ago. A long time to be angry."

"I'm not angry. I was for a long time, but I got over it. If I'd married Dixie I'd have messed that up just like I messed it up with the woman I did marry." His face went slack. "Who'd you say you were with, again? My memory isn't so good these days."

"The Film Preservation Department at UCLA. I'm trying to track down a movie Dixie Day made before she met Red Montana." He'd cooked up the half-lie on the way there from the museum.

"I wouldn't know anything about it. I'd only been going out with her a couple of weeks when I brought her to the set. We met at a party. She came there with a cameraman. I'll remember his name in a minute." His mind wandered. "I hear Dixie's in a bad way."

"The doctors don't give her long to live."

"I'm sorry. She was a good old gal, too good for Montana. I hope that crumb doesn't stuff her like he did Tinderbox."

"The cameraman," Valentino prompted.

"Cameraman?" When the muscles in O'Reilly's features let go, he truly looked old. "Uh. Dick Hennessey. I remember his name on account of Hal Roach bounced him later. It was a big scandal at the time. Cops busted him for shooting stag films on the side."

The only promising-looking Richard Hennessey listed in Los Angeles County ran a production company in Pasadena. He answered his own telephone.

"My father was a cameraman," he told Valentino. "He passed away six years ago."

"I'm very sorry. I'm looking for a film he might have shot back in the thirties."

"For Hal Roach?"

"No, it was something on the side."

"Oh, you mean the porno stuff. Can't help you there. The judge had it all burned after Pop was convicted. He did a hundred and thirty-six hours of community service, a record then. Fatty Arbuckle didn't get that."

Valentino didn't bother pointing out Arbuckle was acquitted.

Hennessey's candor had surprised him. "That must be a painful memory."

"Not at all. Pop opened his own photo-supply store and did all right. His films were tame by today's standards. The A studios shoot steamier stuff all the time and get away with an R rating."

"You *saw* some of his stag films?"

"Better than that. I was his assistant. The only ten-year-old apprentice cinematographer in the business."

Hennessey Productions worked out of an ornate old Queen Anne house on San Diego Boulevard. The film detective tiptoed among the cables and equipment cluttering a large room on the ground floor and shook hands with a thickset man in shirtsleeves standing with a director half his age. Nearby a young couple sat up in bed, the woman smoking, the man having his makeup touched up by a technician. They were plainly naked under the sheet.

Hennessey was a ruddy-faced sixty-something, with gold chains around his neck and his hair dyed glossy black. "We're shooting a two-reeler for the

Playboy Channel," he said. "I'm not doing anything Pop didn't do, but now it's respectable."

He and his visitor adjourned to a break room equipped with a refrigerator and microwave oven. They sat down at a laminated table.

"Valentino. Any relation?"

"My father says no. Let's talk about yours."

"Gladly. I owe everything to Pop. He helped me get set up in business and loaned me money to stay afloat through the last recession."

"You don't think it was irresponsible to expose you to his stag operation at such an early age?"

"I was a Hollywood brat. If you want to hear about exposing, talk to the producer who exposed himself to Shirley Temple in his office at Fox. At least my old man taught me a trade."

"Did that trade include Dixie Day?"

Hennessey showed no surprise. "Your eyes would pop out of your head if I told you the names of the future movie queens who took off their clothes for my father. I could make a fortune off cable if those films still existed."

"One of them does."

"It's true the cops missed one when they raided the studio. It was being developed in a custom lab at the time. I remember Pop saying something about it, but I don't know if Dixie Day was in it. It wasn't among his stuff when he died."

"You said he made you a loan before he died. May I ask how much it was?"

"A hundred thousand dollars."

Valentino dropped his gaze. He didn't want the glint to show. "That was generous."

"You could have knocked me over with a chorus boy. I never dreamed anyone could put aside that much selling Minoltas to tourists."

"Did he keep records?"

"He was anal about it. I've got three file cases in the basement. You can take a look if you'd like."

Valentino said, "I'd like."

The Montana-Day "ranch"—the Circle M—comprised fourteen acres in the Hollywood Hills, a tract that cost as much as a thousand-acre spread in Texas. The house was a rambling hacienda, 10,000 square feet of pink adobe with a red tile roof. The guard at the gate was got up like an old-time lawman, complete with Stetson and sheriff's star. He was expecting Valentino and waved him on through.

A stout Mexican woman in maid's livery led the visitor to a bright sunroom walled in with glass on three sides, where an old woman awaited him in a wheelchair. She spoke quietly to a younger woman in a nurse's uniform, who left the room on rubber heels.

"I met the original Valentino once, when I was seven years old," said the old woman. "You favor him."

"So I've been told. Thank you for seeing me, Miss Day. Or do you prefer Mrs. Montana?"

"Miss Day will do." The reply held a harsh edge. She had aged well, and skillful makeup disguised most of the ravages of her illness. The turban she wore to cover the baldness caused by radiation therapy was an exotic touch, but he could still see in her that well-scrubbed, all-American quality that had won the simple hearts of Depression audiences. The Wild West Show glitter she wore in public was conspicuously absent from her present costume of blouse, slacks, and open-toed shoes. "How is Dick Junior? All grown up and then some, I suppose. His father certainly kept him busy around the set."

Over the telephone, he'd told her he'd spoken with Richard Hennessey. "I was afraid you'd deny knowing either of them," he said.

"You can't make the past go away by pretending it didn't exist. Lord knows I would if I thought it would work."

"I spent two hours in Hennessey's basement going through his father's records. He wrote down everything, even the details of his blackmail."

"That alone proves he wasn't cut out for it. He was desperate to save his son from bankruptcy or he never would have considered it. He came to see me while Red was in L.A., supervising the construction of the museum. He brought a print of the film with him. He offered to show it to me in the screening room, but I said that wouldn't be necessary. I knew what was on it. You saw some of the frame enlargements. I had a good body, don't you think?"

"You were a beautiful woman." He didn't know what else to say.

"Poor Dick. Do you know what he was asking for the film? Ten thousand dollars. I told him he could get ten times that from Red. He said he preferred dealing with me. He was so nervous, and so ashamed. I think he'd have given it to me for nothing if it weren't for Junior's situation. He would have been that glad to be out of it."

"Why didn't you pay him?"

"I couldn't. I don't have any money. The museum, this ranch, all the bank accounts and investment portfolios are in Red's name. I haven't had control of a cent since the day we married. I have to ask him for money to visit the beauty parlor. My husband is a mean, stingy man, Mr. Valentino. And that's not even his worst quality."

Valentino said nothing. He felt he was on the verge of learning something he'd just as soon never know; but the hints Dick Hennessey, Sr., had dropped into his daily journal had started him in a direction he couldn't reverse.

"Red has a violent temper. All our friends think I suffer from migraines. That's what Red tells them when they visit and I'm upstairs waiting for my bruises to heal. In nineteen fifty he threw me down a flight of stairs and told the press I broke my leg when I fell while exercising Cocoa, my mare. I won't go into every incident. It galls him to pay the servants as much as he must to keep them from selling the real story to the tabloids."

"Why didn't you divorce him?"

"Weakness. Pride. Red Montana and Dixie Day is one of the great love stories of Hollywood. Who was I to blow apart the fairy tale? The old studio system made us slaves to our public images. By the time I finally stopped caring, it was too late. You get used to living in hell. That doesn't mean you stop hating the devil."

Valentino had begun to experience the same dizzy sensation he'd felt at the museum. "What are you trying to tell me?"

"I haven't many weeks left," she said. "I suppose it's the time for confessions."

"*You're* the blackmailer?"

"Only indirectly. I told Dick he could squeeze a hundred thousand out of Red easily. I even helped him work out the details. The only thing my husband has is the pure white image of Red Montana and Dixie Day. It's an icon. He's built his fortune on it; it's his ticket to immortality. I knew if Dick succeeded I'd never hear a word about it from Red. I was right.

"Dick offered to split the money with me," she went on. "I didn't want it, but I did ask him for one thing."

"A print of the stag film."

She smiled a Dixie smile, straight off the milk carton.

"You shouldn't sell yourself short as a detective. I'd planned to release it to an exhibitor when Red died, but fate forced my hand. In a way I was glad. Now I'd get to watch him suffer."

"You sent him the frame enlargements."

"A very old friend of mine made them in the film laboratory at Sony. I felt the need to torment Red. They'll drive him crazy until I'm gone. He'll think he's safe then. What he doesn't know is I've arranged for my friend to make additional prints and send them to every sleazy theater and cable station in Southern California. Let Red try to exploit *that* for his own glory the way he did my terminal cancer. The only thing I've had since our wedding that was truly mine."

She balled her fists on the arms of the wheelchair. Beneath the makeup her face was a naked skull. "Think of it. However long he outlives me, he'll bear the stigma of the has-been cowboy hero who married Jezebel. And when he's gone, the world will be only too relieved to forget us both."

Suddenly Valentino found that sun-filled room in the Hollywood Hills suffocating. He wanted to be anywhere else.

His hostess misinterpreted his discomfort. "I'm sorry, Mr. Valentino. Whatever my husband promised you, I assure you he won't honor it when he hears the truth. You'd be better off telling him you failed. Is there something I can do to make it up to you? I'd offer to autograph a picture, but I don't think it will be worth much for long."

Valentino thought of *Six-gun Sonata*, that monument to chivalry and innocence, as thin as the celluloid it was made of. He didn't think he could watch it, or any Montana-Day picture, without seeing a bloated egomaniac and his battered, bitter wife. He shook his head and left. He didn't breathe easily again until he'd descended into the smog and smut of Los Angeles.

Picture Palace

"I wait for you, *signore*," said the taxi driver. "*Signore* Diavolo entertains no visitors."

Valentino paid his fare, including a tip in return for the little man's concern. "That won't be necessary. He's agreed to see me."

"I wait." The driver slid a Florence newspaper from above the sun visor and unfolded it.

Giuseppe Diavolo's villa, perched on a hill overlooking the city of Dante, was very much in keeping with the man's work: earthy but elegant. The columns on the portico were discolored and cracked, like those of an ancient ruin, and the marble facing on the walls had been patched many times with plaster of varying quality that faded in different colors, creating a harlequin effect. Valentino had never before visited a director's home that reminded him so much of his movies.

The woman who answered the doorbell was very tall and looked even taller because of her hair—teased and heavily sprayed so that it resembled architecture, and obviously dyed black. It brought out the lines in her face beneath the thick pancake. She wore a long printed dress of heavy silk. "*Sì?*" She looked down at him along the straight length of a nose that belonged on a Greek statue.

"My name is Valentino. Mr. Diavolo is expecting me."

"No." She shut the door.

He rang the bell again. When she opened the door again, he showed her the letter he had brought. "I wrote Mr. Diavolo back in February that I'd be in Florence at this time and would like an appointment. This is his invitation."

She glanced at the sheet, snatched it out of his hand, and pushed the door shut again.

He rang again. The woman's voice came from inside. "Go away! I call police."

As Valentino approached the cab, the driver folded his newspaper and returned it to its place above the visor. "You see?" He started the motor. "Geniuses, they are pigs. I say to my wife, be happy you married *un imbecille*."

Valentino barely heard him. "Do you know where to find the office of *Celluloide?*"

Celluloide was the cinema magazine with the largest circulation in Florence; which meant the driver had to radio his dispatcher for directions. At length he drew up before a crumbling building in a dilapidated neighborhood, collected his fare and another tip, and was still watching his former passenger anxiously when Valentino looked back from the entrance.

A clanking elevator the size of a coffin lifted the visitor to the third floor, where he found the office behind a door with the magazine's name flaking off the frosted glass.

"Angela Mondadori, please."

The underfed male seated behind the front desk looked up briefly from his ancient typewriter, then leaned back and shouted at the top of his lungs. "Angie!"

The clatter of typewriters that filled the shabby room paused not at all. Soon a tall, slender young woman with black hair shorn close to her skull emerged from behind a partition plastered over with playbills and approached Valentino with her dark brows lifted. She was an elegant figure in such a setting, expertly made up in a tailored pink suit that put him in mind of the young Jackie Kennedy. She might have stepped off the cover of an Italian fashion magazine of the 1960s.

When Valentino introduced himself she smiled warmly. "I've enjoyed your letters. Face-to-face I can't believe you're not Rudolph's grandson." Her English was fluent, although charmingly accented.

"We share the same brand of hair oil." His resemblance to the silent-film star whose name he bore never embarrassed him in the company of fellow aficionados. "May I take you to lunch? I'd like to talk."

"Let me take you."

Her car was tiny even by modern standards, a classic. Riding in it, he felt he'd stepped into a frame of *The Bicycle Thief.* She steered them deftly through a succession of twisting streets jammed with traffic, using her horn more often than her brakes, and parked before a restaurant with a terrace that looked out on most of the city. The waiters addressed her as *Signora* Mondadori. Her guest complimented the wine and pasta.

"My ex-husband and I dined here all the time," she said. "I got custody of the place on weekdays."

"*Salud.*" He clinked his glass against hers and drank. "I tried to see your father today. A woman slammed the door in my face twice."

"That would be Constanza. My dear stepmother."

"I showed her *Signore* Diavolo's letter. It got in; I didn't. Has she always been this protective?"

"Until about two months ago, she was one of the most gracious hostesses in Tuscany. Then suddenly she started turning away visitors. Even I can't get in."

He breathed in the air of Tuscany, redolent of spice and tomato sauce and the dust of Caesars. "Giuseppe Diavolo is one of the greatest *auteur* directors of the postwar period. After you gave me his address, I spent months persuading him to donate a print of his masterpiece, *L'enfanti del Inferno*, to the UCLA archives. I'd rather fall on my sword than return empty-handed."

"Constanza claims he's too ill to see anyone, but she won't say if he's consulted a doctor. I know he was treated for a heart condition several years ago. I've called every physician in the city. None has seen him. Am I permitted to dust off a movie cliché and say I suspect foul play?" She smiled nervously.

"Does she fit the role of *femme fatale?*"

"I always felt she married my father for security rather than love, but that's an ancient and honorable custom in Italy. We got on well enough until I started pressing for details."

"Have you tried the police?"

She toyed with her pasta. "I'm unsure of my ground. My parents separated when I was small. My father never visited; his films were more important to him than his family. I suppose I still resent him for that. When I began reviewing films I used my husband's name and built up a reputation independent of Giuseppe Diavolo's. I renewed contact with him last year more as a journalist than as his daughter. We're practically strangers."

"The police don't know that. You should tell them your suspicions and have them accompany you for a visit."

"I envy you Americans." She smiled again. "You refuse to accept the existence of insoluble problems."

"It's all those movies. Everything is resolved inside two hours. Will you let me know how this comes out?" He gave her the name of his hotel.

"Of course. Movies need endings." She summoned the bill.

Il Circolo Sesto was playing on the television in Valentino's room. He doubted it was coincidence; the city of Diavolo's birth was bound to feature his films on the local station regularly. The archivist, who considered this most famous title in the director's *oeuvre* his most murky and pretentious, enjoyed nevertheless the scene in which the hero arm-wrestles the Devil. He stretched out on the bed to watch it and found himself still riveted half an hour later when the telephone jarred him out of the sequence in the Roman catacombs.

"Valentino." He punched the Mute button on the remote.

"This is Angela Mondadori. My stepmother told the police they are welcome to visit, but that if I come with them I won't be admitted."

"Did she say why?"

"No. The police assume my father and I don't get along. 'It is their home, *signora*; we cannot tell them who they must or must not allow to cross their threshold.' " Her impression of an Italian police official came right out of Vittorio De Sica.

"Obviously he's never seen *Open City.*"

"Will you go in with them? We haven't known each other long, but I trust you more than I do the police. If you say everything's all right, I'll believe you."

"Why would your stepmother let me in after barring you? She's turned me away once already."

"Please? I'm frightened. I know I haven't the right, but I *am* his daughter."

He watched Sophia Loren pleading with an impossibly young Marcello Mastroianni on the black-and-white screen at the foot of the bed. When he agreed to accompany the police to Diavolo's door, he wasn't sure which request was more effective; the one in his ear or the one playing out in silence in front of him. He decided, not for the first time, that he had seen far too many movies.

The police inspector's name was Cabrini. He reminded Valentino of Claude Rains in *Casablanca*, minus the urbanity. The archivist was pretty sure Inspector Renault would not sit behind his desk with his cap on, no matter how jauntily it was slanted, nor conduct an official conversation with the remains of his lunch spread out on his blotter and a napkin tucked inside his uniform collar. The pencil moustache, at least, was authentic.

"You are a detective?" Cabrini was looking at Valentino's business card.

"A historian, actually. That bit about 'film detective' is just to get people's attention. Tracking down odd scraps of celluloid can be like a manhunt sometimes."

"I would not know. I am myself an enthusiast of the opera." He returned Valentino's passport. "Since your papers are in order, you are free to visit any public place in our beautiful city. If, however, *Signora* Diavolo refuses to admit you to her house, I cannot argue the point."

"I understand."

"*Buòno.*" The inspector rose, tugged down his short jacket, and led the way to the door. There he glanced down, and with a sheepish expression went back and deposited the napkin on the desk.

Today, Constanza Diavolo had on a sleeveless dress of maroon velvet. Valentino admired the muscle definition in her upper arms, rare in a woman her age. She had been warned by telephone of the visit, and so did not appear surprised to find an official in uniform standing on her porch. Her eyes hardened dangerously when they shifted to Valentino. His thin hope that she would not recognize him from their brief first meeting vanished.

Removing his cap, Cabrini launched into what sounded like a formal apology in Italian. Valentino heard his name. Again the hard look, longer this time. Presently it flickered. She shrugged and opened the door wide.

The entryway was as large as some houses, with sunlight gleaming off polished marble and a number of life-size statues scattered about like guests at a cocktail party. The visitors followed their hostess through a succession of similar rooms, elegantly furnished in mahogany and silk, onto a back terrace whose view of Florence and the broad, unpredictable River Arno made the vista from yesterday's restaurant look like a faded mural. An elderly man in a white linen suit and Panama hat sat at an umbrella-shaded table reading, of all things, *Variety*.

Valentino's throat caught when the newspaper came down, exposing tanned features behind plain black Ray Bans and a neat white pencil moustache beside which Cabrini's was a silly prop. From the crown of his hat to the unlit cigar propped between the fingers of his left hand, the man was an icon. He made the film detective, who met regularly with international stars, feel like a little boy holding an autograph book.

Diavolo shook the inspector's hand, speaking softly in Italian, then switched to English when he grasped Valentino's. "I have enjoyed your letters. Please sit and share my shade."

Constanza withdrew, to return moments later bearing a tray containing glasses and a pitcher of lemonade. She poured and served, then seated herself beside her husband. Valentino noted that no servant had yet made an appearance.

"This is a beautiful home," said Cabrini.

"*Grazie.*" The director flashed his famous white smile. "My best films began here, in my head. It is less a home to me than a national treasure."

Valentino was charmed rather than put off by his host's frank egotism. It was as emblematic of him as his white suits and cold cigar. "I'm surprised you don't invite more people in."

Diavolo understood the implied question.

"My wife is protective of my privacy. I am writing my memoirs, you see, and concentration is a problem. To spare me interruptions she has appointed herself my Cerberus."

"It is a difficult thing to be forced to lie to one's own daughter." The inspector fingered his cap in his lap.

Constanza muttered something in Italian.

Diavolo sipped from his glass. The hand holding the cigar remained motionless on the table. "You forget she is a member of the press. If she knew the truth, she would be after me to publish excerpts in her magazine. So her stepmother tells her I'm ill."

"When will you finish?" Valentino asked. "The world has waited so long to hear you comment at length on your career."

"Six months, a year. *Chi consta*, who knows? I am old, and no studio is pressing for a release date. I shall tell her when I am receiving visitors again."

"About *L'enfanti del Inferno*—" Valentino began.

Constanza turned to the inspector. "You wanted to know, my husband, is he in good condition. You are satisfied?"

"*Sì.*" He stood abruptly and leaned down to shake the director's hand again. "Thank you, *signore*, for your hospitality. I apologize for this interruption."

"*Prego.*"

Cabrini turned a stony face on Valentino, who had no choice but to follow his lead. *Signora* Diavolo thumped the front door shut behind them with finality.

"I don't buy it!" Angela said. "I don't buy it for a minute. It's bunk."

Despite his sympathy, Valentino was amused by the language of her displeasure. It was obvious she had learned her English from old Hollywood movies. They were standing in the lobby of his hotel, where she had been waiting when he returned from her father's villa. She was wearing another tailored suit, this one powder-blue. She reminded him now of Audrey Hepburn.

"I heard it from his own lips," he said. Another old line.

"Since when is he so susceptible to distraction? All his films were created in the midst of chaos. She's got some hold on him, I know it."

"I had the impression once she was coaching him. That means nothing. A lot of old people take direction from their spouses. Even some young creative types depend on someone to prod them into action. He certainly didn't act as if he was afraid of her."

"You're absolutely sure it was him."

"He's almost as recognizable as his stars. I've seen his *Sixty Minutes* interview at least—" He broke off.

"What is it? You just thought of something."

He shook his head. "Probably nothing. I watch millions of feet of film every week; it's easy to get mixed up. Do you have any of your father's interviews on film or tape?"

"At the office. I have my key with me."

"You take all the fun out of breaking and entering."

Angela's desk was no different from the others at *Celluloide* except for the work piled on top. It stood in the middle of the floor without any partitions to separate it from those of the lowly columnists and copywriters whose labor filled the magazine. When she switched on the gooseneck lamp the cone of hard white light reminded Valentino of the monochrome settings of most of Giuseppe Diavolo's early films.

She rummaged through drawers filled with videotapes in cardboard sleeves, found one bearing the hand-lettered label she wanted, and popped it into a combination TV/VCR on the desk. The tape contained an interview with the director on Italian television. Diavolo sat in a plastic scoop chair on a bare soundstage with his legs crossed and one hand holding an unlit cigar resting on his raised knee. He wore a white suit and black sunglasses, just as he had on his terrace. Only the Panama hat was missing, exposing his full head of snowy hair.

"Shall I translate?" Angela asked.

"Not necessary. Doesn't your father ever light his cigars?"

"No. He only holds them to make that hand look natural. He lost the use of it when the Allies bombed his village during the war."

"That's what I'd heard." He leaned his face close to the screen, then straightened. "Your eyes are younger than mine. Can you read the monogram on his shirt pocket?"

"G.D.," she said after looking. "What did you expect?"

"I wanted to be sure the film wasn't reversed. That happens sometimes, by accident or design. Whenever William Bendix stepped up to the plate in *The Babe Ruth Story*, they reversed the negative so he appeared to bat from the left side, like Ruth. The editors didn't seem to mind that he ran the bases backwards. If the monogram reads all right the film wasn't tampered with."

"What does that have to do with my father?"

When Valentino looked at her, his excitement turned to sympathy. "It means you may have to prepare for the worst."

She parked the little car down the hill from the villa and they got out. It was a clear night; the archivist could scarcely tell where the stars ended and the lights of Florence began. "Do you think you can keep her from slamming the door in your face long enough for me to walk around to the terrace?"

"I can try. Are you sure we shouldn't call the police?"

"With no more than we have to go on, I wouldn't be surprised if Inspector Cabrini fined you and deported me for invading the privacy of Florence's most distinguished citizen."

As she rang the doorbell, he slipped around the corner of the house and waited between two windows, hugging the wall like Cary Grant in *North by Northwest*. When he heard the door open he hurried to the back of the house and stepped onto the terrace.

It was deserted. He tried the back door. It was locked. He sagged against it, cursing every movie he had seen in which illegal entry was so much more convenient. At that instant a latch turned on the other side with a dry rasp. He scrambled behind a tall planter just as the door opened and Giuseppe Diavolo came out.

Except it wasn't Diavolo.

The man in the white suit whom Valentino had met that afternoon wore neither hat nor glasses. His pink bald head gleamed in the light of the electric lamps flanking the door. He had not a strand of the impressive white hair of the man in the television interview. The film detective was still assimilating that fact when the bald man drew a cigar from an inside pocket and set fire to it with a lighter, using both hands.

Valentino stepped out from behind the planter. "Who are you?" he demanded.

The bald man started and turned. Rapidly his expression changed from shock to recognition to a bluff smile.

"*Signore* Chaplin, is it not? I did not hear Constanza announce you."

"The name is Valentino. And yours is not Diavolo. Who are you?"

He puffed at the cigar, obviously framing an argument. Then he looked at the hand holding the cigar, and from that to the other in which the lighter still rested. At that moment he appeared to shrink in upon himself like a balloon deflating.

The back door banged open and Constanza Diavolo tore out onto the terrace. She was still wearing the maroon velvet dress and her face flushed nearly as dark when she saw the hatless impostor and Valentino standing together. Valentino stepped back involuntarily from the flood of harsh Italian that rushed out at him.

Angela Mondadori appeared in the doorway. "I couldn't hold her any longer." Then she saw the bald man wearing one of her father's white suits. "Who are you?"

"I'm waiting for that answer," Valentino said.

Signora Diavolo added gestures to her diatribe, slashing her sharp-nailed hands at the air. The bald man said something in Italian, then repeated it in a louder voice. She stopped in mid sentence, looked from one face to another, and burst into tears. "Rovina! *Imbecille*, you have ruined me!" She stumbled over to the table beneath the umbrella and collapsed into a chair with her face in her hands.

Valentino told Angela to call the police. She turned to comply.

"Wait!"

Angela turned back. The bald man lowered the hand he had raised, and with it the last vestige of his facade. His eyes were gray and watery. Valentino wondered how he could ever have mistaken this beaten old man for an immortal director.

"My name is Lloyd Bugleman." The accent now was eastern American, possibly New Jersey. "I'm an entertainer."

Constanza Diavolo moaned, a heart-rending sound. The film detective ignored her. "Entertain us."

"Believe it or not, I've faced tougher rooms." Bugleman's attempt at humor died in the silence. He cleared his throat. "My impressions didn't go over so well at home, so I came here, where they're not so particular about my Jimmy Cagney. My mother was Italian. She taught me the language."

"She did a good job," Valentino said. "You managed to fool an Italian police official."

"It helps that I look so much like Giuseppe Diavolo. People trust their eyes more than their ears. When Constanza's brother caught my act he was impressed enough to offer me an extended gig for three times what I was making in that ratty little club in the suburbs. All I had to do was study Diavolo's TV interviews, put on the suit, and do my act for visitors who wouldn't go away. He said it was just a job," he added quickly.

"It isn't my brother's fault. Don't blame Roberto."

Angela and Valentino looked at Constanza. She was staring at the flagstones now with her hands limp. There might have been a time when her tears would have added to her fragile beauty. Now they merely made ugly tracks in her heavy makeup.

"Where is my father?" Angela's voice was toneless.

"He died. Two months ago. It was his heart, I think. He went to sleep one night and I could not wake him in the morning."

Valentino said, "Why didn't you call the police?"

"He was dead and cold. There was no use."

"When a man dies, you're supposed to report it," Angela said. She seemed about to say more, but stopped when Constanza raised her head to look at her. She was no longer crying. Her eyes were dead.

"I was born *povero, misero*." She looked at Valentino. "There is no proper word for it in English; *poor* does not answer. Giuseppe willed this house, this property, everything in it, to the government in Rome. For a museum, he said. He didn't care about me. Only his memory. I could not be *povero* again."

"Where is my father's body?" Angela's voice broke.

"Under these stones. Roberto buried him. Do not blame him. He was only helping his sister." Her eyes came to life, softened. "I am so sorry I did what I had to do to you. You were the one person Bugleman could not have fooled."

Bugleman spread his hands. "They didn't tell me any of this. It was just a gig to me. You'll tell the police I cooperated when I found out."

"Not asking the questions you didn't want to know the answers to doesn't make you innocent." Valentino was cold.

Angela said, "Constanza is right."

All eyes were on her. She stood framed in the doorway, a tall, beautiful young woman with not a little of her father's presence.

"If my father cared as much for people as he did for his legacy, this would not have happened. I know how it feels to be abandoned through no fault of one's own. I can't punish Constanza for that."

"The authorities have to be told," Valentino said. "If they find out on their own, it will go a lot harder for her."

Angela went over and sank down on one knee beside her stepmother. "*Celluloide*'s copyright attorney belongs to a large firm. He'll recommend a good criminal lawyer, as well as a probate attorney who will see that you receive a decent settlement from my father's estate. You were with him almost twenty years. There are laws to protect you."

Constanza shook her head. "I cannot afford lawyers."

"The magazine can. I have backers."

"What's in it for the magazine?" asked Valentino.

"First screening privileges on all the Diavolo films that have been in storage for forty years. That is, if Constanza agrees."

"But I do not own them."

"That will be the settlement."

Her stepmother's face filled with wonder. In that moment she looked no older than Angela. "I do not go to *il penitenzario?*"

"I'm the daughter, and the injured party. I'll testify on your behalf. You may have to pay a fine for improper disposal of a body." Angela made a wry face at Valentino. "We can introduce a respected historian from America as a character witness. I think the donation of a print of *L'enfanti del Inferno* to the UCLA archives would be an appropriate gesture of gratitude."

Valentino said, "She's the finest woman I've ever known."

Angela stood and helped Constanza to her feet. The two women went into the house, one supporting the other with an arm across her back. Valentino and Lloyd Bugleman were left alone on the terrace. The entertainer relit his cigar, the flame shaking. He took a puff and let it out with a shudder. "So what happens to me?"

"Back to the ratty little club."

He nodded. Then he narrowed his eyes. "I thought I had my act down cold. What tipped you off?"

"The cigar. You held it in your left hand. It was Diavolo's right that was paralyzed. The cigar was a prop to discourage people from grabbing and shaking it."

Bugleman looked down at his hands. "Constanza told me about that in the beginning. I tried to make the switch, but it just didn't feel right after all those weeks onstage. I didn't think anyone would notice."

"Next time, don't rehearse in front of a mirror," Valentino said.

The Day Hollywood Stood Still

"**K**laatu barada nikto."

"I'm sorry?"

In confusion, Valentino repeated the phrase. "You know," he said. "From the original. If Patricia Neal got it wrong, Michael Rennie was dead. I thought it might break the ice."

Quincy Dundrear, twenty-four, with his head shaved clean as a stone and one nostril pierced with a pearl the size of a thumbtack, scratched his chest through a black T-shirt with a pair of pigs making love on the front. His last two pictures had made a billion and a half for Fox.

"I thought you were remaking *The Day the Earth Stood Still*," Valentino said. "If you've forgotten everything else about the film, you're sure to remember *Klaatu barada nikto.*"

"I'll take your word for it. I never saw the picture. We're going a different direction this time. When the alien stops all the power on earth, the fire engines can't get around and L.A. burns to the ground."

"L.A.? The original took place in Washington, D.C."

The young director wrinkled his nose. The pearl looked like a giant zit. "Washington's so done since *Independence Day*. We're going to blow up the Hollywood Bowl and the Hall of Justice."

"What's Gort doing while all this is going on?"

"Gort?"

"The giant robot. The one Patricia Neal had to persuade to bring Michael Rennie back to life and save the world from destruction."

"Why would she want to do that? No explosions, no box office. You have to wonder how the industry got along before *The Terminator*."

"So no Gort."

"If that's his name. We're making the robot small and cute, like R2-D2. Our villain's scary enough; an oil company CEO who wants to demolish a homeless center in East L. A. so he can drill for crude."

"He shouldn't have to drill too deep in this movie."

Valentino shifted his weight in the beanbag chair. Dundrear's office was done entirely in early seventies, complete with orange shag wall-to-wall and *Charlie's Angels* posters in frames. The director was leaning against one of those clunky dark-veneer-over-chipboard desks with phony chisel marks.

He looked at his watch, a gold Rolex on a chain around his bare neck. "Who did you say sent you?"

"UCLA. I'm with the Film Preservation Department. We have the master print of the 1951 *Day the Earth Stood Still* and we want to strike a new print and digitally enhance the soundtrack for video re-release, to coincide with the premiere of your version. We'll divide the profits with Fox in return for distribution rights. You producer likes the idea, but he suggested I talk to you so we're all on the same page."

"What'll you do with your end?"

"Invest it in film preservation. Did you know ninety percent of all movies made before sound are lost forever? We want to prevent such attrition in the future."

"Why?"

"Well, as a cinematic artist yourself, I'm sure you agree that the classics of the form should remain available for appreciation and study. You must have gone to film school."

"I quit tenth grade to direct rock videos. I went from there to TV commercials. In between jobs, I shot a slasher flick on a ten-thousand-dollar budget. It grossed two million domestic, and here I am."

"Why'd you choose to remake a picture you haven't seen and care nothing about?"

"Financing. All these rich computer geeks sat through it a thousand times. The title alone saved making a pitch. They couldn't turn out their Swiss bank accounts fast enough. From what I hear, there were almost no special effects in the original; that'll add the extra half-hour the running time needs and dress up the trailer. Also there's a babe, an obnoxious kid, and a jerk boyfriend. The casting call will look like an episode of *Entertainment Tonight*."

"Who plays the alien?"

"Jim Carrey's looking for a change of pace."

Valentino needed a change too. "What about the rights to distribute the original?"

"Officially I have no control over that, but if the studio agrees to give them to you, I'll walk. The last thing I need is another property competing with mine."

"That doesn't say much for your property."

Dundrear's tongue came out when he smiled. A silver stud glittered in the ambient light. "When *Godzilla* tanked the first weekend, sales and rentals on the original spiked up forty percent. If the videotape hadn't been available, the new film might have made back its investment Saturday night. I didn't get this job by sitting around letting history repeat itself."

"In that case we have nothing to talk about." Valentino stood.

"Stay in touch. I'll send you two tickets to the premiere."

"No, thanks. I'll wait till it comes out on video."

Franklin Poll, Quincy Dundrear's producer, had changed in the years since his first directorial effort, a gritty crime drama set in his native Chicago, had revolutionized the gangster movie. He'd put on weight, shorn his curly locks, and trimmed his beard, now streaked generously with silver; but the eyes behind the granny glasses were bright, and his voice was youthful. He welcomed Valentino back into his office with a firm handshake and sat him down in his prized Eames chair. The walls were paneled in teak and bare but for a huge original four-sheet poster of *Captain Blood* mounted behind the desk, where his Oscar for Best Direction stood on display. Poll took a seat on the Eames footstool with his hands gripping his thighs.

"What did you think of Quincy?"

"Not much," Valentino said. "He's a snotty kid well on his way to becoming a full-grown jackass."

"Agreed. But a jackass with talent. How he manages his narrative pace without leaving half his audience in the dust is beyond me. In film school, we thought the screwball comedies of the thirties moved quickly, but *Bloodslide* makes *Blonde Crazy* look like *Ivan the Terrible*."

"If you told him, he wouldn't know what you're talking about. He has little interest in cinema history and less respect."

"He's not alone. This new crowd knows only jump cuts and blackouts. They grew up on MTV. But they bring the kids into the theaters, and that's all the studios care about." The adolescent tenor took on a bitter edge.

"He said he'd quit the picture if Fox gives UCLA the distribution rights to the original *Day the Earth Stood Still*."

"I was afraid of that. He wouldn't know it, but he'd be right at home in the old Hollywood with that attitude. We almost lost the Fredric March *Dr. Jekyll and Mr. Hyde* in 1941 because MGM didn't want it to compete with the Spencer Tracy version. They bought up every print and ordered them destroyed. Those old moguls were ruthless businessmen."

"You're not going to let him get away with it, are you?"

Poll spread his hands. His fingerprints had been worn off by contact with miles and miles of safety stock. "I'm up a tree. The industry's in love with Quincy just now. When he has his first flop, I'll get back some leverage."

"He's doing a hack job on one of the most significant pictures of the Nuclear Age. That's his business—and Fox's—but no one has the right to censor a classic for any reason. Especially not when it's for his own selfish ends."

"Calm down, Val. Wait till Quincy's package leaves the theaters. If it's a hit, he won't care if the original shares the video racks with the remake, and if it falls on its face, it won't matter."

Valentino struggled to his feet; the best-engineered chair in the world was almost impossible to get out of. "No pipsqueak Roger Corman is going to stand in the way of cinema art. This isn't the end."

Poll smiled crookedly in his beard. "That line's got whiskers. You ought to get out and see a new movie every now and then. It will brighten up your dialogue."

"*Down to the Loop* was the first great Hollywood film since *Lawrence of Arabia*," Valentino said at the door. "It restored my faith in the industry. I never thought the man who shot it would end up just another schlockmeister."

The smile turned sour. "It doesn't happen all at once It's the death of a thousand cuts."

He had an appointment in Tarzana with a retired U.S. Navy cameraman who claimed to be sitting on 25,000 feet of battle film unseen since World War II, but he called and postponed. For once in his life, Valentino hadn't the stomach to discuss old movies. Instead, he went home to his private screening room and watched the master of *The Day the Earth Stood Still*. By the time Michael Rennie, as the messenger from outer space, broke into the study of Sam Jaffe's Einstein-like scientific genius to correct his arithmetic, Valentino was enthralled and at peace.

His door buzzer sounded just as Rennie was delivering the doomsday speech at the end. Valentino waited until the flying saucer took off, the camera following it into the cosmos, and then the closing credits, while the buzzer razzed again. He turned off the projector and went out to answer.

"Did I get you out of bed?" The flat blue eyes of the stranger on the doorstep took in Valentino's fully dressed condition without expression.

"I was watching a movie. May I help you?"

The man showed a gold badge attached to a pigskin folder. "McPherson. I'm a sergeant with L.A. Homicide. You're Valentino?"

Nodding, he felt a smile coming on. "*Mark* McPherson? Like in *Laura?*"

"Henry. I wish you Hollywood types would get your heads out of pictures once in a while."

"Sorry, I should know better. Has there been a murder in the neighborhood?"

"Can I come in?"

Valentino stepped aside. The sergeant had fair hair and delicate features and was probably routinely carded whenever he entered a bar. His blue suit was inexpensive but fit his slight frame snugly. His gaze swept the living room and alighted on his host. "Where were you this evening?"

"Here. I said I was watching a movie. It *isn't* a neighborhood murder, is it?"

"What makes you say that?"

"If it were, you'd be treating me more as a witness than a suspect. To answer your next question, I've been alone all evening. There's no one to verify I didn't go out. Who's dead?"

"A director at Twentieth Century Fox named Quincy Dundrear. You had a fight with him this afternoon."

Valentino felt shock, then a great emptiness. He didn't mourn Dundrear so much as a life snuffed out so early.

"It wasn't a fight," he said. "He didn't see eye to eye on a matter I thought important. Who'd you talk to, Franklin Poll?"

"Most innocent people would be curious to hear how Dundrear was killed."

"Why should that matter to anyone but the police? I've been involved in homicide investigations before, Sergeant. I'm not as curious as I was in the beginning."

McPherson's eyes were like cheap enamel, without depth. They were unreadable. "I understand you're some kind of film historian. How is it you've been involved in homicide investigations?"

"My business cards identify me as a film *detective*, which describes the main part of my work more accurately. I track down and collect lost films, often in bits and pieces. I travel a great deal, and it's a competitive market. Since videos entered the picture, it's become a lucrative one as well. Where there's money, there's often murder."

"Fair answer. A little glib."

"I watch a lot of movies. The dialogue rubs off."

"Uh-huh. Somebody beat Dundrear to death, probably with a baseball bat, sometime between six-thirty, when his secretary went home, and seven-fifteen, when the janitor found his body. There was plenty of blood."

"My God."

"The autopsy will tell us more. It was definitely a rage killing. You fought with Dundrear over movie distribution rights. When Franklin Poll backed him up, you said,"—he took out a spiral notepad and flipped it open to a dog-eared page—" 'No pipsqueak Roger Corman is going to stand in the way of cinema art. This isn't the end.' Some people would consider that a threat." He flipped the pad shut and put it away.

"I meant I'd go over Poll's head. He doesn't run the studio and neither does Dundrear."

"But you didn't go over his head. You canceled an appointment you had and went home. According to you."

"If you know I canceled an appointment, you checked with my secretary. I told her when I called I was going home. I needed to cool off before I talked to anyone else."

"So you admit you were angry."

"I'm angry now. An arrogant punk like Dundrear is bound to have plenty of enemies. You ought to save some energy for the others. I didn't' kill him, Sergeant."

McPherson stirred, produced a pager, and asked for a telephone. Valentino pointed it out next to the armchair from the *Maltese Falcon* set. The sergeant dialed, listened, said, "Be there in twenty," and hung up. His eyes were still unreadable.

"We'll continue this later. That was an all-units call. We got a bomb threat."

"Where?"

"Fox."

Alone, Valentino turned on the TV. All the local stations were covering the story, but none had details. Cameras on the street captured only barricades and police from the bomb squad suiting up in lead shields and visored helmets that reminded him of Gort the robot in the movie he'd watched earlier. Helicopter footage showed only the roofs of office buildings and sound stages at Fox and flashing red and blue lights on the ground.

After thirty minutes, the scene switched to a room at City Hall, where a police inspector named Harrison, with gold leaf on his cap visor, announced to the press that the threat had been made by an anonymous caller to a nightside employee shortly after nine that evening, and that sixteen soundstages had been evacuated while police conducted a search for the explosive device.

"J.R. Roberts, *L.A. Times*," announced one reporter. "What can you tell us about the caller?"

"The studio employee said it was an adult male voice with what sounded like a Brooklyn, New York, accent."

Another reporter, who introduced himself as Jack Fell from the *San Diego Union*, asked, "What were his exact words?"

Harrison consulted his notes. " 'You have twenty-four hours before one of your sound stages is reduced to a burned-out cinder.' We take that to mean he was referring to an incendiary device."

While the inspector fielded a question about the possible motive, Valentino called police headquarters. He persuaded a sleepy-sounding officer to page Sergeant McPherson and give him Valentino's number. Ten minutes later McPherson called.

"It's just a hunch," Valentino said. "Quincy Dundrear was directing a remake of *The Day the Earth Stood Still*. At the end of the original film, Michael Rennie threatens to 'reduce your world'—meaning *our* world—'to a burned-out cinder' if the earth doesn't stop meddling in outer space. Those were the same words used in the bomb threat. It could be a fanatic fan."

"Probably a coincidence." But the sergeant sounded less irritated than he had a moment before.

"What have you got to lose by beginning your search with whatever sound stage Dundrear was shooting on? Franklin Poll can give you that information."

"Maybe the bomber got the same information from Dundrear."

"He could be the killer."

"He could still be you."

"Not with you as my alibi. You and I were standing in my living room when the bomber called in the threat."

"Don't go anywhere. I'll be in touch."

Valentino went to bed. The telephone in the bedroom woke him at six. It was McPherson. He sounded tired.

"We found it. It was on Sound Stage Eight, where they're building the sets for *The Day the Earth Stood Still*. It was an incendiary with a mercury switch on a digital timer, set to go off at nine P.M. The Bomb Squad defused it."

"Glad I could help."

"We're not making it public yet, and we asked Fox to shut down operations for today to make it look good. If this guy thinks we're still looking for the bomb, he won't think we're looking for him. You should have heard them scream."

"Hollywood. Time is millions. A bomb is just a big noise."

"Yeah. We're tracing the components, but that takes time. What do you know about fanatic fans?"

"Sci-fi buffs often have high IQs," Valentino said. "Their social skills usually aren't as impressive. When they're not attending *Star Trek* conventions, a lot of them live in front of their computers. If this one's aim was to stop a cheesy remake of *The Day the Earth Stood Still*, I'd look for a Web site specializing in pre-sixties science-fiction trivia."

"How many thousands of those can there be?"

"Narrow it down to those you can trace to local addresses."

McPherson paused. "You're still a suspect. You could have rigged the bombing to distract us from the murder investigation."

"Get some sleep, Sergeant. You're starting to sound like Boston Blackie."

The morning news reported no new developments in the bombing investigation. Valentino took the master print he'd watched to UCLA and signed in the reels with the librarian in charge of the vault. Ruth, the ancient Cerberus of a secretary in whose services he held part interest, intercepted him outside his tiny office and told him he had a message from a Sergeant McPherson at police headquarters. "Been stealing office supplies again?"

"That was one roll of splicing tape, ten years ago," he said. "Do you ever forget anything?"

"Only every time Harry Cohn tried to get me on his casting couch. He says he'll pick you up downstairs in ten minutes."

"Who, Harry Cohn?"

"Funny guy. I don't need this job, you know. If I ever decided to open my mouth, I could own MGM."

"Forget it, Ruth. Everyone you could blackmail is dead."

"Serves me right for being discreet."

He stepped outside just as an unmarked green Chrysler drove up and McPherson told him to get in. The sergeant looked older and drawn, but he'd changed into a gray suit. As they took off, Valentino asked him if he'd managed to rest.

"I went home and took a shower. Know anything about computers?"

"A little. I'm no hacker."

"I am. These days everyone has a specialty. I figure what you know about fan Web sites can help. Does the name Ernest Sizemore mean anything to you?"

"Not a thing."

"He's got a site devoted entirely to *The Day the Earth Stood Still*. We traced it to an apartment on Sepulveda. We've got men on the scene. Landlady says he works days, but she doesn't know where, always comes home around three. Wait till you see his place."

"He can't be the only one who's crazy about that film. Even in L.A. I could yell out '*Klaatu barada nikto*' on any street and get a positive response."

"Yeah, well, you remember the guy who called in the bomb threat had a Brooklyn accent? According to the landlady, Sizemore moved here three years ago from Flushing."

"That's promising."

"It gets better. We checked him with Social Security. Until he got fired last year for showing up late too many times, he worked in Special Effects at Twentieth Century Fox. He's a demolitions expert."

"Step on it," Valentino said. When the sergeant turned his head to scowl at him, he grinned. "I always wanted to say that."

The apartment was on the fourth floor of a building whose elevator had been out of order since Governor Brown. It was one room with a pull-down bed and dozens of reproduction posters and original lobby cards, in frames, advertising the 1951 version of *The Day the Earth Stood Still.* There was a cramped water closet, a hot plate, and a Macintosh computer with a bullet-shaped monitor and a seventeen-inch screen. The screen saver looked like a revolving agitator from a washing machine, but was actually the spangled interior wall of the circular corridor in Klaatu the alien's saucer-shaped spaceship.

McPherson had left instructions with a plainclothesman in the lobby to call him on his walkie-talkie in five minutes. It crackled. He unclipped it from his belt and spoke into it. "Working. Hit the button when anyone starts upstairs. Let 'em pass." He returned the radio to his belt and rattled some keys on the computer board. When the Web site appeared, the eerie theremin score from the movie came out of the speakers on the sides. Animated icons of Gort, Klaatu in his flight suit, and the flying saucer jigged across the screen.

"Most of the pages are filled with trivia questions and answers," said the sergeant. "He's got a file blocked out by an access code. I could run some at random, but I thought you might have some specific ideas, knowing the film."

Valentino sat in the office chair before the monitor. "It's a little long, but I'll try *'Klaatu barada nikto.'*" He pecked out the phrase.

A box appeared onscreen with the words ACCESS DENIED— INCORRECT PASSWORD inside.

He tried each of the three words separately and got the same message. "Gort" failed next. "Carpenter," Klaatu's alias when posing as a human, was equally disappointing. He tried the names of each of the major characters. He was glad he'd watched the film so recently. When the last, "Bernhardt," didn't work, he tried "burned-out cinder," then each of the three words separately. Nothing.

He sat back, chewing the inside of a cheek, while McPherson checked his watch. What was it Klaatu had said to the robot when he wanted to go into the saucer? The word made him think of a dance: Mambo? Samba? Surely not Lambada. He closed his eyes, willing himself out of the tiny apartment and into the movie. After a moment he smiled. "Meringue."

"What?"

He shook his head and manipulated the keys: MARENGA. The icons continued to jig for another second. Then the screen switched images. The new one resembled a blueprint.

"Floor plan," he said.

"It sure is." McPherson leaned close to the screen. "Only someone who worked at Fox or spent as much time in the building as I did last night would recognize it. It's Sound Stage Eight."

The walkie-talkie crackled. He turned it off, drew a flat pistol from the holster on the other side of his belt, and told Valentino to step into the little water closet and shut the door.

"The city's high on good relations with the studios." Waiting for the light at Cahuenga to change, McPherson rubbed his bloodshot eyes. "Franklin Poll wants to thank the men responsible for collaring Sizemore, so instead of going home to sleep, I get to run you over to Fox and collect a pat on the head."

"I heard Sizemore confessed," Valentino said. A day had passed since the arrest on Sepulveda. The bomber, a small man with a prematurely bald head, had submitted without resistance.

"To planting the bomb and making the threat. He was a disgruntled employee, plus he'd heard when he was working there that Quincy Dundrear was going to hack the remake. He decided to take his revenge *and* strike a blow for the original. He sounds a little like you. You can see why you made a good suspect."

"He hasn't taken the blame for Dundrear's murder?"

"Not yet. He will. A lot of perps cop to the lesser charge first."

"I hope you're right. I can't help wondering why he'd bother to plant the bomb after killing the director. That would have shut down the project just as well."

"So he's the careful type. Belt and suspenders."

"Then why make the call? He'd killed once; why give Fox the chance to evacuate the rest of its employees?"

"If you keep asking questions you'll talk yourself back into being a suspect." The light changed. McPherson drove on.

Franklin Poll's outer office was filled with visitors, all of whom glanced up from their magazines and manicures when the intercom buzzed. There had been a subtle shift of power in the studio, Valentino could tell; Poll had once again become The Man to See. The attractive Asian receptionist smiled up at the newcomers and told them to go on in.

Poll sprang up from behind his desk and vaulted across the room to shake McPherson's hand and then Valentino's. He looked nearly as youthful as he sounded. The only grave thing about him was the black armband stitched to his right sleeve.

"Splendid job, gentlemen," he greeted them. "Quincy is a great loss, but I don't mind telling you how good the morale is around here since you put that animal behind bars so quickly."

McPherson said, "We caught a couple of breaks. One of them was Valentino here."

Poll shook a finger at Valentino. "I know what *you'd* like, and it's yours. When *The Day the Earth Stood Still* is in the can, UCLA will have exclusive distribution rights to the original. Mind, I don't know when that will be. We have to find a new director, and when a major studio is forced to stop production for an entire day, there's no telling how long it will take to get back up to speed."

"Congratulations, Franklin. Looks like you're back in charge."

"I'm a survivor. So's Quincy, in a way. The new film will be dedicated to him, of course, and there's talk of naming a special award for him at the Academy."

That was it. Valentino had been aware that there was something different about Poll's office. He'd thought it was the mood of its occupant, but now he knew. "Where is *your* Oscar, by the way?" The desk was empty of everything but the telephone and intercom.

"I took it home. It seemed disrespectful to keep it on display after what happened to Quincy." Poll spoke quickly.

"Maybe it just needs cleaning."

"Cleaning? No." The producer looked away.

Valentino said, "Sizemore's a demolitions expert. When it came to shutting down the studio, he'd go to his strength. Bludgeoning a director to death is an amateur play. Something a desperate producer might do when he sees all his authority passing into the hands of a punk who ought to be shooting dog-food commercials."

"Sergeant McPherson, has anyone from a studio asked you about becoming a technical advisor? It pays well, and you won't have to give up your job with the city."

McPherson was wide awake. "I think I'd like a look at that Oscar. The M.E. found traces of gold in Dundrear's skull."

For a moment it looked as if Poll were undecided whether to call his receptionist or bolt for the door. The sergeant drew his pistol.

Valentino went over and put a hand on the producer's shoulder. "It's bad casting, Franklin. You can't bring it off."

A string seemed to snap inside Poll, then. Valentino caught his weight and maneuvered him into the Eames chair.

"Get that bottle!" McPherson shouted.

The producer had taken a plastic prescription container from an inside pocket. Valentino clawed it out of his fist and read the label. "Valium." He put it in his own pocket.

"I'm an old fool." Poll was sitting now with his head tilted back, gripping the arms of the chair tightly as if to avoid slipping to the floor. "I took the Oscar with me to his office. I thought I could shame him into doing honor to a project that would bear my name as producer. It didn't mean anything to him."

"How could it?" Valentino asked. "He didn't pay his dues, like you."

"He said he knew a shop on Sunset where he could have one made for twenty bucks and put any name he wanted on the plaque. '*Deep Throat*,' he said. 'Best Performance by an Orifice.' I didn't even know I was hitting him until the statue got so slippery it slid out of my hands. I picked it up and walked out of his office. It's there, in the bottom drawer of my desk. I didn't even try to clean it."

Valentino stepped that way and opened the drawer. He looked at McPherson and nodded.

"Call headquarters," the sergeant said. "Ask for Lieutenant Carl Decker. Tell him I need a couple of uniforms."

Poll's eyes rolled Valentino's way. He looked old behind the granny glasses. "I'm sorry, Val."

"You shouldn't meddle outside your sphere." Valentino lifted the receiver.

Greed

Max Fink's very public dream of 1927 turned into a hangover in 1929, but by then everyone else was too busy taking aspirins to notice. Fink had lucked into millions in 1912, when he rented out his candy store in Brooklyn evenings and weekends for the exhibition of silent motion-picture shorts. When he came by one night after closing and saw how many people had lined up to pay to see painted Indians chasing a train across the New Jersey countryside, he evicted his tenants, bought a projector, struck a deal with a local distributor, and went into show business.

The movie colony migrated to southern California. Fink followed, pausing at choice locations across the continent to purchase vaudeville theaters in trouble and convert them into movie houses. Fifteen years after he stopped selling candy, he invested his profits in the stock market and used his credit to build a chain of motion picture palaces from coast to coast, saving the jewel in the crown for Los Angeles.

The Oracle was designed as a Balinese-Turkish-Grecian temple, with a slight Polynesian influence. Seating was planned for 5000, with space in the pit for a 100-piece orchestra. Fink commissioned a four-manual Wurlitzer pipe organ, a half-ton crystal chandelier, and plaster Pegasuses to flank the grand staircase leading to the mezzanine. When word reached H. L. Mencken, he said it showed what God could do if He had bad taste.

Then *The Jazz Singer* opened to delirious throngs at Grauman's, and overnight Hollywood shut down all its silent productions, built sound stages, and wired its sets so audiences could hear their favorite matinee idols speaking lines instead of having to read them on title cards. All this retooling sparked a recession in California. Reluctantly, Fink told his contractor to reduce the size of the orchestra pit and reconfigure the auditorium to seat only 1,800. Construction in six cities was postponed until the industry caught its second wind.

In spite of the cutbacks, the completed Oracle was a wonder. Its marquee towered forty feet into the sky, lit by 16,000 electric bulbs, with colored searchbeams swiveling and crossing far above the rooftops. The attendance at the premiere of *The Hollywood Review of 1929* shattered every record set since *Ben Hur* in 1926. But six months later, Max Fink was broke.

After Wall Street crashed in '29, Fink was forced to sell his theater chain to avoid bankruptcy. It was a temporary reprieve. In 1933 he shot himself to death in a dollar-a-week hotel room within sight of a line waiting to get in to see

Mae West in a personal appearance at the Oracle. Nearly seventy years later, it was rumored Max Fink's ghost still roamed the aisles of his beloved picture palace.

If so, the dust and mold spores must have kept him too busy sneezing to rattle his chains.

This time, when Valentino stepped onto the sidewalk before the theater, there were no crowds, no colored lights, no bulky cops in double-breasted tunics to hold back hysterical women. Partly it was because this Valentino was not the star of *The Sheik*; mostly it was because the Oracle was a wreck. Time and competing forms of entertainment had not been kind to the place. The fabulous marquee was long gone, the Deco fluting and baroque flourishes that had decorated the building's facade chipped and pigeon-stained and blackened with soot. Plywood covered the box-office windows and a palimpsest of spray-painted gang signs coated the sandstone to a height of eight feet all around. When he entered the lobby, Valentino left footprints an inch deep in the dust on the linoleum that covered the marble floor. Nothing remained of the friezes and statuary. Insulation hung like entrails from a ceiling ten feet lower than the original.

"It's what you'd call a fixer-upper," said the real-estate agent, Anita Somebody. She was a carefully preserved blonde in her forties, and Valentino knew her story without asking: She'd come out from Des Moines or someplace like that twenty years ago, hoping for a shot at *Dallas*, and when that missed the mark and she couldn't get work in commercials, it was either realty or prostitution. Prostitution didn't come with a health plan. She looked obscenely well pressed in her agency blazer and tailored skirt among the rat droppings.

"I barely know one end of a hammer from the other," Valentino said. "Why are you showing me this place again? I'm looking for a place to live."

"It's the closest we can come to your budget, unless you want to commute from Oxnard. The neighborhood's zoned commercial and residential. No one's sure where the break is. You could put in twenty years before they figure it out."

"I can't afford it. I don't mean the purchase price. If I bought this place, I'd feel obligated to restore it to its original grandeur. Did I mention I'm on salary at UCLA?"

Her lipstick smile told him she hadn't capped her teeth. "Why don't you postpone your decision until you've seen the projection booth?"

But he was in trouble long before he got there. The path led through the auditorium, crushed red velvet seats and gilt sconces, strung with cobwebs but no less charming for the neglect than Egyptian treasures half-buried in Sahara sand. He felt the same tingle he'd felt when his mother took his hand and led him into a movie theater for the first time. But that had been only a square blockhouse in Fox Forage, Indiana. This was Max Fink's fabled Oracle, home of *Hell's Angels, 42nd Street,* and *Anna Christie.* He could almost hear Garbo's smoky voice, saying—

"There's a hidden staircase here."

"What?" He had to put on the brakes to keep from colliding with Anita the realtor. She'd stopped to pry with her fingers at a seam in the drywall. A six-foot-tall rectangular section came away, revolving on parched hinges. Dusty light lay on a flight of steep narrow steps leading upward.

"They seem to have gone to a lot of trouble to keep the customers from finding the projection booth," she said.

"Illusion."

"I beg your pardon?"

"They called Hollywood the Dream Factory," Valentino said. "A dream won't work if you know where it's coming from. They cared about that kind of thing back then."

"Before my time, I guess. I just like to pop a tape into the VCR and veg out on the sofa in my sweats."

He smiled. "Bet you liked *There's Something About Mary.*"

"Oh, yes. It was hilarious! Now, follow me carefully. I'm sure these steps aren't up to code."

In the stairwell he thought he smelled stale popcorn and Moxie. It was probably dry rot, or else phantom Fink having a snack. Valentino had to turn sideways to avoid rubbing the walls with his shoulders.

The booth was actually a spacious loft, with a square opening overlooking the screen, or what remained of it behind a burlap-colored fire curtain. He remembered the Oracle had been one of the last L.A. theaters to show 3-D films back in the fifties. That required twin Bell & Howell projectors, each the size of a VW Beetle. They'd have needed plenty of room, but not this much. He could have put all the furniture in his present quarters into this space.

Anita sensed his curiosity. "There used to be a wall there. On the other side was a sort of lumber room where they stored posters and props. They had live shows onstage during the Depression, to entice people who wouldn't ordinarily spend the money on a ticket. In the sixties this was a hippie commune." She was chanting like a tour guide. "There's a bathroom through that door, which the projectionist used. It's a comfortable bachelor arrangement."

"What's behind *that* door?" He pointed. This one had curved corners, set into a gasketlike frame. It had a broom handle.

"Believe it or not, it's a vault. We're supposed to keep it locked so kids can't get in and suffocate. That's where they kept the films. There's nothing in there now, just empty cans."

He asked to look. She produced a ring of keys and undid the deadbolt. The enclosure was four feet wide and six feet deep. Anita held the door while he stepped inside. He was glad he hadn't said what he thought of *There's Something About Mary.*

The air was stale but dry and cool. There was no light fixture. He peered through the dimness, groping at built-in racks holding jumbles of flat film cans that made a tinny empty sound when he moved them. A built-in bench allowed him to sit while he tugged at one of a row of cans standing on edge on the bottom rack. Something thumped inside. He rattled the next three or four in line. He was sure they contained reels of film.

Many disappointments encountered in his years with UCLA's Film Preservation Department had taught him not to get excited. He'd probably stumbled on someone's long-forgotten pornographic library. He lifted a can off the rack and turned it toward the light outside, squinting at the yellowed label.

He returned the can to the rack—his hand didn't even shake—and stepped outside, dusting off his palms. "If I buy this place, everything comes with it, right?"

Anita frowned prettily. "You mean mineral rights? I'm—"

"No, I mean all the contents of the building."

"Of course. A sale is a sale."

Valentino smiled. "Where do I sign?"

"*Greed?* You ought to open a window in your screening room. You've been breathing acetate."

Kyle Broadhead pronounced Valentino intoxicated in the ringing tone he used in his classroom to declare Robert Altman a hack. The Film Studies professor lay almost supine in his ergonomic office chair with his feet propped on the drawleaf of his desk, unscrewing and screwing back together the pieces of his favorite pipe, which he was no longer allowed to smoke on campus. With his eyelids at half-mast and his chin drawn into the loose flesh around his neck, he resembled a trimmed-down Alfred Hitchcock; a director he admired up to a point.

"I don't blame you for thinking that," Valentino said. "You've forgotten more about cinema history than I'll ever know."

"Flattering, but inaccurate. I've forgotten nothing."

Idle braggadocio, in anyone but the author of *The Persistence of Vision*, the bible of film preservation. The book chronicled Broadhead's thirty-year quest for the original 1912 version of *Quo Vadis?* produced in Italy; a quest interrupted by the three years he spent in a prison in Yugoslavia, accused of spying. He was Valentino's only mentor.

"I thought *I* was a buccaneer," Broadhead continued. "I never signed an agreement to buy a house on the evidence of a label on a film can I didn't open."

"I didn't want to open one under those conditions. You know how unstable that old nitrate stock is. For all I knew, the next person she showed the place to might have been with MCA or Turner. Or worse, some real-estate developer who wouldn't know Stroheim from Streisand and threw it all out. I had to jump."

Broadhead pursed his lips, Hitchcock fashion. "You've been day-dreaming for years about buying one of these broken-down picture palaces and fixing it up. You just wanted an excuse."

"Partly. I didn't imagine seeing that label. And there were enough cans on the rack to suggest it's a complete print."

Valentino let him ponder while he breathed in the cramped academic atmosphere. Books crowded the floor in careless stacks, an arrangement that contrasted sharply with the orderly shelves of videotapes, DVDs, and sixteen-millimeter prints in dustproof cases. He knew he was coming off faintly ridiculous, like a tourist waving a map he'd bought from a street hustler, thinking he possessed the key to the Lost Dutchman. Preservationists and silent-film buffs had been looking for Erich von Stroheim's directorial masterpiece since 1925, when his horrified superiors at MGM slashed its twenty-four reel, four-hour running time by more than half and, apparently, threw away the deleted footage. Valentino calculated that over time he'd wasted an amount equal to the department's annual budget chasing rumors of fragments and entire reels awaiting rescue from junk shops in Vienna, Alaskan landfills, and the cellars of eccentric private collectors.

"Everything's against it, including timing," Broadhead said. "The film was four years old when the Oracle opened. By then you couldn't give away tickets to a silent feature, so what was it doing in the vault? I think your realtor salted the mine. She probably did her homework on you after you made the appointment."

"That's diabolical, even for California."

"Von Stroheim chose the title *Greed* for a reason."

"Anyway, it can't hurt to check it out. I have to fly to San Francisco this afternoon to look at B trailers. Also I'm nervous about handling eighty-year-old stock. Can you take a look?"

The professor blew through his pipe. "Maybe it's time we laid this grail to rest. It's consumed too much money and far too many careers, starting with von Stroheim's."

"In other words, you don't want any part of it."

"Who said that? My God, man, it's *Greed*. Give me the keys."

In San Francisco, Valentino was working for the enemy. A retired RKO flack had died there of complications from a broken hip, leaving fifty thousand feet of promotional trailers from 1940s programmers to his daughter, and Viacom wanted an expert evaluation before buying them to dress up some re-releases on video. The company's pockets were so deep its board of directors didn't realize it had been in competition with UCLA for the world's dwindling supply of classic films for years. But in return for Valentino's advice, the megacorporation had promised to donate a percentage of the profits to the Film Preservation Department.

The department could use the cash, and after his impulsive action that morning, the archivist needed the job security. The mortgage on the Oracle would eat up everything he stood to gain from the sale of the house he'd outgrown in West Hollywood, and he was looking at a couple of hundred thousand dollars' worth of renovations that would take years to complete. What had he been thinking?

His elegant room at the Drake—courtesy of his temporary employers—helped him forget for a time his commitment to a steady diet of peanut-butter-and-jelly sandwiches, and the trailers, which were in pristine condition, allowed him to lose himself in the era of snap-brim hats and mink stoles. But the trolley-car trip back downtown after the screening only reminded him of the location shots for *Greed*. Von Stroheim, mad genius that he was, had insisted upon filming every line of Frank Norris's novel, *McTeague: A Story of San Francisco*, tracing the descent of a good-natured, slow-witted dentist into insanity and murder, all for a cache of money his wife had hidden from him. Valentino had been appalled and fascinated by the butchered version he had seen, and was obsessed with the opportunity to experience the director's original vision.

The auteur's dream had been, like poor old Max Fink's, grandiose and doomed. He had started out with fifty reels—*eight hours* of flickering celluloid—and edited them down to a feature that was still eighty minutes longer than *The Birth of a Nation*. Von Stroheim had hoped that people would come to see the first two hours, adjourn for dinner, then come back for the rest. The idea was decades ahead of its time; too early for the studio brass. It was the beginning of the end for him as a director. Soon he was supporting himself as an actor, playing a succession of Prussians and Nazis for audiences to hiss at until his swan song, as the loyal butler and ex-husband of Gloria Swanson's Norma Desmond in *Sunset Boulevard*, the role for which he was best remembered. Ironically, the character was a former great director reduced to menial servitude.

Valentino had room service on Viacom and ordered a movie on Pay-Per-View, but lost interest after twenty minutes: There were no drunken-brute dentists, no Death Valley confrontations, no ZaSu Pitts. He left a wake-up call for six o'clock—his plane was at eight—and went to bed.

"*Herr* Valentino, you haff had your rest, *ja?*"

He started awake, he thought. A swatch of moonlight lay on the carpet like a gauntlet flung through a gap in the curtains covering the window. A dark figure stood in the shadows to one side with feet spread thirty inches apart.

Valentino's heart bumped. He couldn't speak. Had he double-locked the door? He remembered putting on the chain.

"You vill safe *mein Kind, ja?* I am counting on you."

The intruder's Teutonic accent was as hard to follow as his German. Valentino had the wild thought that his room had been broken into by a neo-Nazi skinhead. "What do you want?" he asked hoarsely. "My wallet's on the bureau. Take it and go."

A bitter laugh escaped the shape in the shadows. "Vot do I vant vit your money? I spent more than you earn in a month on one dinner at the Trocadero. I vant *mein Kind*."

The Trocadero hadn't existed for fifty years. *Mein Kind?* He tried to remember his high school German. *My child.* "I think you've mistaken me for someone else." That sounded weirdly comical, even to him.

"*Du lieber Gott.*" The stranger stamped his feet twice, propelling himself sideways into the shaft of cold light.

Valentino's breath caught. The man was decked out head-to-toe in the uniform of an imperial Austrian officer. A visored cap perched at an arrogant angle above his shaved temples, his white tunic was buttoned tightly to his throat and sparkled with medals, and riding breeches were stuffed into the tops of gleaming black knee-length boots. In one hand he held a pair of gloves, in the other a leather riding crop, its thong handle resting against his shoulder. A monocle glittered in one eye. He was the living image of Erich von Stroheim in *Foolish Wives*.

The archivist's shock gave way to annoyance. He was the victim of a prank. Kyle Broadhead had gotten some actor friend to put on a costume and frighten him out of a night's sleep. *Greed* had turned out to be a wild goose chase and this was his way of getting back at Valentino for the waste of his time.

"Tell Kyle you accomplished your mission," he said. "What did he do, promise you a part in Mel Brooks's next—"

"*Silence!*" The riding crop whistled through the air and struck one of the shining boots with a report like a pistol shot. The crop pointed at him. "You vill safe *mein Kind!*"

Valentino forced himself to meet the iron gaze. It seemed to him that the eye not covered by the monocle was moist.

Something burred. "Von Stroheim" looked up as if hearing an air-raid siren, then vanished. The shaft of moonlight was empty.

The burring continued in bursts, with brief silences between. Valentino stirred from under the covers and lifted the receiver off the telephone on the nightstand. His "Hello" was hoarse.

"You need to get out of San Francisco. You're starting to sound like a foghorn."

"Kyle?"

"Did I wake you?"

"No big deal. I was having a stupid dream." Only as he said it did he realize it *was* a dream. He switched on the lamp, dispelling the last wisp of phantasm from the room. "What's in the cans, the director's cut of *Showgirls?*"

"Nope. I only risked a peek, but I think it's the bonanza. I'm calling from the Oracle on my cell. We might have the full eight hours here. And something else we didn't count on."

I am counting on you, von Stroheim had said. Valentino regretted ordering prawn from downstairs. "What?"

"A skeleton."

Valentino had taken a cab to LAX on his way out. Broadhead met him with the hybrid electric car he drove whenever he felt like irritating the department head, a conservative sourpuss who leased SUVs that increased in size in direct proportion to the amount of fuel they consumed. Valentino wedged his bag into the backseat and folded himself into the passenger's side in front.

"How were the trailers?" Broadhead spoke above the ticking of the motor.

"A little foxed. Nothing serious. What kind of skeleton?"

"Human, I'm pretty sure. I'm not an anthropologist. It was crammed under the seat."

"What seat?"

"That bench in the vault. It made a hollow sound when I laid one of my cases on it. I groped around until I found the edge of the lid. I may be the first person to discover that extra bit of storage space since the place was built. Or the second. Someone had to have put the skeleton in there."

"Cases?"

"My invention. Aluminum carriers, with vacuum pumps to seal them airtight. Prevents oxidation while the film's in transport. I should apply for a patent. It'd mean a cool twelve bucks in royalties annually, film preservation being the growth industry it is." He puffed on his burning pipe, filling the vehicle with noxious gases.

"How long do you think the skeleton's been in there?"

"Forty years, anyway. I called your realtor. To satisfy my curiosity about the film, not the bones. The vault was plastered over when they bought the theater in 1961. Plaster started falling a month ago and they tore the rest down. They had to have a key made for the vault. No one knew it was there."

"Did you call the police?"

"It seemed wise. I took the liberty of moving *Greed* to the university first. Care to see it?"

"Do you think the police will let me in?"

The professor looked over at him. "I meant *Greed*."

Broadhead, who had a class to teach, left Valentino at the Oracle and ticked away. A woman named Sergeant Franks allowed the new owner into the secured area. She was tall enough to have played basketball in college, and not long ago. She stooped to shake Valentino's hand on the landing outside the projection booth. "I see the resemblance," she said. "Grandson?"

"No relation. You seem young to know Valentino at all."

"I thought he was a fashion designer until my lieutenant set me right." She brushed a dangling shard of plaster away from her teased-out hair. "You sure bought yourself a wreck. Planning to raze and develop?"

"Actually, I hope to restore it." Valentino gave her a card.

" 'Film detective.' That's a bureau I never saw downtown."

"It's a jazzy name for a procurer. I'm a preservationist."

"Theaters?"

"Movies. This started out as a search for a new house with a better screening room."

"Well, I bet it's bigger. Did you know a corpse came with the place?" Franks smiled girlishly. But her eyes were sharp.

"If I had, I'd have tried to bargain down the price."

"Mm-hm. I understand you were out of town when it turned up."

"I had a business appointment."

The sergeant consulted a notebook with a red cover. "A Professor Broadhead called it in. Interesting man. Said you asked him to come in and poke around?"

"He's an expert on old film stock. There were some specimens in the vault. They can be volatile. I didn't want to touch them until after he'd had a chance to inspect them."

"Volatile like explosive?"

"If exposed to flame. In this case I should have said fragile. Before the nineteen fifties, when safety stock was introduced, motion-picture film contained silver nitrate. It deteriorates rapidly if not properly stored, just as silver corrodes. Half of all films made before nineteen fifty have been lost for that reason; ninety percent before nineteen twenty. All we retain of Theda Bara, for instance, are a few dozen production stills. Her career has vanished."

Franks wrote something in her notebook, possibly *Theda Bara*. "This stuff valuable?"

"To film history. It doesn't compare to, say, a Rembrandt painting. Colleges and film societies can't afford to pay as much as a syndicate of Japanese tycoons." Valentino smiled. Did she suspect him of a forty-year-old murder? If it was murder.

"Mm-hm. Man who's seen as many pictures as you, I guess you're not squeamish."

"I still flinch when Lon Chaney's mask comes off in *The Phantom of the Opera*."

"That one I know. I saw the road show when it played L.A. Come in and take a look. Maybe you can give us a positive ID, ha-ha."

A photographer tripped his flash just as Valentino entered the oversize booth behind the sergeant. The timing, as if on cue for the first take of a criminal-investigation scene, made him feel as if he'd stepped onto a live set. He had the sensation that the man with the camera, the uniformed officer scribbling in his report book, the pair of technicians mixing and applying their powders, the woman in the green smock bent over something inside the open vault, had all been running their lines and primping only a moment before.

"Ms. Johansen, a minute?" Franks said.

The woman in the smock sat back. She wore a cuplike mask over her nose and mouth. When she took it off, Valentino was struck by the perfection of her features. She was a shorthaired blonde with elliptical blue eyes, clear and unflawed. Her nose was straight and she had a generous mouth that looked as if it might contain a smile as bright as a klieg. She wasn't smiling.

"A minute is an hour," she said. "What's so important? Oh, hello." She noticed Valentino and moderated her scowl.

"Hello. I didn't know bacteria was a problem."

"What? Oh, the mask. I'm allergic to dust." She sneezed.

Franks said, "Mr. Valentino owns the building. Harriet Johansen. She's with the criminal-science division."

"Forgive me for not shaking hands." She held up a miniature whiskbroom in a rubber glove.

He looked past her. A drop cord clipped to one of the racks inside the vault shed halogen light into the low bench, whose top was tipped back to expose the recessed interior. In that moment he realized he'd never seen a human skeleton "in person," and was mildly surprised to learn that it didn't look much different from those he'd seen in movies. The leering skull and hooplike ribs wore a fine coat of gray dust. He should have been horrified. Many thousands of feet of Universal and Hammer shockers had desensitized him to this basic symbol of mortality. There was a musty odor that reminded him of old magazines.

"He was a little dude," Harriet Johansen said. "Couple of inches taller and he'd have had to be folded."

"How do you know it was a he?" Valentino asked.

"Shape of the pelvis. Also I caught him looking down my blouse when I bent over."

He grinned. "Was it murder?"

"Tell you when I finish dusting, maybe. If there was bone trauma, a skull fracture, or a blade or a bullet nicked a rib, yes. Without that, or a loose slug somewhere in the box, all we've got is improper disposal of a body." She sneezed again. "Excuse me."

"Gesundheit. Was he naked?"

"No sign of even the remnants of clothing. That indicates homicide. Attempt to foil identification. Did you do it?"

"I have an alibi. They walled off the room before I was born."

Franks said, "Who told you that?"

"Kyle Broadhead called the realty company." He knew he'd made a mistake even before he finished speaking.

"Inquisitive type, isn't he?" The sergeant's tone was flat.

He straightened from his crouch, as if his back were sore. He was stalling. "He wanted to know how long the films had been in the vault."

"I'd like a look at those films."

"Actually, it's only one. Forty or fifty reels. And it has to stay in a stable environment. I don't think the police evidence room qualifies."

"It's evidence in a homicide. I can get a warrant."

"You don't even know if it is a homicide." Valentino exhaled. "I'll try to arrange a screening. It takes time. A new negative has to be struck from the original, and a positive made from that onto safety stock. The film is almost eighty years old. Running it through a projector would destroy it."

Franks snatched a ribbon of cobweb away from her face. "I'll give you three days."

Johansen sneezed. Valentino and Franks said, "Gesundheit."

"You need to have new cards made." Broadhead ran a pipe cleaner through the barrel of his pipe. "You've got *detective* on the brain."

Valentino said, "You know and I know we can't transfer eight hours of vintage celluloid in three days. If the case isn't wrapped up before then, we can say goodbye to *Greed* for the second and last time."

"If the police haven't been able to solve the case in forty years, what makes you think you and I can?"

"They didn't know there *was* a case before today. Anyway, you found *Quo Vadis?* and that went back a *lot* further."

"It took me thirty years."

"You didn't have me to help."

"You're an arrogant young fool."

"And you're a pompous old crotch. Where's the film?"

"In the cooler, where else? I had to move *Ivan the Terrible* to make room for it. I hope *Ivan* gets along with *Battleship Potemkin.* They're sharing a rack." Broadhead pursed his lips Hitchcock fashion. "You know, it's only a movie. Not worth prison time."

"I haff to safe his *Kind.*"

"What?"

"That stupid dream. I can't do it without you, Kyle."

"You can't do it *with* me." He laid the pipe on his desk in two pieces. "Where do we start?"

"When Max Fink sold the Oracle."

"That was in nineteen twenty-nine!"

Valentino looked at his watch. "You're right. We'd better get started."

They divvied up two of the four estates. Broadhead took Government, Valentino the Press. While the professor pored over the Los Angeles County property records at the Civic Center, the film detective visited the microfilm room in the library downtown and scrolled through ancient numbers of the L.A. *Times.* After a while he stopped mooning over the advertised premieres of films that no longer existed and confined his attention to the local news sections.

Four hours later, squinting against the glare of the 21st century, he met Broadhead in their downtown hangout, a micropub with four-sheets on the walls of W.C. Fields playing poker, Errol Flynn in tights, and Marilyn fluttering too close to the flame. Valentino was famished and ordered the Fatty Arbuckle Burger. Broadhead, parched and smelling of old plat books, drank a pitcher of stout.

"The theater changed hands three times between twenty-nine and thirty-seven," Valentino said. "The last time was to a guy named—"

"Warren Pegler," Broadhead finished. "He sold it in fifty-six to a film society. They showed Fellini to college students until they couldn't afford to support the hobby. That's when your realty firm bought it and rented it to hippies. They didn't care if the toilets flushed."

"The *Times* did a human-interest piece on Pegler when he took over. He was a double amputee, lost both legs in an accident in the developing lab at Metro, where he worked. Invested his compensation check in Warner Brothers just before *The Jazz Singer*, pulled out of the stock market two months ahead of the twenty-nine crash."

"Your reading was more interesting than mine."

"Trade you places," Valentino said.

"You mean you drink, I eat?" Broadhead refilled his glass from the pitcher.

"I mean I only read up to nineteen forty. I need you to check the papers from just before Pegler sold the Oracle until it changed hands again. The vault was already plastered over when the realty firm acquired it. Whoever did that must have known about the body inside."

"Redecorating projects don't always make the papers."

"Disappearances usually do. Whoever was using that skeleton dropped out of sight suddenly. I'm assuming someone missed him and reported it to the police."

"And what will you be doing while I'm working up an appetite looking for corpses in the *Times*?"

"Pegler interests me. Country records should tell me if he has any heirs. They might know something."

"Why bother with the heirs? Talk to the man himself."

"He'd be a hundred if he were alive," Valentino said.

"Ninety-six." The professor fished a spiral notebook out of an inside pocket. "Last January, a district judge ruled him incompetent to care for himself and committed him to a nursing home in San Diego. Here's the address."

A tasteful sign at the end of a broad composition driveway identified a low brick building surrounded by trees as the Autumn Leaf Elder Care Facility. Valentino parked in a small lot that still had plenty of room for visitors and tapped on an open door marked OFFICE inside the foyer. A young woman in a USC sweatshirt with her hair in a ponytail looked up from her desk. He introduced himself and said he was there to see Mr. Pegler.

"Warren." She smiled. "Is your first name Eric?"

He hesitated. "No."

"I'm sorry. Warren has his bad days. When he's not entirely lucid, he keeps asking for someone named Eric. I thought it might be a family member. He never has visitors, so I assumed—" She shrugged. "Are you a relative?"

He gave her a card. "I'm a film archivist. I understand Mr. Pegler worked in the developing lab at MGM in the twenties. I wanted to ask him some questions about early Hollywood." He was pretty sure "about a murder" would not result in an interview.

"You've told me more about his background than he's ever told any of us, except when he's regressing, and that's usually a jumble. From some of the things he's said, I thought he had something to do with pictures. He's having a good day today. He'll enjoy a visit. Room eighteen."

He passed some bent elderly people pulling themselves along a rail in the hallway and stopped before eighteen. A loud argument appeared to be going on inside. Then he recognized Humphrey Bogart's raspy lisp, inviting the coppers to come up and get him. Valentino knocked loudly to make himself heard above the TV. The shouting stopped and a voice told him to come in.

"You don't look like you have any pills for me. Come to rob me?"

The old man seated in the wheelchair next to the bed had a full head of white hair and lively eyes in a thin, pale, pleated face. He wore a white dress shirt that looked freshly ironed and loose tailored slacks, cut off and sewed neatly at the knees, below which there was nothing. He pointed his remote control at Valentino as if it were a gun. On the TV screen atop his bureau, Bogie was shooting it out with the police in silence.

Valentino said no and held out a card. Pegler moved his lips over what was printed on it. His ninety-six-year-old eyes appeared to be in good working condition.

"What the hell's a film detective?"

Valentino explained, then added, "I just bought the Oracle Theater. I wanted to ask you some things about it as a former owner."

"You bought yourself a money hole, how's that for starters? Cost you a lot less just to hang a sign around your neck saying ROB ME. Patrons, the tax man, studios, even my own projectionist took everything that wasn't bolted down. Then Washington took everything that was. I was all set to sell to Paramount when Antitrust told the studios they couldn't own theaters anymore. That was in forty-seven. The next nine years broke me and I finally let the old trap go to real-estate sharks for less than I owed in back taxes."

"Why didn't you sell *Greed?* Plenty of collectors would have made you a handsome price even then." He watched closely for Pegler's reaction.

The old man's face was blank. "Sell greed? I didn't think that was something you sold. Folks are generally born with it."

"I'll get to the point, Mr. Pegler. A man's skeleton was found in the film vault at the Oracle, along with some reels of old film. Do you know anything about it?"

"What vault? I stored all the pictures I rented in the basement."

"The realty firm tore down a plaster wall that was covering the vault. I thought you might know who put it up."

Pegler scowled at his remote, as if he might wipe Valentino out by changing channels. "You're asking me to take a lot at face value. *If* you're who you say you are, *if* you own the Oracle, *if* there's a skeleton and film in a vault, that wall was there when I bought the place. You'll have to ask Max Fink. You'll find him in Forest Lawn under six feet of California."

Valentino didn't press the point. "I understand you were a film technician at Metro."

"Don't make it sound so grand. I was an assistant developer. Young squirt that I was, I planned to run the studio one day, take Thalberg's place. Then some damn fool left a cigarette burning next to some fresh film stock. When the flames hit the chemicals, the dark room went up. Me, too. They had to cut me in half to save what didn't burn." He thumped one of his stumps with the hand holding Valentino's card. The card slipped from his fingers and fluttered to the floor. It reminded Valentino of a cinder.

"I'm sorry."

"Not necessary. I was going to direct, then produce, then buy the studio. Instead I bought a theater. Folks needed a place to go to forget when times got hard. It was good living right up till I got robbed."

Valentino thanked him for the information and grasped the doorknob. "Who's Eric?" he asked.

"Eric?" The old man shook himself out of the past. "These kids around me gossip like old women. I get confused sometimes. Eric was my first dog. Smartest Great Dane you ever saw. Hell, he's dead ninety years. Coal wagon run over him."

"I thought it might have been Erich von Stroheim. You both worked at Metro."

"That old fake. I'd hear him snarling at my boss outside while I was developing. You couldn't print a frame fast enough to bring a smile to that fish face. Said he once belonged to Franz Josef's Imperial Guard. I bet he shoveled out the stable."

"He was a great director, though."

"So was DeMille, and *he* knew how to work inside a budget. You know von Stroheim shut down production on *Merry Go Round* three days waiting for delivery on Austrian Army underwear that never showed up on screen? He broke the bank finally. That's when Mayer bought the studio and fired him."

Valentino was about to point out that things hadn't happened quite that quickly when Pegler lifted his remote and flipped the TV sound back on, just in time for Bogart to catch a bullet in the back and plummet to his death. The film detective left. On his way out he leaned into the office. "I'm afraid Mr. Pegler didn't enjoy my visit after all."

The woman in the ponytail smiled sympathy. "A little thorny, was he? That's how you know it's one of his good days."

Kyle Broadhead was teaching an evening class when Valentino got back to UCLA. Valentino went to his own office to wait and found his message light blinking. Sergeant Franks had called and left her number at Homicide. He thought about putting off returning the call—she might have decided to rescind the three-day reprieve and demand immediate delivery of *Greed*—but worrying about disaster was as bad as the disaster itself. He dialed the number.

"You academic types keep police hours," Franks said. "Ever hear of a director named Castle?"

He hesitated. "William Castle. He shot horror flicks on the cheap during the '50s and '60s. He used gimmicks to heighten the reaction: battery-charged seats to shock the audience, painted sheets on wires to send spooks flying over their heads, actors in costume running up and down the aisles. Early experimental theater."

"That checks. Department computer shows him answering a public-nuisance complaint in nineteen fifty-eight for scaring an old lady half to death during a showing of something called *The House on Haunted Hill* at the Oracle. Care to hear the particulars?"

He said yes. He felt a tingle, as if he were sitting in one of Castle's electrified seats.

"Seems a wire or something broke thirty minutes in and a certain object dropped into the old lady's lap. She wet her pants and screamed for a cop. Guess what it was."

"A human skeleton."

"Maybe you *are* part detective. Well, this Castle is a skeleton himself now, so we can't grill him. But if no dental records turn up suggesting otherwise, which is a crapshoot anyway after all this time, we may safely consider Mr. Bones an alumnus of some medical-school anatomy class and redirect our energies toward murders that took place in this century."

"What does Harriet Johansen say?"

"About what, the case or your perfect cheekbones? I'm not a dating service."

"She said I had perfect cheekbones?"

"Don't assume you're off the hook," the sergeant snarled. "I don't close cases on the evidence of convenience. You've got sixty hours to deliver that old film." The connection broke.

Broadhead's office was locked. Either he'd gone straight home from his class or had stopped in and come back out, assuming Valentino was still in San Diego. The film detective went home. This time he dreamed von Stroheim was dancing with a skeleton.

"If you're determined to rot your brain, make sure the tripe you write about is entertaining," Broadhead said. "When you return *Dumb and Dumber*, rent a Blondie film and write about Penny Singleton."

The student shuffled out in his baggy pants and *Scary Movie* T-shirt, carrying his paper rolled up with the scarlet *F* inside.

"He compared Jim Carrey to Chaplin." The professor buckled his briefcase and scowled at Valentino as if he were responsible for the student's lapse. "Good morning. You look conflicted. Did the canary you swallowed give you heartburn?"

Valentino told him about William Castle.

"I knew that," Broadhead said. "The incident made the front page of the Entertainment section in fifty-eight."

"Is that all you found?" Valentino accompanied him up the steps of the lecture hall.

"Nope. I almost stopped looking after March nineteen fifty-six. That's when the projectionist at the Oracle disappeared."

Valentino stopped with one foot on the top step.

Broadhead switched on his desk lamp and handed Valentino the printout from the *Times* City section:

POLICE SEEK THEATER EMPLOYEE

The Fugitive detail of the Los Angeles Police joined the Missing Persons bureau today in the search for a projectionist who vanished between his home and his job at the Oracle Theater Sunday afternoon. Theft and flight are suspected.

Albert Spinoza, 21, a film student at the University of Southern California and a part-time licensed projectionist, was reported missing Monday morning by his mother, with whom he lived, after he failed to return home Sunday night from his job at the Oracle on South Broadway. Oracle owner and manager Warren Pegler told police that Spinoza did not show up for work Sunday afternoon. Pegler, who is supervising a remodeling project inside the theater, said that a matinee showing of *The Ten Commandments* had to be canceled, as no replacement could be found who was licensed by the Motion Picture Projectionists' Union.

This morning, Pegler reported to police that the box-office cash receipts were missing from Saturday night's premiere screening of *The Ten Commandments*. He told officers an estimated $1,000 had disappeared from a safe in the projection booth. Police believe that Spinoza may have fled with the receipts.

The article took up five inches at the bottom of a column. "Anything else?" Valentino asked.

"Couple of items rehashing the same information, then a two-inch piece at the end of April announcing the police had abandoned the investigation. No leads."

"Pegler said something about his projectionist robbing him, along with the government and everyone else. I thought he was just ranting."

Broadhead gave him his Hitchcock look. "There's another explanation for Spinoza's vanishing act. Did you read the whole article?"

"I caught the reference to a remodeling project. You think that's when the wall went up?"

"A safe was mentioned, but no vault. You'd think that with a man missing, the police would ask questions about fresh plaster."

"Maybe Pegler answered them. He was past fifty even then, a legless man in a wheelchair. Probably told them some salty stories about early Hollywood. Without anything else to go on they might have written him off as a harmless old character."

"L.A. police were just introducing computers then," Broadhead said. "Your Sergeant Franks brought up a nineteen fifty-eight complaint. If the department's in the habit of erasing obsolete files to make room on the hard drive, nineteen fifty-six might take awhile. It's somewhere, though. When she finds out about Spinoza, the Castle theory goes to the back of the closet."

Valentino shook his head. "The theft of a thousand dollars seems cheap for a murder motive, even by Eisenhower-era standards."

"Who says theft had anything to do with it? Pegler's the only source for the information there even was a theft. It helped make the idea of a voluntary disappearance more plausible, to cover the fact that Spinoza was already on his way toward becoming a skeleton in the vault. The real reason would be a lot juicier. Any one of the seven sins would do. One especially."

"*Greed.*"

"Which would mean Franks was right after all," Broadhead said. "The film's involved."

"Which means we're back where we started. We have to make the case before the film winds up as confetti on the floor of the police evidence room."

The professor stood and charged his pipe from a humidor shaped like Oliver Hardy. "I don't have another class until three. If we leave now we can beat the San Diego traffic both ways."

The woman in the ponytail wasn't smiling. She had on yesterday's sweatshirt or one just like it. "I'm afraid Mr. Pegler's having one of his bad days. The conversation's apt to be one-sided."

Valentino said, "My friend's closer to his age. Maybe he can draw him out."

Broadhead glowered.

"I didn't mean you'd be doing all the talking," the woman said. "When Warren's like this, he goes on and on about obscure things. Most of the people he talks about are probably dead."

"Good."

She glared at Broadhead.

"He means we're good listeners," Valentino said.

"Eric, that you?"

Broadhead, closing the door of room eighteen behind them, glanced from the man in the wheelchair to Valentino, who shrugged. "He says it was his dog."

"Poppycock. I heard an *h*."

"How can you hear an *h* in Eric?"

"Erich?"

This time Valentino actually heard the *h*. He had an insane idea. He coarsened his voice. "Varren? Varren Pekler, iss dat choo?"

"Easy on the accent," Broadhead muttered. "He's senile, not stupid."

"Erich, you old fake. Still wearing that monocle. I bet you're blind in both eyes by now. I heard you were dying."

Valentino paused. Von Stroheim had died in France in 1957. He'd been dying when Albert Spinoza disappeared. "I am not dead yet, you drugstore developer. Vhere is *mein Kind?*"

"Speak English, you damn kraut. What kin?"

"*Greed.*"

Pegler wore what appeared to be a fresh white dress shirt and a different pair of tailored slacks. Today, however, he was huddled deep in his chair, looking shrunken beneath a heavy afghan across his shoulders on a warm California day in late spring. His eyes still shone, but were moist, not sharp. He clearly didn't understand.

Valentino played a wild card. "Don't act schtupid. You developed every frame of the original fifty reels. I know you didn't destroy dem when T'alberg told you to. I vant *Greed!*" He barked the last word. Broadhead jumped.

Pegler didn't. His face became more wizened. It took on a sly cast. "You'll have it when I give it to you, not before. Until then you can go on paying me."

"You are *blackmailink* me?" In his excitement, Valentino wasn't faking the accent. He *was* von Stroheim. He tightened one fist, grasping an imaginary riding crop.

"Don't swing that monkey-stick at me," Pegler said. "I'm charging you storage. You can croak right here in the booth if you want. I don't care. I'm not Spinoza."

"What about Spinoza?" Broadhead asked. Valentino nudged him. He was afraid a strange voice would break the spell.

The old man didn't seem to notice. "He got to snooping in the vault. When he found *Greed*, he wanted to send the reels to France so you would have them before you died. My fault for hiring a film-school student. He thought you were a great artist. He didn't know he was working for a greater one. How could he? He wasn't born when my legs burned off."

Valentino and Broadhead were silent. The thin old face bent in the middle, making a smile as sharp as a lance. "Still smoking, Erich?" he asked.

Harriet Johansen wore a blue dress to the private screening. It brought out the startling color in her eyes. Valentino told her the smock she wore on the job didn't do her justice.

He took her on a tour of the Oracle. Most of the debris had been cleared away, but years and many tens of thousands of dollars of work remained before the theater would begin to resemble a shadow of its early self. He had borrowed one of the university's big Bell & Howell projectors and with Kyle Broadhead's help had installed it in the booth. Broadhead, who was a licensed projectionist, came down to shake the criminal specialist's hand, then went back up to thread in the first reel. It would be the first showing of the restored *Greed* on safety stock outside the Moviolas at UCLA.

Valentino, wearing a burgundy smoking jacket that had belonged to John Barrymore, poured the wine and escorted Harriet to the only two adjacent seats in the mezzanine that retained their original upholstery. Sapphire light trickled into pools on the faded carpet from the wall sconces. They'd been rewired only that morning.

"Are you going to live here?" she asked.

"Where better, for a professional film buff?"

"You'll never get away from the movies."

"The movies are where you go to get away from everything else."

She shook her golden head. "I have a confession to make. I've never seen a silent movie."

He touched her glass in an unspoken toast to the experience. "You'll have to promise to see it again when it's scored. Silent films were never really silent. When it premieres in public, I hope to have funding for a full orchestra. That's if the renovations don't put me out in the middle of South Broadway."

She looked up at the ceiling, gutted of its frescoes and chandelier. "A skeleton isn't going to fall in my lap, is it?"

"If it did, you'd probably just dust it off. I imagine you told Sergeant Franks the bones weren't William Castle's property."

"Skeletons used for demonstration purposes are linked together with wire," she said. "That had never been done with Albert Spinoza."

"You've identified him positively?"

"The FBI lab in Sacramento ran the DNA from marrow samples. I doubt the evidence will be used in court. Warren Pegler's in a bad way, I heard. They moved him from the prison ward to the ICU."

"If he does make it to trial, Franks can have the nitrate print for evidence. We have a fresh negative in the can and two positives on safety stock in the cooler."

"It sounds like the film was in better shape than the murder victim."

"Film isn't flesh," he said. "Different conditions apply."

"So it was Erich von Stroheim's careless smoking that ended Pegler's dream to direct. I've seen pictures of the German with a cigarette holder clamped between his teeth."

"Austrian. Anyway, who knows? Pegler believed it. He had to have already struck off an extra print of *Greed* and removed it from the Metro lot, to save it from destruction. He knew film and probably recognized a masterpiece. After the fire, it gave him the chance to revenge himself on the man he held responsible for his tragedy. Not to mention a great deal in ransom not to destroy the film. The cash from von Stroheim sweetened Pegler's investments in the stock market. That's how he managed to buy the Oracle."

"Spinoza's skull was fractured," she said. "Pegler must have hit him with something from behind, probably when he turned toward the vault to steal the film. After he fell inside, the rest was easy. Pegler stripped the body to stall identification, dumped it into the storage space, shut the vault door, and walled it up, just like Edgar Allan Poe." She brightened. "Got any Vincent Price pictures?"

"Next time," Valentino said.

"So vengeance was the motive."

"And greed."

"Hold your horses." Broadhead sounded testy in the booth. "This isn't like operating a VCR, you know."

The film began rolling. Ten minutes into the first reel, caught up in the story of the dullard dentist whose animal needs draw him into the abyss, Harriet snuggled close to Valentino and intertwined her fingers with his on the swan-shaped arm of the seat. He smiled at her and used a corny old movie line. "Where have you been all my life?"

"I know where I'll be the next eight hours."

Bombshell

Beata Limerick had turned her back on stardom and fallen into a fortune. She'd been getting the big buildup at MGM in 1967 ("Not since Marilyn . . .") when she walked out on her contract, offering no explanation. The studio sued, then withdrew its suit when she handed the head of production a cashier's check for the entire amount she'd been paid while on salary. The money was accepted, but not before someone actually said, "You'll never work in this town again."

She never did; but then, she never had to.

Six months after she quit, she married the chairman of the board of the corporation that built Century City. When he died, shortly before their fifth anniversary, he left her forty million dollars in cash and securities and an additional sixteen million in real property, including four hundred feet fronting on Rodeo Drive in Beverly Hills.

By then, Beata had become a force to reckon with at Hollywood parties. Coat-check girls who wanted to be starlets, starlets who wanted to be stars, and stars who didn't want to be coat-check girls laughed at her jokes and gushed over her diamonds, then came away uncertain whether they should worry more about Beata discussing them behind their backs or Beata not discussing them at all.

Valentino—who was related neither to the silent-screen actor nor the clothing designer—had no wish to star in anything, and so he enjoyed Beata's company thoroughly and without fear. She in turn enjoyed his, having tested him and found that he wanted nothing from her. In addition, they shared a reverence for Hollywood's rich and gaudy history. For his part, it was his job: He was an archivist with UCLA's Film Preservation Department. For hers, it was a passion: She was the foremost collector of movie memorabilia on the West Coast. It was said that with one bid at Sotheby's—$250,000 for the drapery-dress Vivien Leigh had worn in *Gone With the Wind*—Beata Limerick had upped the ante on everything from Mickey Rooney's Andy Hardy hat to the chariot Charlton Heston had raced in *Ben Hur*.

She and Valentino encountered each other frequently. Both were regulars at auctions and estate sales where newly discovered reels of film and motion-picture props and wardrobe shared the block. They rarely competed; Valentino was more interested in movies than memorabilia, and Beata's preference ran toward items she could exhibit without having to set up a projector. Often they lunched afterward, celebrating their victories and commiserating over their defeats.

"I don't consider it a secret why I left MGM," she told him on one such occasion. "It's just easier to refuse to answer the question than it is to repeat the same story over and over. I was afraid of the curse."

"The curse?"

She smiled, accentuating the striking beauty of her sixty-year-old face. Time, not surgery, had been kind to the woman whom Hedda Hopper had declared "Hollywood's Alice Roosevelt Longworth."

"The *curse*, foolish boy. Thelma Todd. Jean Harlow. Marilyn. It was still around for Sharon Tate. All the great blond bombshells came to an early end. I was twenty-five; if I wasn't going to be great, the hell with it, and I didn't want to die. When that truck took off Jayne Mansfield's head, I got the message. I didn't walk away from my destiny. I ran for my life."

"She wasn't really decapitated, you know. It was just her wig they found on the hood of her Buick."

She patted his hand.

"I was being picturesque. I own the wig. I'd own the Buick, too, if Spielberg hadn't outbid me."

"You seriously believe there's a curse on blondes in Hollywood?"

"I believe in astrology, tarot cards, and voodoo. It's my birthright. I'm a native Californian."

They were serious rivals once only, years before they became friends. Beata had annihilated him in a battle over a rare unedited print of *The Sandpiper* at Vincente Minnelli's estate auction. That was the first day they'd had lunch; her treat.

"I couldn't resist," she said. "I doubled Liz Taylor in that one—it was my brunette period—and it's all I have to show for my career in pictures, such as it was. Anyway, you're better off without it. It's a stinker."

"Stinkers have a way of making money. UCLA could have exhibited it in revival houses and made enough to restore half a dozen better films."

"I'll make it up to you one day."

"One day" was fifteen years coming. Valentino had been very young at the time of his disappointment, an assistant to an assistant. In the years since, he had been instrumental in the recovery of many motion pictures long considered lost. Along the way he'd acquired character lines in his face, while Beata, at threescore, could still pass for forty-five. But she hadn't forgotten her promise.

"I'm cleaning house," she told him over the telephone. "Bring your checkbook and I'll let you have *The Sandpiper* for what I paid."

The film, he knew, had doubled in value since she'd bought it. But Valentino had learned never to display eagerness in a business negotiation.

"I'll need to screen it. Those old Metrocolor features are prone to bleeding."

"So are old actresses. However, I'll forgive you for stabbing me in my aged heart if you'll agree to sample my chicken cordon bleu during intermission. Two o'clock Tuesday?"

At the hour mentioned, he came off the elevator opposite Beata Limerick's penthouse apartment in Beverly Hills and read a sign written in a hasty hand, thumbtacked to the door.

V.—

Let yourself in and sit down on something. I'm putting on my face, and no man should be left standing that long.

Love, B.

He placed the package he'd brought under one arm to open the door. The two flat cans bound in gift paper contained Beata's MGM screen test, which he'd acquired in a blind lot along with some more commercial items, and had been saving for a special occasion.

Most of the apartment was one huge room, partitions having been removed to create space for some of the artifacts his hostess had collected over the years. Opposite the groaning shelves and display cases, a vast picture window looked out on West Hollywood and most of the Valley. A forty-year-old Bell & Howell projector in excellent condition stood on a stout table facing a portable screen.

Valentino set his package on an eight-foot chaise that had appeared in *Samson and Delilah* and examined the label on one of the film cans stacked on the floor beside the table. It identified *The Sandpiper* as the contents, along with the production number and a stern warning that it was the property of Metro-Goldwyn-Mayer.

He was accustomed to dining earlier. The aroma of the chicken dish coming from the kitchen made his stomach grumble. Music floated through the door of Beata's bedroom. He distracted himself from his hunger by trying to place the melody. It was "Diamonds Are a Girl's Best Friend," Marilyn Monroe's show-stopping production number from *Gentlemen Prefer Blondes*.

Of all the storied bric-a-brac in Beata's collection, he found two items most amusing: Margaret Hamilton's pointed witch's hat from *The Wizard of Oz* and Fred MacMurray's crutches from *Double Indemnity*. Only someone of her eclectic tastes would assign equal prominence to props from a fairy-tale classic and the darkest of *films noir*. He put down Francis Lederer's ruby ring from *The Return of Dracula* and looked at his watch. 2:21. Beata was rarely more than five minutes late for an appointment. She would have no one calling her a diva.

The smell from the kitchen turned acrid. A loud, razzing noise drowned out Marilyn, who seemed to be singing on a continuous loop, returning to the beginning of "Diamonds" immediately after the closing bars. It was a smoke alarm.

He pushed through the swinging door to the kitchen, eyes stinging, found the oven control, and turned it off. Tipping open the oven door, he groped for a potholder and swung the smoldering pan from the rack to the top of the range. He switched on the fan in the overhead ventilator.

Soon the smoke dissipated and the noise stopped. Marilyn was still singing.

Valentino passed through the living room and rapped on the bedroom door. There was nothing wrong with Beata's hearing, he knew; she must have been aware of the alarm.

He tried the knob. The door was locked. He banged again, harder, and called out her name. No response.

Well, the worst that could happen was he'd catch her wearing only one eyelash and she'd accuse him of watching too many John Wayne movies. He backed off two steps and threw his shoulder against the door. It didn't yield as easily as doors did onscreen. Two more tries and one giant bruise later, the frame split and the door flew open. He stumbled in and almost sprawled across Beata's king-size bed, which already contained Beata herself.

She lay on her stomach, diagonally across the satin comforter, clutching the receiver of a white French-type telephone (*Ninotchka? An American in Paris?*) at the end of one outstretched arm. Her hair, which she'd continued to bleach against relentless graying, was disheveled as in sleep, obscuring her profile. There were age spots on her shoulders and her skin sagged in places, but she was in remarkably good condition for a woman even much younger. A CD player built into the wall facing the bed continued to belt out Norma Jean Baker's anthem for gold diggers from concealed speakers, but Beata wasn't listening. She was dead, which was shocking enough. Even more shocking, she was stark naked.

The detective lieutenant who arrived behind the uniformed police was an unexpected sight. Ranking investigators in Beverly Hills knew how to wear Armani and which gold clip went with which hundred-dollar tie. Ray Padilla wore pumpkin-colored polyester and a bowling shirt.

"Valentino, huh?" Instead of commenting on the name, he barked at a young officer in a trim uniform to turn off the CD player. He needed a haircut, and the dead pipe clamped between his teeth managed to observe the department's smoking ban while violating its spirit.

"Lab rats don't like us touching anything," said the young man.

"Use your elbow. I'll be humming that damn tune for a week."

Marilyn stopped singing abruptly. Valentino answered Padilla's questions and watched him scribble in a tiny memorandum book with a short mechanical pencil. The lieutenant wandered the room, recording details. An empty bottle of barbiturates on Beata's nightstand took the better part of one page. Something about the scene reminded Valentino of something, but he couldn't think what. It nagged him.

Padilla leaned one ear close to the telephone receiver clamped in Beata's hand, straightened. "This thing squawking when you broke in?"

"Squawking?"

"You know, that irritating noise telling you the phone's off the hook. Ma Bell hates spending her monopoly money on a dial tone."

"All I heard was music," Valentino said.

"Makes sense. The noise cuts off after a minute. Her skin's cool. She'd been dead awhile when you say you showed up. What is it you do?"

"I look for movies."

"That shouldn't take long in this town."

"Beverly Hills?"

"Hollywood. The Monster That Ate Southern California. You can't sit on the john without seeing Natalie Wood on a monitor in the stall."

"The movies I look for haven't been seen in decades. I'm a preservationist, and in some small way a detective."

Padilla turned his bleak eyes on him. "She seem depressed when she called you?"

"Anything but. So you think it's suicide?"

"No. I'm looking for a reason not to rule it out. I don't like that she left dinner in the oven, or that she chose a time when she was entertaining, or that she's naked. The telephone in her hand could mean she changed her mind and was trying to call for help when she lost consciousness, but it looks like set dressing to me. Also, I'm in some large way a detective, and I notice when something's missing. How about you?"

Valentino looked around, but the lieutenant wasn't a patient man.

"No glass, Sherlock. You can swallow a lethal dose of sleeping pills without water, but I don't know why you'd want to. Why not hang yourself? I mean, as long as you're making it uncomfortable."

"Marilyn Monroe."

"Yeah, that damn song. I can still hear it."

"I mean the missing glass. I'd wondered why all this seemed so familiar: the telephone, the pills, the nudity. It matches the situation in Marilyn Monroe's bedroom when she was found dead. There was no glass there, either. The case was ruled a suicide, but to this day a lot of people are convinced she was murdered."

"Some think it was the Kennedys," Padilla said. "On account of her relationship with Jack and Bobby. I really needed a nutball homicide. It's been a week since the last one." He took a Ziploc bag out of his pocket. It contained the note Valentino had found on the door and had given to the uniformed officer. "Would you swear she wrote this?"

"I never saw her handwriting. It sounds like her."

"I'll give it to the department graphologists. There ought to be samples in the apartment. Older woman living alone should know better than to leave her door unlocked. Was that normal?"

Valentino smiled through his sadness. He and Beata weren't close, but she was a bright daub of color in his often-gray academic life.

"I've never heard 'Beata' and 'normal' used in the same sentence. But I wouldn't say she tempted fate. She was superstitious." He told Padilla about her belief in the curse of the blond bombshells.

"Ironic; I don't think. I wonder who else she told."

"I suppose I'm a suspect."

"If this happened anywhere but the land of fruits and nuts, I'd book you as a material witness. Where else would two grown people spend a sunny day indoors, watching an old movie on a creaky projector?"

"A *bad* old movie," Valentino volunteered.

Padilla ground his teeth on his pipestem. "I wonder if 'Diamonds Are a Girl's Best Friend' was part of her CD collection or the killer brought his own? You gave this young man your contact information?"

Valentino said he had.

"Good. Now all I have to do is call up Ted Kennedy and ask him where he was this afternoon."

Valentino spent much of the next two days on the telephone, tracking down Beata Limerick's executor and asking how he might bid on *The Sandpiper* before her estate went on the block. As an antidote to all the diplomacy involved, he devoted the rest of the time arguing with his contractor. He was in the midst of construction at the Oracle, which was the abandoned movie theater he'd bought to serve as his living quarters and private screening room. On the third day he attended Beata's memorial service.

Lieutenant Padilla plunked himself down on the adjoining seat. He had on the same combustible suit he'd worn to the crime scene, but had traded his fiery madras necktie for a sober black knot. "If I were half the people here, I'd think twice before going to a funeral. The ushers might not let them leave."

The film archivist surveyed the sea of white heads. "Thirty years ago, you'd have had to pay admission to see them. You don't often find this much Hollywood history gathered in one spot."

"Thirty years ago they'd all have been suspects. I don't see a set of muscles strong enough to force those pills down even an old woman's throat."

"Was it the pills that killed her?"

"M.E. says yes. She put up a fight; lesions and contusions and a fractured skull. No other Marilyn CDs on the premises, by the way, and no box for the one that was playing when you found her. No prints, either. And that wasn't her handwriting on the note. Prints are yours."

"If I'd known she was dead, I'd have worn gloves when I took it off the door. What about Kennedy?"

"Introducing a bill on the Senate floor at time of death." He grinned joylessly at Valentino's expression. "Did you think I was joking about calling him?"

"I was just wishing I could have been on the extension."

"I never figured to make captain anyway. I'm not here about the Limerick woman. Where were you last night between ten P.M. and midnight?"

Valentino felt as if the back of his seat had turned to icy metal. He'd heard some version of that question on the soundtracks of countless crime movies, but had never expected to have to answer it himself.

"I was at home, going over construction bills. What happened?"

"Anyone who can verify that?"

"An electrician in Tarzana, though he might not admit it. I called him at his home around eleven to ask why it cost six hundred dollars to install a dimmer switch."

"You won't need him if phone-company records check out. Did you know a woman named Karen Ogilvie?"

The chill spread to Valentino's face. "I know her husband, Morris. He's a major contributor to UCLA, including my department. Karen used to do television a long time ago; she was Karen Earl then. She quit acting when she married Morris. Has something happened?" An old woman seated directly in front of him, whom he recognized from a half-forgotten commercial for Spic and Span, turned her head and shushed him.

The lieutenant lowered his voice. "Palm Springs P.D. faxed these over this morning." He slid a manilla envelope from his saddle pocket, removed the contents, and passed them to Valentino.

The pictures were smudged and grainy, but the face of the dead woman was familiar despite the depredations of age. Karen Earl Ogilvie was slumped over a steering wheel with her hair disarranged and dark smears on her forehead, chin, and the collar of her fur coat. Her eyes were open, her lips slightly parted as if to ask the photographer to wait while she fixed her lipstick.

Padilla took back the sheets. "She dined out with girlfriends last night. Husband was in New York on business. When the maid came in at seven A.M., she heard a motor running and looked in the garage. This is what she found."

"Carbon monoxide?"

"They're testing. That's blood on her face and coat. Someone cracked her a couple times with a blunt instrument. Her Porsche was undamaged, so she wasn't in an accident. Palm Springs cops think the killer was waiting for her in the garage, which meant he had access, and probably to the house as well."

"Did Ogilvie tell you he knows me?"

"We missed him in New York. He's in the air, on his way back to a surprise."

"Then why are you here? Am I the suspect of the week?" Valentino raised his voice, and got a chorus of geriatric shushes for his indiscretion.

"I'm not finished. Mrs. Ogilvie wasn't wearing the same clothes she'd had on when she left her friends. They said she was wearing a two-piece suit and no coat. Maid says the coat was hers, but she hadn't worn it in years, on account of all the controversy about animal rights; kept it in a storage bag in a closet. The lab rats are pretty sure someone put her in a dress after death. They found the two-piece suit crammed into a hamper. The extra flourishes made me think of Beata Limerick, and Beata Limerick made me think of you."

"If he changed her clothes after death, how did blood get on the collar of the coat?"

"It wasn't a spill, it was a smear. Pattern's different. Maybe the killer got blood on him and wiped it off."

"Maybe he did it deliberately."

"Why would he do that?"

"Why would he change her clothes?"

"Good point. There's more. The side door to the garage was bolted from the house side. He must have let himself out that way, but it's odd he bothered to bolt the door behind him."

Valentino experienced an eerie rush of déjà vu.

"The dress she had on," he said.

"Yeah?"

"Was it blue?"

"Thelma Todd," Valentino said.

"Never heard of her." Padilla looked at the black-and-white photograph of the beautiful curly-haired blond woman with the huge eyes and pert pointed chin as if he were committing a suspect's features to memory.

Valentino took back the book and returned it to its shelf. They were in the oversize projection booth of the Oracle, which the new owner had converted into temporary living space while the rest of the theater was in upheaval; a square opening looking out on the auditorium showed coils of exposed wires like spilled entrails and jagged sections of old plaster heaped on scaffolds. The crew was eating lunch, oblivious to the mustard and pickles dropping onto the vintage upholstered seats. The pair had come there straight from the memorial service. Valentino drew a tattered paperback from another shelf and ran his finger down the table of contents.

"She was before your time," he said. "Mine, too. Todd was a glamour queen and a fine comedienne, like Carole Lombard, who was another doomed blonde for Beata's curse."

"You'd think they'd learn to lay off the bleach." Padilla looked out at the carnage. "So you live here?"

"Just barely. I went apartment hunting and wound up in a gilt palace, minus most of the gilt. They'd have torn it down by now if I hadn't bought it."

"Sounds like a good excuse to pass it by."

Valentino found the chapter he wanted and skimmed. "Todd lived a wild life even for a movie star of her era, including a relationship with Lucky Luciano. In nineteen thirty-five her maid found her in her garage, slumped over the wheel of her Packard convertible. The ignition was on, there was blood on her face and fur coat, the door to the garage was barred on the other side. Death by monoxide poisoning. She had on a blue dress under the coat."

"This scumwad knows his trivia."

"Maybe he's read this book." Valentino held it up. It was titled *Hollywood's Unsolved Mysteries*.

The lieutenant surveyed the rows of books, which took up most of the space on the shelves not devoted to videotapes, DVDs, and reels of raw film. "I hope, for your sake, your alibi floats. You're a honey of a suspect."

"Good luck finding a motive. I liked Beata, and I never saw Karen Earl outside old episodes of *The Untouchables* and *Peter Gunn*."

"What's good motive? These days, all you need is a truck-stop waitress who short-changes you to take it out on the first meter maid you see." Padilla maneuvered his way around a plaster Buddha on his way to the stairs.

Throughout the next week, Valentino drew all his information on the murders from *E.T.*, *Access Hollywood*, and the *Los Angeles Times*. Details linking the slayings to the cases of Marilyn Monroe and Thelma Todd had been suppressed, but he learned that Karen Ogilvie had whiled away the afternoon before her dinner with friends watching old footage of herself in her screening room, a staple in the motion-picture community every bit as crucial as swimming pools and tennis courts; apparently there was a smidgen of Norma Desmond in even the most well-adjusted retired siren. Valentino himself was not mentioned, to his relief, but Lieutenant Padilla was quoted often, saying that whoever had killed the two women was probably known to and trusted by them, in order to have obtained access to their homes and proximity to their persons. Even without the connections to infamous Hollywood fatalities, news that a serial killer was targeting old-time actresses filled columns and airtime. Little was left to cover the death in an automobile accident of Geoffrey Root, a popular female impersonator who played local nightclubs. For years he'd skewered— and sometimes amused—such flashy femmes as Dolly Parton, Zsa Zsa Gabor, Cher, and Madonna with his dead-on impressions of them in sequins and heavy makeup. *E. T.* sandwiched accident-scene footage between the latest on the Limerick-Ogilvie murders and Jennifer Lopez's romance of the month. When the camera panned to the accordioned hood and what lay upon it, Valentino muted the sound and snatched up the telephone.

"Congratulations," Padilla greeted. "You're no longer my prime suspect. Your electrician backed up your story."

"What do you know about Geoffrey Root's accident?"

The lieutenant put him on hold for ten minutes.

"Highway Patrol says a jogger found his Acura folded up against a tree in Laurel Canyon at dawn," he said when he came back on. "Apparently Root lost control on a curve, went through a guardrail, and bounced down a ravine. He wasn't wearing his seatbelt. His head punched a hole in the windshield." He chuckled mirthlessly. "He was headed to a charity benefit, which was canceled when he didn't show; had a bunch of costumes in the car. There were pink feather boas and high-heeled pumps scattered all over."

"I'm more concerned about the wig," Valentino said.

"Which one? CHiPs said it looked like an explosion at the Hair Club for Men. Or rather, Women."

"The wig on the hood of the car. Do you know anything about the Jayne Mansfield case?"

Padilla swore and told the archivist to meet him at police headquarters.

Whoever decorated lieutenants' offices in Beverly Hills had taken pains to keep them from looking as if they were occupied by police, and Ray Padilla had done his best to fill his up with cop. For every African violet and Miró print he had inherited, he'd installed a bowling trophy or a cartoon clipped from *Parade.* That day he was actually wearing a leisure suit, powder blue with a clip-on tie. He wasted no time on handshakes, waving Valentino into the plastic scoop chair facing his littered desk.

"My first partner worked the Mansfield case from this end," he said. "Kept bending my ear about it till he retired. Jayne was running around with a mob lawyer at the time, named Brody. He represented Jack Ruby, the guy that shot Lee Harvey Oswald. Seems these sex kittens couldn't keep away from gangsters and Kennedys. Anyway, she, Brody, and her teenage son were killed in June nineteen sixty-seven when her Buick rear-ended a truck on I-90 in Louisiana, on their way to do a TV interview in New Orleans. To this day, a lot of people think Jayne was decapitated. She wasn't. Her wig flew out through the broken windshield and landed on the hood and a gawker saw it and leapt to the most sensational conclusion, as gawkers will, especially when a movie star's involved. I called Highway Patrol again after I spoke to you. There were no pieces of shattered glass in Geoffrey Root's wig, which means he wasn't wearing it when his head hit the windshield. Someone had to have placed it there after the accident."

Valentino said, "I think at this point we can stop calling it an accident."

"Dollars to Ding-Dongs he was knocked out or dead before his car went down that ravine. Our boy aimed it at the guardrail, put it in Drive, jumped clear, and climbed down afterwards to dress the set. Same basic M.O., except his first two victims were women."

"Female impersonators come close; that's the whole idea." Valentino stood and paced in a circle. The office was too cluttered with stacks of file folders to encourage any more movement than that. "I can't help thinking this character got all his ideas from Beata. When I asked her what she meant by the curse, she mentioned Thelma Todd, Marilyn Monroe, Jean Harlow, Sharon Tate, and Jayne Mansfield. Three of those have already served as models for the crime scenes."

"That checks with the profile. The victims had to have known and trusted the killer for him to get so close. Trouble is, by the time we finish questioning all the friends, servants, personal assistants, and presidents of fan clubs, this maniac will have died of old age."

Valentino considered. "Did Root live alone?"

"He had a companion, fellow named Sheridan. What their relationship was isn't police business these days." Padilla straightened his clip-on. "It's a place to start. Let's go."

"Why me?"

"You speak entertainer. I need an interpreter."

Padilla drove better than he dressed. Half an hour later they entered the driveway of Geoffrey Root's Frank Lloyd Wright house in the Hollywood Hills. The late performer's partner, Evan Sheridan, let them inside. Tall and graying with a slight stoop, he was obviously composing himself with effort. The visitors apologized for intruding and said they wanted to ask about Root's activities before the accident.

Sheridan showed them into the sunken living room, where he said he and his companion had been relaxing before it was time for Root to leave for his charity benefit. It was done in tasteful colors with modern furnishings. An Impressionist-inspired painting of a premiere at Grauman's Chinese Theatre decorated the chimney above a fieldstone fireplace. Valentino noted a pair of tiny, state-of-the-art speakers propped on the ends of the granite mantel. He asked if the room was a home theater.

For answer, Sheridan bent and activated a switch hidden beneath the marble top of a huge coffee table. The painting above the mantel slid up noiselessly into a pocket, exposing a canvas screen.

"Rear or front projection?" Valentino asked.

"Front." His host pointed to a square aperture high in the wall opposite the screen. "Geoffrey preferred film to DVD and videotape, using a professional-grade projector. I said we were relaxing, but actually he was working. He always prepared for a show by watching footage of the women he impersonated. Yesterday we saw excerpts from *Some Like It Hot*, *Red-Headed Woman*, and *Will Success Spoil Rock Hunter?* You know: Marilyn, Jean Harlow, Jayne. Will you gentlemen please excuse me?" He left the room hastily, tugging a white handkerchief from a pocket.

"Interviewing the widow's the worst part of this job." Padilla spoke without irony. "Harlow was one of the blondes the Limerick woman mentioned. Did she die violently?"

"No. Kidney failure took her at age twenty-six."

"Not promising. From a killer's point of view."

Sheridan returned. "I'm sorry. It's very hard answering all these questions. Is it common in accident investigations?"

Valentino turned aside the inquiry. "Which one of you operated the projector?"

"Neither one of us. Geoffrey was adamant about observing union rules in work-related situations. He always employed a professional projectionist."

The archivist and the detective exchanged glances. Padilla spoke first. "Who'd he use yesterday?"

"Oh, the same one as always, Arthur Augustine. For a young man he's one of the best in the business."

"Who left first, Root or Augustine?" Padilla asked.

"They left together. Geoffrey was his ride home. But he won't be able to give you any information about the accident; his house is between here and

Laurel Canyon. Geoffrey would have dropped him off several miles short of where—he ended up." Sheridan swallowed.

"One more question," Valentino said gently. "Where is his house?"

"Stupid," Padilla said, driving. He gripped the wheel tightly in both hands.

Valentino was startled. "Who, me?"

"Me. I'm paid to be a detective. These are all pros, and they were all screening or about to screen films the day they were killed. It stands to reason they'd hire a projectionist, one they knew and trusted. That's how he got into their houses. They let him in."

"We didn't know Root was screening until just now. The other two could have been coincidence. I didn't see it, either; and I know the procedure; screening's a big part of my work. It shouldn't be hard to find out if Augustine ran projectors for Karen Ogilvie and Beata." Valentino stared out the window, at the same scenery Geoffrey Root had seen on his way to death. "How do you think he killed Root?"

"Probably at some lonely stop sign, or else he made an excuse for Root to pull over. This guy likes blunt instruments. With Root dead or unconscious, he slid him over and drove him to the top of the ravine. You know the rest."

"Everything but why."

"Why's the prosecutor's problem. Right now I'm wondering what next. Who was the other blonde Beata Limerick mentioned?"

Valentino hesitated. "Sharon Tate."

Both men fell silent, and Padilla pressed the accelerator. They were old enough to remember the lurid details of the blond actress's murder in 1969; a ritual slaughter, along with three friends, in a bungalow in Bel Air by the Charles Manson "family" of devil-worshipers. They'd been stabbed multiple times and Sharon's blood used to smear the word "Pig" on the front door. That sun-drenched drive seemed as bleak as midnight.

The house was an anomaly in twenty-first-century L.A.: white clapboard with a steep peaked roof and a picket fence, held over from the forgotten days before the movie colony was founded. The door was opened by a woman in her fifties, with skin brown and crinkled by too many tans and a head of fried hair, aggressively peroxided. She was dressed too young, in a tight pink halter and canary-yellow Capri pants that squeezed her bare midriff into something resembling a bicycle inner tube. The rest was rouge, mascara, and vermilion on her fingers and toes.

"Arthur Augustine." Padilla held up his shield.

"Artie's at work. I'm his mother. May I take a message?"

"Where's he working?"

She drew in her chin and turned to Valentino. He pulled a sympathetic face. "It's important we find him."

"He works all over; he's very popular in his field. He never tells me where. He hasn't been in an accident?" She touched her throat, a theatrical gesture.

"He causes accidents," Padilla growled.

Quickly, Valentino said, "We just want to ask him some questions. Could we see his room? He might have an appointment book."

"He rents an apartment upstairs. Artie's no mama's boy. You won't disturb anything? He's particular about his things."

The lieutenant let Valentino mouth the comforting response, and she stood aside. The front parlor (as it would have been called when the house was new) glittered with professional-quality photographs of a young Mother Augustine in silver frames: cheesecake shots in two-piece swimsuits, glamour poses in evening wear, tough-girl tableaus with a pistol and a dangling cigarette. She'd chosen to display her aspiring-actress portfolio.

"You've learned my secret," she said. "I tested for everything in town, from soap operas to deodorant commercials. I finally landed a part opposite Bobby Darin, but I got pregnant and had to bow out. Sandra Dee stepped in. I tell Artie it took my little man to knock the stars out of my eyes."

"Tease him a lot, do you?"

She tipped back her head and looked down her nose at the lieutenant. Valentino wondered if she'd had it bobbed. "He pretends to be annoyed and I pretend to think he's ungrateful, after I gave up the bright lights for him. We laugh."

"Where's his room?" Padilla said.

"Apartment." She led the way up a narrow staircase and flicked her bright nails in the direction of a closed door. Padilla tried the knob.

"He keeps it locked," she said with satisfaction. "As if I'd pry."

He produced a ring of assorted keys from a polyester pocket. "Okay if I try these?"

"Knock yourself out." She sounded sincere.

He was halfway through the ring when the latch clicked.

"Oh, my stars." The woman's voice was a squeak.

Posters leapt out from the walls when the door was opened. Some were pricey originals, others reproductions: Marilyn sprawled before the falls in *Niagara*, Jayne's vapid face grinning between her cotton-candy hair and her ice-cream breasts in *The Girl Can't Help It*, Thelma Todd looking fetching in a lobby card for one of her comedy shorts, a chilling rendition of Sharon Tate wielding a bloody stake in *The Fearless Vampire Killers.* There were other four-color images, all of them tragic blondes: Jean Harlow, Carole Lombard, Dorothy Stratten, Inger Stevens—the long, sad Parthenon of yellow hair, gaudy lives, and early death. Someone had taken a four-inch brush and slashed scarlet paint diagonally across every lovely face.

Oh, my stars, indeed.

Augustine's library was a miniature version of Valentino's, apart from its emphasis on the Industry's dark side: *Hollywood Babylon, Fade to Black, Hollywood's Unsolved Mysteries, Helter Skelter.* An empty CD box atop a Sony player caught his eye: a single of Marilyn singing "Diamonds Are a Girl's Best Friend."

Padilla called to him. He joined the lieutenant at a small writing table, where yesterday's *L.A. Times* lay folded to a gossip column, with a check mark beside the fourth paragraph:

> . . . Holiday O'Shea, popular road-company star of *Hello, Dolly; Gypsy;* and *Gentlemen Prefer Blondes,* celebrating her 55th with husband and friends with a private screening of a local cable documentary of her life at Orson's Grill Friday . . .

Padilla looked at the archivist. "What day is today?"

Orson's Grill, in a defunct Burger Chef on Cahuenga, featured posters and memorabilia—the latter locked inside shatterproof glass cases—relating to the life and career of Orson Welles, with a menu engineered to replicate the late actor/director's expansive waistline in its clientele. The maître d' pointed Padilla and Valentino toward a private room in back. The lieutenant drew his sidearm, towing a chain of gasps through the crowded common room.

"Has-beens, also-rans, and wannabes," he said. "Those are his targets. Life would be simpler if these twisted jerks would just kill their mothers and be done with it."

Valentino said nothing. He was tense and his throat was hoarse from arguing in favor of his civilian presence at the showdown. He'd finally compromised, agreeing to hang behind in order to avoid being trapped in the crossfire between Padilla and the backup he'd ordered for the rear entrance.

A burly waiter stood before the door to the back room. "Sorry, fellows. Private party. Not even staff's allowed inside till after the movie."

"Whose orders?" Padilla showed him his gun and shield. The waiter blanched.

"Why, the young man's, sir. He said he was the projectionist."

"You see a projector?"

"He was carrying a big black case like one comes in."

"How long ago?"

The waiter shrugged. "Twenty minutes."

Padilla told him to stand clear.

The door was locked from the other side. The lieutenant clasped his automatic in both hands, raised a foot, and threw his heel at the latch. The door was more cooperative for him than Beata's had been for Valentino. It swung open and banged against the wall inside the room.

"Police! Drop it!"

Valentino craned his neck to see inside. Four middle-aged people in formal dress sat around a linen-covered table, eyes wide above gags tied around their mouths. One was a woman in her middle fifties with a chrysanthemum head of improbably butter-colored hair. Their hands were out of sight; tied, Valentino supposed, to their chairs.

A reedy young man in cords and a tweed sportcoat stood this side of the table with his back to Padilla, looking over his shoulder at the source of the interruption. Annoyance was plain on his narrow features, which were a younger version of Mother Augustine's. He'd stopped in the midst of drawing a collapsible steel baton—the kind police used in place of nightsticks—from a black case standing open on the table. The case was filled with long-bladed knives and coils of nylon rope.

Just then a door on the other side of the room burst open and two policemen in uniform sprang through, one standing, his partner dropping into a crouch. Their sidearms were trained on the young man holding the baton.

His head spun that way. Then his shoulders sagged and he let his weapon fall back into the case.

Padilla barked another command. Arthur Augustine turned to face him and folded his hands on top of his head.

"Pigs," he said.

Holiday O'Shea whimpered through her gag.

The "Curse Killer" stained front pages and breaking newscasts for two weeks, complete with its familiar back story of parental neglect and adolescent jealousy. It made Valentino feel sorry for Augustine, until he thought of Beata Limerick. Ray Padilla was forced to buy a new suit to wear before the cameras. When Augustine was declared mentally unfit to stand trial and remanded to the maximum-security ward of the state mental hospital in Camarillo, the entire episode began to fade, joining the shockers of Hollywood past.

Beata's print of *The Sandpiper* went to auction. Valentino, remembering her now without sadness, topped Ted Turner's bid and claimed it. The restoration experts at UCLA put it on the list behind *Charlie Chan's Chance* and two hundred feet of Theda Bara's *Cleopatra*, which was all of that silent feature that had ever come to light.

Six months after the arrest in Orson's Grill, ABC announced plans to tape a TV movie about the murders. The producers didn't lack for fair-haired has-beens, also-rans, and wannabes to fill the cast.

Shooting Big Ed

There's nothing rarer than an East L.A. millionaire. That paradox might have been enough in itself to pique Valentino's interest, without the added incentive of acquiring a lost film from the first decade of talking pictures for the UCLA Film Preservation Department, free of charge; together, they compelled him to cancel his day's appointments and brave the gangs and carjackers to pay the old man a visit.

Sometime in the late 1940s, Ignacio Bozal had suddenly appeared in Acapulco with a bankroll big enough to buy and renovate a broken-down resort hotel and open for business just before the birth of the Mexican Riviera. Rumors persisted that he'd made his stake harboring Nazi war criminals in Argentina, or had been a member of the Perón government and looted the treasury, but no serious investigation was ever made, and Bozal's claim of a silent partnership in a gold mine in the Sierra Madres was accepted as plausible by his American investors. Thirty years later, having doubled his fortune many times over, he'd sold out to a corporation and emigrated to California.

There, scorning the mansions of Bel-Air and Beverly Hills, he'd bought a city block of modest houses in the largely Mexican-American suburb of Los Angeles. A wall went up around it, sheltering his middle-aged children, grown grandchildren, and great-grandchildren under his benevolent eye. He kept his fleet of mint-condition classic automobiles in the attached garages and converted the basement of his personal dwelling to store his huge film collection. He told interviewers of his sentimental attachment to the American cinema, which he said had taught him his English. Visitors were amused by the 1930s American slang that peppered his speech; he looked like an old Spanish grandee and talked like a combination of Wallace Beery and Roscoe Karns. At ninety-six he was said to be in good health and better humor. He was a frequent contributor to the film program at UCLA.

The gateman, a thirty-year-old Hispanic in a tailored gray uniform who referred to Bozal as Grandpapa, found Valentino's name on his clipboard and told him where to park. The compound reminded the newcomer of a street in *The Godfather*, if it had been filmed south of the border: tawny children in baggy swimsuits frolicking in the spray from open fire hydrants, heavyset women in light summer dresses sitting on porches, slick-haired *hombres* in bright sport shirts smoking cigarettes and conversing in rapid Spanish on the sidewalks. There was plenty of family resemblance to go around.

"Ever hear of a mug named Van Oliver?"

Ignacio Bozal, it developed, had little patience for small talk. The question, delivered in a refined Spanish accent incompatible with the vocabulary, came two minutes after a white-coated houseboy (who also called him Grandpapa) led Valentino into a sunken living room and left him alone with his host.

"Old-time picture actor," Valentino said. "He was murdered. Another one of Hollywood's unsolved mysteries."

The old man jerked his chin, approving. He was a small man and ancient, but erect, and his thin build gave the illusion of height. His gold Rolex and cuff links looked too heavy for his fragile wrists. But his eyes were bright behind huge glasses and he had a full head of fine white hair like Cesar Romero's.

"At least you know more than that punk I talked to on the phone. He thought Garbo was a brand of mouthwash."

Valentino winced, knowing who'd answered. All the other archivists in his department had interns who were film school grad students. His had gone to see *Scooby-Doo* fourteen times.

He came to the young man's defense. "We can't all be buffs. Most people wouldn't know Oliver. He only made one movie." He wondered, with a little thrill, if that was the film Bozal was offering to donate.

The old man kept him in suspense. "Officially, he just disappeared. My bet is they buried him up in the hills, or rowed him out past Catalina and dumped him overboard in a cement jacket. In those days, you couldn't convict anyone of murder in the State of California without a corpse. It was almost a double murder, if you can call a movie studio a victim. It drove Warner Brothers close to bankruptcy."

"They shelved the film without releasing it," Valentino said. "Publicity couldn't promote it properly without a star to interview and show up at premieres. That was in nineteen thirty-one. They might have recut and reshot to build up one of the other players and brought it out later, except the Catholic Decency League shut down gangster films."

"Protecting the nation's youth." Bozal snarled out of the side of his mouth. "Nothing's changed in seventy years except the width of the lapels. Anyway, the picture was eventually lost. Nobody cared about preservation back then; rereleasing hadn't caught on, and there was no TV or home video. They remade it in 'thirty-seven as a musical with George Brent in the lead. It tanked, natch. You know the title?"

"*Big Ed.* Oliver played a gangster loosely based on Al Capone. Only he didn't play him like Edward G. Robinson in *Little Caesar* or Paul Muni in the original *Scarface*. The few insiders who saw the final cut said he had an entirely new take on the character. Had the film made it into theaters, it might have changed the history of the gangster movie."

"Not just gangster movies. Acting. Robinson was nasty, Muni played psycho. Jimmy Cagney in *Public Enemy* was like a bomb about to go off. Oliver kept his cool, like James Dean twenty years later, and Al Pacino in *The Godfather*. He may have been the first actor to play to the camera instead of the back row of the balcony. A lot of the production is what you'd expect of the transitional period between silents and talkies: stagebound and static, chained to those damn hidden microphones, but his performance would stand up beside anyone's today."

Valentino's thrill became a cozy hum. Bozal wasn't parroting something he'd read or heard; he spoke as someone who'd seen the evidence firsthand, and recently. "Where'd you find it?"

"Former Warner Brothers splicer died last year. I bought his estate."

"I can't believe I missed a sale like that. What was his name?"

"You wouldn't recognize the name. He was out before the industry gave film editors screen credit. It was a private deal in Europe."

Valentino was sure this rapid-fire response was a lie. He assumed the millionaire was protecting a favorite fishing hole. "Is *Big Ed* the film you're donating? I'd sure like to see it even if it isn't."

"It is. Screening room's downstairs."

They went down to the basement. Bozal used the handrail, but the stairs didn't slow him down. He seemed fit for any age past sixty. The lower level appeared equal in square footage to the rest of the house, with thousands of film cans stored like wine in racks on the walls, three rows of theater seats upholstered in green plush, and a nylon screen framed by an Art Deco proscenium. Three steps led up to a platform at the opposite end, where the houseboy who'd admitted Valentino had the gate open on a Bell & Howell projector of 1930s vintage. "No problems, Ernesto?"

"Ready when you are, G.P.!"

"Cut that out." Bozal indicated a seat up front and sat next to his guest. "Half my family is in pictures and the other half wants to be. If we were in Mexico, it would be artichokes."

Ernesto slammed shut the gate, switched off the recessed lights in the ceiling, and started the feature. As the numerals thrown onto the screen counted down from ten, jumping a little because of broken sprocket-holes, the sound track popping and crackling, Valentino felt the delicious anticipation he'd known the first time he saw a movie in a theater when he was a boy. The millions of miles of celluloid he'd studied in the course of his job had failed to dim its silvery luster; and to know that he was about to see a nearly seventy-five-year-old feature for the very first time made him almost giddy. But he was apprehensive as well: What if he didn't like it?

Five minutes in, his fears vanished.

His host had been right about the creaky production values. The talking-picture revolution of 1927 had looted the Broadway stage of actors who could really act, and some of the players were wooden and unsure of themselves emoting before a working crew instead of a rapt audience; rooted as they were to the vicinity of the primitive microphones, concealed in potted plants and prop telephones, they were unable to gesture widely or roam the soundstage, and the camera's soundproof booth had put a temporary end to pans, zooms, and dollies. It was like photographing an amateur theatrical production. There was no background music to enhance mood, just some scratchy Stravinsky under the opening and closing titles; in 1931, the studios worried that audiences would wonder where the music was coming from. *Big Ed* had, in fact, every disadvantage of its time.

But from the moment Van Oliver made his entrance, stepping down off a train from New York and pausing, only his eyes moving as he stood on the platform with one hand inside his long overcoat, searching for friends or enemies, the movie became unique, and all his. He was a lean man in his early twenties, with dark Mediterranean features under the curled-down brim of his fedora, piratically handsome. When he opened his mouth to speak his first line, Valentino half expected an exotic accent. Pure American came out instead, in a casual baritone that took on an ominous edge when he met resistance. He acted balletic rings around stage professionals and more than held his own against seasoned character actors from Warner Brothers' rich reperatory stock—Murderers' Row, *Variety* called it. All the time he was on camera he was mesmerizing, and scenes in which he did not appear crackled with tension, anticipating his entrance. He seemed to have *star* tattooed on his forehead.

The action scenes—Oliver disarming a rival with one hand, punishing him with a backward swipe of the other, police cars barreling around corners, the inevitable montage of clattering tommyguns, crashing sedans, exploding storefronts, illegal alcohol gushing into glasses stacked in sparkling pyramids—were exciting and fresh with the adolescent inspiration of the period. Valentino's back seldom touched the plush back of his seat. Even the love scenes between Oliver and Madeleine Crane, a striking brunette with enormous, expressive eyes, seemed to set the screen afire; within two years of its filming, the Motion Picture Code would bar such raw sexuality for the next three decades.

The ending electrified. Oliver's death scene was defiant, not contrite. Had the picture been released, his curtain line—"You and what army?"—would have made every reference book on great movie quotations. Valentino found himself applauding when the closing credits sprang onto the screen.

The lights came up. Ignacio Bozal, lounging in the adjoining seat with legs crossed, observed Valentino's expression with a smirk. "Quite a show, eh? Bogart wouldn't have got a chance at *The Petrified Forest* if Oliver had stuck around five more years. He'd've finished out his career saying, 'Tennis, anyone?' on the Great White Way, just like he started."

"Whatever happened to Madeleine Crane? She looked familiar."

"She had bit parts as wisecracking secretaries in a couple of programmers before *Big Ed*. Her real name was Magdalena Carvello; she was Puerto Rican. She could turn the accent on and off. When the Roman Catholic lobby shut down gangster pictures, Warners didn't renew her contract. RKO offered her a long-term deal, but that would've meant sleeping with Howard Hughes, so she turned it down. She married some joker and moved to Europe."

"Too bad. For moviegoers, I mean."

"She'd've been out of work in a couple of years anyway. Can you see her as the long-suffering wife of some philanderer played by Chester Morris? The Hays Office wouldn't have let her play anything else."

"For someone who came here late in life, you know a lot about inside Hollywood."

The old man blew a raspberry. "Everybody who was anybody wintered at my joint in Acapulco. You hear a lot of gossip when you mingle. See a lot, too. Garbo went skinny-dipping in the indoor pool." He leered.

"What did you hear about Van Oliver?"

"Nothing you probably didn't read. It's part of industry lore. He was just what you saw on the screen, though I don't know if he ever shot anyone. He ran errands for the Capone mob in Chicago, and came out here to scout a new racket when the actors started talking union. Jack Warner liked his looks and offered him a screen test. Well, you can see the impression he made. The studio changed his name from Vincent Olivera and signed him for three pictures.

"Rumor was it didn't sit well with Chicago," he went on. "Maybe they didn't approve of moonlighting, or Big Al wasn't flattered by his characterization. The fat bastard had spies on all the sets; we know that from George Raft's experience when he worked on *Scarface*. Maybe Oliver fell for his own publicity and told the mob where to go. Anyway, he dropped out of sight the day after the picture wrapped. People don't just disappear, except in Universal horror films. When his resumé came to light, the truth wasn't hard to figure out."

Valentino pondered. In the background, he heard Ernesto removing the last reel from the projector and placing it carefully in its can. He knew the sounds better than the beating of his own heart. "A rediscovered classic of this quality *and* an unsolved disappearance. I can hear our man in Information Services rubbing his hands together over the publicity. This gift is beyond generous, Mr. Bozal. There may be an honorary doctorate in it for you."

"A mug like me, with 'Doctor' in front of his name? Don't make me laugh." The old man's snicker carried traces of Allen Jenkins and Torquemada. Then his face grew thoughtful. "I'd be tickled down to the ground if you could swing a print of *Greed.* My sources tell me you stumbled over von Stroheim's original full-length version."

"You'll have it if I have to bootleg it myself," Valentino said.

"God, I love foul play!"

Henry Anklemire leaped up from behind his desk next to the boiler room. "Our man in Information Services" was an evil cherub in a toupee a shade too dark for his vintage and a checked suit (size portly), polka-dot tie, and striped shirt that made a cataclysmic statement Valentino thought could not have been coincidental. His face glowed as from a strong shot of whiskey.

"We'll keep that between ourselves," Valentino said. "My department head thinks Sherlock Holmes was a sociopath."

But Anklemire was on a roll. "Look at Marilyn Monroe; not one-tenth the talent of Judy Holliday, but she had the good sense to get murdered by the Kennedys. You ever see Judy Holliday on a T-shirt?"

"There's some question about whether the Kennedys were involved. And you wouldn't know Judy Holliday from Doc Holliday if I hadn't forced you to watch *Born Yesterday* on DVD."

Anklemire had offered his expertise to the university after a year of retirement on top of forty years of advertising cigarettes, automobiles, and feminine hygiene products for a venerable agency on Madison Avenue, on condition that his salary wouldn't threaten his Social Security benefits; twelve months of shooting golf and playing canasta with his next-door neighbors in Tarzana had made him desperate for any activity that didn't involve listening to anyone's blow-by-blow account of his prostate operation. The director of Information Services had assured him that low pay was no obstacle to his employment.

Most of Valentino's academic colleagues loathed the bouncy little flack, for the very reasons that the archivist liked him. He was an aggressive promoter who knew the common denominator that shook loose money from every area of society, and he had no patience for questions of propriety or prestige. Give him a salable commodity and he'd sell it. He knew nothing about movies or their history, but he knew how to turn silver nitrate into gold.

"*Born Yesterday.* Great flick. They ought to colorize it. What you want to do, you want to send the picture on tour, book the revival houses, pass the hat for donations. Then you bring it out on DVD. This outfit sure can use the cash." He raised his voice above the banging of the water pipes next-door. "What we do to get them in is play up the mysterious-disappearance angle and the Capone connection. That didn't hurt Geraldo one little bit, even if he did come up with bupkus from Al's secret vault."

"We found a great movie that's been missing for most of the last century. Isn't that worth anything?"

"Boring. Strictly third paragraph. Nobody cares."

"Nobody but the people you and I work for." But he didn't put up an argument; Anklemire's opinion sadly reflected the majority's. "What do you need from me?"

"You're the archaeologist. Start digging. I can't write copy without material."

"Archivist, not archaeologist."

"What's the difference? Do some homework. Interview people. Get me color: big hats, gun molls, armor-plated Cadillacs, rat-a-tat-tat!" He mimed firing a submachine gun. Anklemire was a living video arcade.

"Who do you suggest I interview? Capone's been dead almost sixty years, and time hasn't been any kinder to the cast of *Big Ed.* Wait." Valentino took out his notebook, into which he'd scribbled his impressions after the basement screening. "Roy Fitzhugh's still around. He played one of Oliver's henchmen. He lives at the actors' home up in Woodland Hills."

"He must be a hundred."

"Not quite that bad. He always played older than he was. He had one of those faces. I hope his memory's still good."

"I'd send a photog with you, but the flash might stop every pump in the place. Try to keep him on topic. We want to know what happened to Oliver, not how many football teams Clara Bow went to bed with."

Valentino laughed. "What do you want me to do, solve his murder?"

"If it isn't too much trouble."

The archivist was still shaking his head when he dropped by the lab to see how the technicians were coming with the film he'd brought back from East L.A. A young expert in a Haz-Mat suit—everything but the hood and latex gloves, which he would don before approaching fragile, volatile celluloid—told him there were several films to be duplicated before *Big Ed*, but that it had been moved up the list by order of the head of the Film Preservation Department. Valentino, who knew quite a bit about what was involved in striking off a new negative from an ancient positive, then making a new master print from the negative, kept his impatience to himself and went from there to the library. UCLA kept an impressive, although incomplete, collection of fan magazines, beginning with the silent cinema and continuing through the 1950s, when the voracious competition from television lured readers in droves from *Photoplay to TV Guide*. Much of the material had been committed to microfilm; much had not, and Valentino wore a path through the linoleum between the drawers where the microfilm spools were kept and the shelves of thumb-smeared magazines in their tattered cardboard file boxes. In among the ads for Packards and Lucky Strikes, he found some production and preproduction material on *Big Ed*, which was mostly photographic: stills of the actors in and out of costume, horsing around on the set, pretending to menace one another in tableaus similar to the scenes they'd shot. Few people studying such pictures in film books realized they were looking at fake publicity stills and not actual frames from the films. By and large they were posed and shot by legitimate artists of the photographic medium; Valentino sometimes wished the movies themselves looked as good as their advertising.

Van Oliver, it appeared, was quite chummy with Roy Fitzhugh, "Big Ed" 's right-hand man in the motion picture. The pair always seemed to have their arms around each other's shoulders, trading mock punches and grinning, and messing each other's brilliantined pompadours with impudent hands. The archivist knew that such carryings-on were often a ruse to disguise deep mutual dislike. However, there were rather more of them than the average. He was inclined to believe the two were close.

Big Ed vanished from the puff columns in June 1931—its announced month of release—as thoroughly as its star had dropped from sight weeks earlier. Under normal circumstances, the feature would have been mentioned everywhere at that time, with cover articles on its leading players in *Modern Screen* and *Liberty*, billboards splashed throughout Los Angeles, press kits sent out, and advertisements in newspapers in key cities across the country. Instead, the story moved to the city section of the *L.A. Times*, where burly detectives assigned to Missing Persons and Homicide were photographed grilling hapless suspects raked in from the local underworld.

As Van Oliver's sinister origins became general knowledge, the focus of the investigation shifted from Where is he? to Where is his body? A plainclothes sergeant was sent to Chicago to interview Big Al himself, who showed him the hospitality of his Hawthorne Hotel headquarters, gave him tickets to a Cubs game, and assured him he had no memory of ever meeting Vincent Olivera. He said he was flattered by what he'd heard about Olivera's impersonation of him on camera. A picture of the sergeant with Capone and Roger Hornsby at

Wrigley Field appeared on the front page and the sergeant came home to find himself back in uniform, directing traffic at Hollywood and Vine.

It was the kind of publicity the nascent motion-picture industry paid millions to avoid. Less than ten years had elapsed since the unsolved murder of director William Desmond Taylor, a sordid episode involving drugs and sex, and with pressure from organized religion and the puritan public for Hollywood to clean up its act, Warner Brothers' first move was to shelve *Big Ed* and hope the scandal would go away.

It didn't work, of course; such measures never did.

The next year, Howard Hughes released *Scarface: Shame of a Nation*, the Church banned it, and a ton of letters from outraged parishioners forced the studios to shift the heroic emphasis from criminals to crimebusters for most of the next two decades. There was no telling how many potentially classic films were banished, unseen by the world, to underground vaults during this period, and eventually lost through attrition and neglect. It was only through employee theft (for even a condemned film is studio property, not to be removed from the lot without permission) and the generosity of an elderly collector that Van Oliver's performance had survived. Whatever unsavory practices he'd provided the mob, his artistry deserved recognition.

Emerging from the building, blinking against the toxic beauty of the Southern California sunset, Valentino looked up a number in his notebook and used his cell phone to call the Motion Picture Country Home in Woodland Hills.

"You ready to check in?" greeted Kym Trujillo, his contact in Admissions. "A creaky old-movie buff like you ought to be able to hold his own in the conversation in the cafeteria."

"Ask me again next year. I'd like to arrange a visit with one of your residents. Roy Fitzhugh."

"I know Roy. I admitted him myself. He's a hoot. Hang on." She came back on the line three minutes later, sounding subdued. "I talked to one of his nurses. He's an Alzheimer's case, has his good days and his bad. Today's not so good. He's usually at his best mornings."

He thanked her and said he'd call in the morning. Standing there holding the telephone, he felt again the humming sensation he'd experienced in Ignacio Bozal's screening room; he was hooked. He called the L.A. Police Department and asked for Lieutenant Henry McPherson in Homicide.

McPherson remembered him from the Dundrear murder at Twentieth Century Fox. Valentino had helped him break the case, but the lieutenant's goodwill evaporated when he learned what he wanted.

"The mainframe hard-drive has enough to remember without a seventy-year-old murder investigation," he growled. "The file would be in the subbasement, if it didn't go into the incinerator under Eisenhower. Why should I send a uniform down there to dig through the boxes with two new cases on my desk this morning, and four left over from last week?"

"Show me where they are and I'll dig through them myself. It's what I'm trained for."

"There was something in *my* training about not letting civilians monkey with open cases."

"It's just research, Lieutenant. I'm not looking to bring anyone to justice, even if whoever killed Oliver is alive and getting around without bottled oxygen. There's an acknowledgment in it for the L.A.P.D. when we go public. I thought you chief might appreciate the good press."

"Well, I'm not letting you into the basement. I'll send a man down when I can spare him. Next week, maybe."

"If you could do it before tomorrow morning, I'll credit you as a consultant. I'm interviewing a surviving witness then and I'd like to go in with all the information I can get."

McPherson broke the silence on his end. "If you're asking me would I like to be in pictures, the answer would be 'Over my dead body,' except we don't sling that one around in Homicide. You'll get it when you get it."

That evening, Valentino kept his adrenaline pumping by screening his favorite gangster pictures. He watched Robinson, Cagney, and Muni riddled with bullets in close succession, then reacquainted himself with the Coen brothers' retro *Miller's Crossing* (complete with the best, if ballistically impossible, machine-gunning scene on film) and Francis Ford Coppola's *The Cotton Club*. Long past midnight he switched off the projector in the booth where he kept his apartment in the Oracle Theater, his combination home and screening room in West Hollywood, and went to bed.

He dreamed he was riding in a beer truck with a pistol under his arm. The cases in the back contained reels of film, not beer. He was bootlegging them across the border between the past and the present, and Father Time was waiting for him at a roadblock with a tommygun that ticked like a clock when he squeezed the trigger.

The buzzer downstairs had been going for some time when he stirred. The first thing he saw was a ball of exposed wiring hanging like a deserted bird's nest through a hole in the ceiling. Renovations had laid claim to most of his princely academic salary since he'd bought the building two years earlier and would continue to do so until the rich aunt he didn't have in Sacramento died and left him beachfront property in Monterey.

The uniformed officer on his doorstep looked less disheveled than Valentino in the bathrobe he'd flung on, but just as sleepy. He shoved a fat insulated mailer the size of a pillow into Valentino's hands and stuck out a clipboard. "You have to sign for it. Lieutenant McPherson said to come back for you with the siren if you don't return it by four o'clock."

Someone had scribbled V. OLIVERA on the big envelope with a thick black felt-tip. Valentino balanced it under one arm and signed the receipt. "What's the rush after seventy-plus years?"

"Hey, you're the one who woke up the bureaucracy." The officer sneezed violently, fished out a handkerchief. "Dust." He left on weary legs.

Valentino put on a pot of coffee in the kitchenette he'd installed in the little room where the week's features used to be stored and read the file, a thick sheaf of reports and statements typewritten on yellow sheets in a dusty cardboard folder bound with rubber bands. He found two photographs sandwiched between pages: a publicity shot of Van Oliver, smiling in a beautifully tailored suit with wide lapels, and a front-and-profile mug of Vincent Olivera, not smiling, taken at the time of an arrest in Chicago in 1927 for the illegal transportation and sale of alcoholic beverages. It appeared to be the only arrest on his record, and he'd been released for lack of evidence. His physical description, printed beneath the mug, revealed he was shorter than he appeared onscreen, a mere five foot six.

The director, a former studio hack named Melvin Fletcher, told police he'd last seen Oliver "tying one on" at the cast party Fletcher threw at his house on Sunset after the end of principal photography on *Big Ed*, but didn't see him leave, and never saw him again. The officers spent considerably more time interviewing Madeleine Crane, Oliver's costar, but she, too, claimed to have lost track of him in the crush at the party; she dismissed rumors of an off-screen romantic involvement as PR hooey. Valentino remembered Bozal saying she'd married not long after and gone to live abroad.

Roy Fitzhugh told detectives he'd accompanied Oliver out to the curb and put him in a cab that was waiting there. He'd assumed the star had called for it, as he was too drunk to drive and had declined Fitzhugh's invitation to take him home. When Oliver failed to report to Warner Brothers the next day to discuss publicity, a flunky was sent to his home, where he found the front door unlocked and Oliver's bed made. There was no sign of disturbance, but also none to indicate he'd gone home after leaving the party.

That made Fitzhugh the last person known to have seen Van Oliver/Vincent Olivera alive. Everyone, the host included, denied ordering the cab, and none of the local companies or gypsies had any record of the fare. Consequently, Fitzhugh had been interviewed twice more, the second time at police headquarters after it was discovered he'd been detained in Mexico in 1925 on suspicion of smuggling firearms across the border from the U.S. He told Homicide he'd been with his late father, an Irish rebel, and that the guns were intended for Free Staters fighting in Belfast. No firearms were found in their possession, and they were escorted out of the country. Roy had been only ten years old, but he could never return to Mexico.

He stuck to his story, however, and since in those days the department had no shortage of Irish-Americans who were in favor of Home Rule, he got the benefit of the doubt.

Robbery-murder was considered. Oliver had been paid $2,500 per week for twelve weeks of shooting, and since he had no bank account under either of his names and the cash was never found, it was possible he had the entire $30,000—a fabulous sum in that third year of the Depression—on his person when he left the party. But the prevailing opinion, stated in interoffice memos, was that the mob, or some old rival from Chicago, had abducted him in a phony cab and taken him for the well-known ride. Bodies disposed of under such circumstances were rarely found.

The fates of the others involved, Valentino remembered, were varied. Madeleine Crane, *née* Magdalena Carvello, quit show business, presumably for wedded bliss; Fitzhugh went on to play a one-man repertory company of second-tier hoods, tired desk sergeants, and, yes, cab drivers, until his retirement; other cast members appeared in other features, successful and not; director Fletcher was yanked early from his next assignment over "artistic differences" and replaced, and took his own life sometime in the 1950s when the only work he could get was directing second-unit crews for TV Westerns. Valentino could only speculate on what might have happened to all of them had *Big Ed* ever seen the light of day.

He finished his coffee over a plate of eggs and called Kym Trujillo at the Motion Picture Country Home. Roy Fitzhugh, she reported, was in fine fettle that morning. He was looking forward to Valentino's visit.

The old character actor had a cheerful room with a fine view of the Santa Monica Mountains and a TV set with a forty-eight-inch screen where the guests on an all-female talk show clucked in merciful silence. He wore a crisp flannel shirt buttoned to the neck, navy sweats, and the chirpy air of a man fully prepared to spring out of his wheelchair and dash around the neighborhood. Valentino saw in his faded eighty-eight-year-old features the horse face and jug ears of slang-talking sidekicks in a hundred movies and dozens of TV shows.

"You've brought me a great deal of happiness over the years, Mr. Fitzhugh. I've seen all your films."

"Not all."

The old thespian's lips pleated when he smiled. His dentures did the rest of his grinning, in a glass of water next to his tidy bed.

"Every one. Even *Big Ed.*"

This drew no reaction. "I got a new one opening next week at Sid Graumann's. I'll get you a pass."

Valentino hesitated. "A new one?"

"Some screwball comedy thing. I forget the title. Jim Stewart's in it, and that dish Lombard." He growled lecherously.

His visitor understood then. Kym had told him Fitzhugh's memory, shaky about things that had been said or done a few minutes previously, was rock-steady when it came to events of a half-century and more ago. On occasion, he confused the past with the present. Medical policy was to humor him rather than try to correct him and cause distress. That suited Valentino's purposes, as Ignacio Bozal might say, "down to the ground."

"Thank you. I can't wait to see it. But it's *Big Ed* I wanted to talk about."

Fitzhugh frowned. "That swish Fletcher. Said I talked through my schnozz, I should take voice elocution lessons. I said, 'Mr. Warner's been paying me for a year to talk through my schnozz. Go to MGM if it's Jack Barrymore you want.'" The smile returned. "I made four pictures since December. I can afford to sit out a suspension."

"You were pretty friendly with Van Oliver."

"Vinnie's swell. From the beginning he tells me to lay off that Van stuff. He was a smuggler, just like me da'." Suddenly his expression changed. "What's a college egghead want from an old dropout like me? I ain't worked since they canned me from *Hawaii Five-Oh* for blowing lines. That never happened before."

Valentino adjusted to the time shift. "We found a print of *Big Ed.* We're planning a big publicity campaign to honor the film and fund the Film Preservation Department. Anything you could tell us about the production would be a big help."

"That swish Fletcher said I talked through my schnozz."

"What about Madeleine Crane?" Valentino said patiently. "What was she like?"

His scowl lifted. "Maggie was a doll. She had a beautiful voice, used to sing old Spanish songs on the set. She was Puerto Rican, but you wouldn't know it except when she sang or got tired and forgot her voice lessons. She died."

Valentino stiffened.

"I heard she got married and moved out of the country," he said.

"I mean after, long after. But still too soon. She never got to see her grandchildren."

"She had grandchildren?"

"Her *grand*children had children. She missed 'em all."

"Are you saying you kept in touch with her after she went to Europe?"

He tried to keep excitement out of his voice. Until now, Madeleine Crane's vanishing act had been as complete as Van Oliver's, if not as dramatic.

"Europe? Who said she went to Europe?"

Valentino realized then he'd had only one source for the Europe story. Everyone else had merely said she'd left the United States. Something inside him began to hum. "Where did she go? Who did she marry?"

He'd pushed too hard. Fitzhugh changed again. "Listen. Do I sound like I talk through my schnozz?"

He swallowed his impatience. "The night Oliver disappeared, you put him in a cab outside Fletcher's house. I guess you didn't get a good look at the driver."

"Who needs cab drivers? I played one so many times I could drive anyone anywhere. Almost anywhere."

"Did *you* drive Oliver?" He tried to make it sound casual. If the 1931-model Fitzhugh mistook him for a detective, he'd clam up or switch gears back to the present. Alzheimer's was an effective defense mechanism in the old actor's case.

"Not all the way. The rest he had to get out and walk. I couldn't even visit him and Maggie."

Him and Maggie.

Vincent Olivera and Magdalena Carvello.

Van Oliver and Madeleine Crane. Married and gone to—

"Mexico," Valentino said aloud. "You couldn't cross the border, because you'd been told to stay out."

Fitzhugh said nothing. He gripped the arms of his wheelchair, fighting to maintain his hold on the present.

Valentino tried something. He wasn't proud of it. He was taking advantage of an old man's sickness. He put on a Spanish accent and said, "You're a stand-up guy, Roy. Too good for a mug like me."

The old actor grinned, showing his gums. "You're the only one visits from the old days, Vinnie. Quite a hike for an old bird from East L.A."

On his way out, Valentino stopped by Kym Trujillo's office. She was a pretty, sharp-witted brunette of thirty who had turned down a modeling job for *Sports Illustrated* to study for her MBA. Her smile turned disapproving when Valentino asked for a look at the Visitors' register he'd signed on his way in.

"Privacy Act," she said. "No can do."

"If I give you a name, can you at least tell me if he's been here to visit?" he asked. "I won't even ask who he came to see."

She thought for a second, then nodded.

He spoke the name. She nodded again.

A black sedan with the longest hood Valentino had ever seen outside a movie boated into the curb as he came out of the building. It had running boards and headlamps that stuck up from stalks on the front fenders. He hesitated, half-expecting a submachine gun to poke out the window. Instead, the rear passenger's door popped open and Ignacio Bozal leaned out.

The elderly collector wore a sharp pinstripe suit that would have cost two hundred dollars in 1931, a dove-gray fedora with the brim turned down over one eyebrow, and matching spats on his shiny patent-leather shoes. Store-bought teeth shone in a grin. "Get in the car."

He made it sound gruff, like a henchman in an old gangster film. There was no trace of Spanish accent.

"I drove my car here," Valentino said.

"'S'okay. We'll just drive a little. You never rode in a car like this. I own nine Cadillacs and this is my favorite." He spoke out of the side of his mouth, Chicago fashion.

Valentino got in. He recognized the driver. He'd traded his white houseboy coat for a chauffeur's uniform. "Where to, Grandpapa?"

"Couple times around the lawn, Ernesto. My daughter Magdalena's boy," he told his guest. "You met him yesterday."

Ernesto turned back to the wheel and they pulled ahead smoothly. The mohair upholstery molded itself around Valentino's back as if a drawstring had been pulled. "You named her after your wife," he said.

"Maggie died in Peru in 'forty-six; cancer. That's why I left for Acapulco. We had fifteen good years, but there were too many memories there. The kids were my first staff when I opened the hotel. They learned good manners and passed them on."

"You're Vincent Olivera."

"I ditched that name when I quit the mob. Never could get used to Van, though; sounded like a delivery truck. I knew you'd figured it out this morning when I called to see if Roy was up for a visitor and they told me he was expecting one. It had to be you. No one else comes to see him since the Alzheimer's."

"I only put it together during the visit. Your name on the register confirmed it. Ignacio Bozal had no reason to shoot the breeze so often with an old character actor. Van Oliver did."

"Roy's losing ground. In the old days he wouldn't've said help if he was drowning."

"He's still cagey. All I got out of him was you and Madeleine Crane went to Mexico, and that only indirectly. You were the only one who said she went to Europe after she got married. You misdirected me that way twice. You said you got *Big Ed* from an estate sale in Europe."

"I didn't lie about getting it from the splicer. I slipped him a thousand to strike off an extra print before I lit out back in 'thirty-one. Just a sentimental souvenir. I met Maggie on that set."

"You're forgetting the thirty thousand that came away with you, too. No wonder there are so many rumors about where you got your financing."

"I earned that money!" Bozal's cheeks showed color for the first time; he never looked more like Big Ed from the film. "I wasn't about to kick back half to that fat bastard Capone."

Valentino watched the cool green lawn slide past as they circled the composition driveway. The motor sounded like marbles sliding on Teflon. "So that's why you left."

"The mob thought they owned me, just 'cause they bought my train ticket West and paid my expenses till I signed with Warners. I offered to pay it back with interest. I turned down their counter-offer: fifty percent of everything I took in from then on. I might've been more polite about it, but that wouldn't have made them like it any better. If they knew how much I made from coffee and mining during the war, they'd blow a gasket."

"Madeleine coached you well on your Spanish accent. Sicilians and Mexicans have the same coloring. As long as you stayed in character, anyone who recognized you years later might have doubted his own judgment."

The old man rested his hat on his knee and ran a brown hand through his white hair. "I had a couple of close calls. But by then Capone was dead. I upgraded the mugs' rooms, tore up their bills, and they decided they'd made a mistake. Also I had some pull in Mexico City. It didn't pay to blow any whistles."

"You sound just like Big Ed."

"You might say I was the first method actor. I been playing Bozal so long, I had to put on this suit to pull off Van Oliver. I figured you earned a second feature. You call yourself a film detective. I had to see if you lived up to the billing."

"That's not why you called me."

"No. If it wasn't for this phony town, I'd've would up on a slab in Cook County or making gravel in Alcatraz. I only done two things right in my life. You got to see what came of them both. Now it's the world's turn. But I'd like to be in the ground before my great-grandchildren find out I'm a phony, too."

"What about Ernesto?"

"He figured it out the first time he screened *Big Ed* for me. He's a damn fine projectionist, and he'll be a great cinematographer when he graduates film school. He's got the eye."

Ernesto smiled from the rearview mirror. "Thanks, G.P.!"

"Cut it out and drive."

Valentino said, "None of the others know?"

Bozal shook his head. "They'll forgive me when I'm gone, but I worked a hell of a lot longer getting Bozal right than I ever did Big Ed or Van Oliver, and any time you watch an actor put everything into a role and tell him what a good actor he is, it means he's failed. I'd rather not get bad reviews from my flesh and blood."

The archivist made a decision.

"I've got a born-again classic, and an enduring Hollywood mystery to promote it. At this point, a solution would only gum up the works."

The old man reached out a hand and took Valentino's knee in a grip that would crack iron. "My whole film collection goes to UCLA two minutes after I croak."

Valentino was moved, despite the block in his circulation. "When that day comes, I'll make the arrangements to have it picked up."

Van Oliver gave him a sinister smile. "You and what army?"

Garbo Writes

"I want to be alone," Harriet said.

"Vant," Valentino corrected, emphasizing the V. "It's 'I *vant* to be alone.' Your accent needs work."

"No, I mean I really want to be alone. My bra came unhooked."

He'd misinterpreted her fidgeting under the off-the-shoulder velvet gown as a seductive dance, in keeping with the dress and the bejeweled contraption on her head, a reproduction of an outfit Greta Garbo had worn in *Mata Hari*.

"I think the ladies' room is behind that column." He pointed.

She excused herself and went that way, leaving him alone among two or three dozen women dressed as Garbo in her various movie roles: disguised as a not-very-convincing young man in boots and jerkin from *Queen Christina*; hauntingly amnesiac in platinum-blond hair and elegant evening dress from *As You Desire Me*; gung-ho Stalinist in severe suit and cloche hat from *Ninotchka*. He counted no fewer than five Anna Christies and as many Mata Haris, although none as bewitching as Harriet Johansen wearing that outfit. She bore an amazing resemblance to her inspiration, a fact Valentino hadn't noted until she'd revealed herself in costume.

There were fat Garbos, old Garbos, black Garbos, an Asian Garbo, and one or two Garbos wearing powder over what looked like five-o'clock shadows. Among the escorts was one very good Erich von Stroheim, several John Gilberts, and three Charles Boyers attempting to look Napoleonic in *Conquest*. Valentino himself wore an imperial Russian uniform and a think Ramon Novarro moustache, cemented with spirit gum to his upper lip. He'd have preferred to go as John Barrymore, but that would have been the wrong movie.

The fancy-dress couples drifted to and fro across the ballroom of the great Beverly Hills mansion, sipping from glass flutes and spilling champagne on the glittering parquet floor. The walls and columns were ornamented in a relentless Art Deco motif, with original and reproduced posters from Garbo's most famous films and glossy black-and-white stills of that iconic face blown up ten times life size among the clamshells and stylized swans. The party had been convened to celebrate the 100th anniversary of the star's birth.

"Let me guess," said a familiar voice. "Lieutenant Alexis Rosanoff."

Valentino turned to shake hands with the host. Matthew Rankin was a trim, erect eighty in a beautifully cut tuxedo with flared 1930s lapels, white shirt, tie, and hair all of a piece and interrupted only by his aristocratic face with its carefully topped-off tan. He might have been an older version of the Melvyn Douglas who had played opposite Garbo three times.

"Right on the nose," Valentino said. "I doubt three people in this room can match the filmography you carry around in your head."

"I've Andrea to thank for that. She was a fan of Greta's for years before they were friends. They died the same day, you know."

His guest nodded sympathetically. Fifteen years had planed away only a little pain from Rankin's tone. "Did you know Garbo well?"

"I never met her. She and Andrea went back to before we were married. They'd visit whenever Andrea made a buying trip to New York, but after Andrea retired, they kept in contact through the mail. She burned the letters at Greta's request, not long before she and Greta died. Some of her other so-called friends had begun to sell her letters at auction."

"Mrs. Rankin was a real friend. The people in charge of the Swedish Military Archives are offering a large reward for the return of several stolen Garbo letters."

"As it happened, I'd just returned from Stockholm when the story broke. I attended a reception for a researcher friend who was sharing the Nobel Prize with another fellow. People will steal anything these days. They aren't content just to hound living celebrities into armed compounds to protect their privacy; now they've begun to prey on the dead ones as well."

Rankin's bitterness seemed justified. A former chemist with a hefty respect for technology, he'd computerized his late father-in-law's department-store chain and built new stores in Europe, Japan, and Australia. His highly visible executive presence, often accompanied by his equally aristocratic wife, had made them public figures, with all the unwelcome press attention that entailed. Since Andrea's death, Rankin had retreated into virtual seclusion, emerging only for such events as this, in respect to her friendship with Garbo and his keen interest in classic films in general.

Valentino had benefited from the latter. As an archivist with the UCLA Film Preservation Department, he'd been pleased to accept generous donations from Rankin to update equipment and purchase rare prints of motion pictures long considered lost. He'd accepted with alacrity the invitation to attend the Garbo party with a guest.

His motives weren't entirely social. Somewhat disingenuously—for he knew the answer, from rumors—he asked his host how Garbo and his late wife had come to be friends. The anger evaporated from Rankin's face. "They met in one of Andrea's father's stores," he said. "My dear girl was working there to prepare herself for an executive position. Greta was a salesgirl, you know, in Sweden; made her debut, in fact, in a promotional film for the store, *How Not to Dress*."

"That footage has been missing for many years," Valentino prompted.

"Your avarice is showing, young man. I'm sure you've heard the story that Greta made her a present of her own print, one former department-store clerk to another. It wouldn't have offended me if you'd come out and asked if I still have it."

"I'm sorry. My cards say *Film Detective*; 'Archivist' makes people's eyes glaze over and they don't hear my pitch. Sometimes I get to believing my own publicity and try to be slick. I won't bother you about it again." His face felt hot with shame.

Rankin laughed boomingly, drawing curious glances from some of his milling guests. "I was paraphrasing Andrea's father. If I'd asked him directly for her hand, he'd have had me thrown out of his house as a golddigger. I've waited fifty years to turn someone on the spit the way he did me that day, just before he agreed. UCLA's in my will. You'll have those reels by and by."

"Thank you, Mr. Rankin. You don't know what that means."

"A second disc on the DVD re-release of *Flesh and the Devil*, probably, and a lot of hyperventilating on the part of a select group of cinema geeks. These days, old movies and department stores suffer from the same apathy on the part of mall rats and Adam Sandler fans. Call Roger. He'll arrange a screening."

"I'd like that very much."

"It's been stored under ideal conditions. I think you'll be pleased." Suddenly Rankin's face went white beneath the tan. "Good Lord!"

Valentino turned, following the direction of his gaze. Harriet was approaching. The legendary head shot of Garbo, full face, in the identical Mata Hari headdress hung on the wall behind her and she seemed to be coming straight out of the frame. All at once she stopped, her plucked brows rising. When Valentino turned back, Rankin was no longer standing before him. He lay on the floor, pale and unconscious, with a crowd beginning to gather around him.

The doctor, dressed as John Barrymore in double-breasted *Grand Hotel* blazer with a coat of arms on the handkerchief pocket, was summoned into Rankin's study, where Valentino and another male volunteer had carried the tycoon and stretched him out on a leather sofa. The patient had come to, but the doctor had insisted on listening to his heart.

He smiled, removing the stethoscope from his ears. "Just a faint, I'd say. You might try a looser collar next time you play dress-up." His trim moustache, unlike Valentino's, was genuine, but appeared to have been retraced with an eyebrow pencil much darker than his thinning hair. His wife, whom Valentino had seen with him in the ballroom, had looked big-boned and awkward in a ballerina's frilly tutu—although no more so than Garbo in that film. Fortunately, she'd worn more becoming outfits in most of her scenes.

"It wasn't the collar." Rankin looked at Valentino. "Who was that woman? I thought it was the guest of honor back from the grave."

"Harriet Johansen, my date. She doesn't look that way most of the time. She's a criminal expert with the LAPD. I'm sorry she gave you a start."

"Make sure she's still here when we give out the prize for Best Garbo Look-Alike. Phyllis won't mind, will she, Ned? I'd hate to lose my personal physician over a social gaffe."

"She has a sense of humor. I told her she looked like one of those dancing hippos in *Fantasia*. She didn't hit me where it shows." The doctor snapped shut his bag and rose from the sofa. "Just to be sure, why not schedule an appointment? We won't have nearly as much fun dressing up for your funeral."

Rankin assured him he would. At the door, the doctor made room for Roger Akers, Rankin's personal assistant, to enter. He was a lean, high-shouldered, narrow-faced man of forty, a high-strung, nervous type whom Valentino had dealt with often in his relations with his employer, and for whom he'd formed an instant dislike. There was something of Uriah Heep in his demeanor. He wasn't in costume. Valentino had not seen him at the party.

"I came as soon as I heard," Akers said.

"I'm sure you did. Did you finish those letters?" The older man sat up and buttoned his shirt.

"Of course not. They said you'd collapsed."

"Well, I didn't die, so you're still employed. Help yourself to a drink, since you're here, but I expect those letters here on my desk in the morning."

"Have I ever failed?"

"You've never been one to overlook a detail—or an opportunity. Now, please leave. I've something to discuss with Valentino."

Spots of color the size of quarters glowed high on Akers' otherwise sallow cheeks, but he turned and left without comment.

"That was fairly unpleasant," Valentino said.

Rankin stood and refastened his tie before an antique mirror. "His concern was real. If I die, that man will have to live on an assistant's salary."

"If you dislike him so much, why do you keep him on?"

Thirties dance music drifted in from outside while Rankin fussed with the tie. "Your stunning date," he said. "Did you say she's a police officer?"

"Not technically. She's a criminalist. She collects and analyzes evidence, but she doesn't arrest or interrogate people or carry a badge or a gun, like on TV."

"Nevertheless I assume she's required to report unlawful activity. Can you come back tomorrow morning, without her, and without telling her we're meeting? I don't want to put you in a position of having to duck awkward questions."

Valentino hesitated. "Something tells me this has nothing to do with my job responsibilities."

"It can, if you agree to my terms. You pose as a detective, which suggests you have a talent for investigation. I know you've been instrumental in bringing many lost films to light. How would you like to exercise your gift and incidentally add Greta Garbo's first appearance on screen to that list? Immediately, I mean. Not after I expire and my will crawls through probate."

"I like the part about getting *How Not to Dress* for UCLA. The other part sounds illegal."

"I want you to dig up something on Roger Akers. Something embarrassing, and preferably intimidating."

"That *is* illegal."

"Only if you break the law to obtain it. What I do with it isn't your concern."

"It is if you're considering some kind of blackmail. That makes me an accomplice."

"There was only one blackmailer in this room, and he's left. I want to use the information to stop him before he cleans me out."

Valentino had no intention of investigating anyone's sordid past, but he had a movie buff's desire to see what happened next. Matthew Rankin, the wily old CEO, had sensed that, and refused to elaborate that evening. His guest agreed to the appointment, but rebelled against the terms by telling Harriet they were meeting in the morning.

They were at her door. She lowered her Best Garbo Look-Alike prize from her face—a nearly priceless period majolica vase fashioned into a full-length likeness of the actress—and fixed him with her Mata Hari-like gaze, primed to wring secrets from the unwary male gender. "If he wants to adopt you as his heir, don't let him. Department stores went out with miniskirts."

"He's kept his going a decade longer than most. Anyway, my birth parents might object."

"Why are you being so mysterious? Remember, you're talking to a police specialist."

Already he'd begun to regret taking her that far into his confidence. "You know I've been obsessed with that earliest Garbo footage for years. He's invited me to a screening." Which wasn't a lie.

"Not an answer. It's no mystery you love movies more than people."

"Not in every case." He kissed her. "Where are you going to put your prize?"

"You'll find out the next time you try to change the subject."

"I'm sworn to secrecy."

"About a screening? What is it, a skin flick?"

"A porno film starring Greta Garbo would be the find of the century, but I'd never show it in public for the same reasons I'm not going to betray Mr. Rankin's confidence. Some things should be kept private."

She didn't pry him any more for information. She also didn't let him kiss her again. He stared at the door she'd closed in his face, feeling a little like John Gilbert must have when Garbo left him at the altar in real life.

Matthew Rankin's mansion wore a grim aspect under a heavy slice of morning smog. Valentino, shorn of false moustache and dressed for work in the California uniform of sport coat, T-shirt, jeans, and running shoes, let the housekeeper lead him to a front parlor to wait while she went to see if her master would receive him. He was contemplating an oil portrait of Garbo in late life—a gift, no doubt, to her friend Andrea Rankin—when a door slammed at the other end of the house.

The noise was followed by a chandelier-rattling scream; and Valentino knew that was no door he'd heard.

The shortest route to Rankin's study led through the ballroom, where a team of invisible servants had removed all traces of the party that had taken place only a few hours before. He pushed past the housekeeper, frozen inside the open door with her hands covering her face, and put on the brakes just in time to avoid tripping over Roger Akers.

Rankin's assistant lay on his back, spread-eagled, as if he'd been knocked flat by a sudden gale. The front of his suit coat was stained dark, and a stain of the same color was spreading around him on the valuable Persian rug.

"Is he dead?"

Valentino looked at the speaker. Matthew Rankin stood on the other side of the great carved desk where he conducted business. The squat revolver smoking in his right hand clashed with his conservative gray suit.

Rankin didn't wait for the answer to his question. "He was a madman. He came at me with that." He pointed.

A marble bust lay on the rug inches from Akers' right hand. It appeared to be a naturalistic rendering of Garbo at the height of her beauty. The wooden pedestal it had occupied stood empty nearby.

The housekeeper raised her head from her hands. Her expression was distorted but she appeared to be regaining composure. When Valentino told her to call the police, she nodded and withdrew, closing the door behind her as from habit.

Rankin looked down, seemed to realize for the first time he was holding a gun, and dropped it on his desk. He sank into his chair. "He wanted more money than I'd been paying him to keep quiet. When I refused, he went into a rage. I've kept this gun in the drawer for years, for my protection. I don't even remember picking it up. He had that bust raised above his head and I knew he meant to split open my skull with it."

As Rankin spoke, Valentino felt Akers' wrist. There was no pulse. Anger or surprise twisted the dead man's face. "It will have to come out now," Valentino said. "What was he blackmailing you over?"

The top drawer was open; presumably, it was the one that had held the revolver. A befuddled-looking Rankin rummaged through its contents and laid a sheet on the desk. With a shudder, Valentino stepped away from the corpse and picked up the sheet.

It was a handwritten letter reproduced on common copy paper. There was no signature, and the text was written in a foreign language he identified as Swedish. "*Liebe* Andrea," read the greeting.

"A friend of mine paid a lot of money at auction for a rare Garbo autograph," Valentino said. "It looks like her writing. Did she write this to your wife?"

"Can you read it?"

"A word here and there, from my high school German, which is close. It appears to be a very tender letter."

"Andrea's mother was Swedish. They spoke in that language when they didn't want anyone eavesdropping; it was another bond between Andrea and Greta. I picked up a little over the years, by osmosis." He drew a deep breath and let it out in a rattle. "It's a love letter."

"Did they have a sexual relationship?"

"Not that I ever knew, but the letter's explicit. Aren't you shocked?"

"Lesbian rumors followed Garbo her whole life. Even her best biographers haven't been able to track down any hard evidence. How did Akers get hold of this?"

"Snooping, how else? He must have found it somewhere in the house. It must have meant a lot to Andrea or she'd have burned it with the others. He gave me this copy: a souvenir, he said. I assume the original's in a safe place."

"We're enlightened these days. It wouldn't be that big a scandal."

"It would be to me. My wife was a very private woman, much like Greta. I'm betraying her memory just by showing you the letter." He sat up straight. "Give it back. I'm going to destroy it."

"If you do, you may stand trial for murder. It's hard to make a case for self-defense without establishing a motive on the part of the deceased."

Rankin's expression was stony; his earlier confusion had evaporated. He scooped up the revolver and pointed it at Valentino. "Give it back, I said."

"It won't do any good. The police are bound to find the original when they go through Akers' things."

The stone cracked. Rankin laid the gun on the desk and lowered his face into his hands. As the first siren came into earshot, Valentino nudged the weapon out of Rankin's reach.

"It's Swedish, all right," Harriet Johansen said. "Would you like a translation? My father was proud of his homeland. He made sure we all knew the language."

They were seated in the break room outside the forensics laboratory at Los Angeles police headquarters. He'd come there straight from Beverly Hills, where he'd given his statement to local detectives. He'd been looking forward to a social visit, to take his mind off the death scene and the picture of Matthew Rankin being taken away in a squad car. "Since when does your jurisdiction extend beyond the city limits?" he asked.

"We've got the best facilities in the State of California. It's a reciprocal thing: L.A. goes to Beverly Hills when we want to know what wine to serve with the veal at the commissioner's banquet." She took a folded sheet out of a pocket of her smock and spread it out on the table. He recognized the Garbo letter. A glop of mayonnaise fell from her tuna sandwich onto the text, smearing the ink when she brushed at it.

"What kind of way is that to treat evidence?"

"Relax. We ran off a half-dozen copies from the fax they sent us. This is a recap of a liaison Mrs. Rankin had with Garbo in New York in nineteen forty-nine. Pretty steamy stuff. You want it grope-by-grope or just a summary?"

"Neither. If the handwriting checks out, it backs up Rankin's story and answers a question gossips have been asking for decades. I'm relieved for him, but it would be nice if just one star were left to shine untarnished in the firmament."

"You sound like a homophobe."

"If I were, I'd have to be a masochist, too, to live in this town. These days a person's sexuality isn't supposed to matter, but of course it does, or the columnists and talk-show hosts wouldn't whisper and giggle so much whenever someone famous gets outed. I like my *Titanics* unraised, my Jack the Rippers unidentified, and my Garbos mysterious."

"But not your shootings."

"I've got a personal stake in this one. If Rankin goes to prison, my department won't get its hands on *How Not to Dress* until he dies and his heirs finish fighting over the will." He told her then the reason for his meeting with Rankin.

She regarded him in silence for a moment. Without the exotic headdress to cover her short ash-blond hair she looked less like Garbo, but shared her sphinxlike expression. "If you'd told me he was being blackmailed, Akers might still be alive and in police custody."

"I promised I wouldn't."

"Don't pull that noble act on me. You had your eyes on that film, and you were willing to help blackmail a blackmailer to get it."

"Guilty, but only of the first charge. I thought if I knew the details I might be able to suggest a better solution. And I'm prejudiced in Rankin's favor. His wife died of a sudden heart attack just when they were planning retirement together. Then the bottom fell out of the department-store business, but instead of bailing out he invested his personal funds to drag the chain into the computer age at a time when most industries were still looking askance at it. His was one of the first businesses to sell merchandise online. Then he used some of the profits from the turnaround to help the film-preservation program. I'd have offered to help even without the added inducement."

"You're still not out of the woods, buddy. But I suppose I'll forgive you, if you promise not to make a habit of keeping secrets."

"I do, from you." He smiled.

She finished her sandwich. "The fingerprint people in Beverly Hills are pretty good. They matched some prints on the bust to the victim, so that part of Rankin's story checks out."

"If your graphologist confirms that letter was written by Garbo, he should be released."

"I spoke to him just before you came. He Googled her and hit paydirt in Stockholm. The Swedish Military Archives has the most extensive collection of her letters in the world. They're faxing samples for comparison, but our guy already has his doubts."

"How can he, without the samples in hand?"

She swiveled the paper on the table and slid it toward him.

"Anything about this strike you as odd?"

He frowned at it, then shook his head. "I'm no expert, except where her films are concerned, and I don't know enough Swedish to order from a smorgasbord."

"You don't order from a smorgasbord; you help yourself. People are imperfect creatures. They seldom write a character in cursive the same way twice. The shape and slant vary, and so does the thickness of the line. But look at this." She used a coffee stir-stick as a pointer. "All these s's are identical. Same goes for the *t*'s and *y*'s and the rest of the alphabet. Even the commas are the same, and don't get me started on the umlauts."

"By all means, let's not discuss the umlauts." He took a closer look. "It's obvious, when you point it out. I'm impressed. I knew you had a good eye, but—"

"Stop trying to butter me up. I'm still mad at you. It was the graphologist who noticed it. One of our computer nerds came up with the explanation. Did you know it's possible to create your own font, even from something as personal as handwriting? All you have to do is scan it in, and if you're handy with a mouse you can sculpt the alphabet in upper-and lowercase and all the punctuation, type it up, and print it out."

"Akers was Rankin's assistant. He must've spent a lot of time at the computer, typing letters and running errands. Experience is a great teacher." Valentino bit his lip—the only thing he ever bit into in that room. It was too close to where autopsies were conducted to trust the menu. "But anyone can see the difference between a printout and the real thing. A pen makes an uneven texture you can feel with your fingers."

"All Rankin ever saw was a photocopy. There never was an original."

"Rankin knows his way around computers. You'd think he'd have noticed the suspicious consistency of the characters."

"*I* didn't, until it was explained. Neither did you, and we're both trained to spot fakes. He was predisposed to accept it as genuine, based on his wife's close ties with Garbo and his own fears for her good name." She scrutinized the coffee spots on the paper, then crumpled it and used it to wipe her hands. "One snag. In order to forge this letter, Akers had to have had access to something fairly lengthy written by Garbo in her own hand, providing him with a complete alphabet and punctuation. You'd be surprised how many letters you can write without using everything. I know *I* was, when the graphologist told me."

"Rankin said his wife burned all of her Garbo letters at her request. Of course, he also said this one might have escaped the fire to fall into Akers' hands."

"Too convenient."

Valentino sat up, jerked taut by a sudden certainty. "A number of Garbo letters went missing from the Swedish Military Archives earlier this year. Rankin told me he'd just returned from Stockholm when the news got out."

"Was Akers with him on the trip?"

"He didn't say."

"We'll ask him. If they can place his assistant in Sweden at the time, and if he spoke a word of Swedish during his visit, they can close the file on this one. No jury would convict Rankin for defending himself against a confirmed blackmailer." Her face softened. "You gain, too. Your goddess's reputation is intact."

"It is," he agreed, and reached across the table to squeeze her hand.

Airline and hotel records and eyewitnesses agreed that Roger Akers had accompanied Matthew Rankin to Stockholm shortly before the theft of Garbo's letters was reported. Further testimony and the discovery of Berlitz tapes in Akers' West Hollywood apartment indicated that he could have forged a letter in convincing Swedish. Then bank records showed monthly deposits of several thousand dollars in Akers' account and matching amounts withdrawn from Rankin's. The district attorney, a stubborn man with eyes on Sacramento, refused to dismiss charges, but abandoned his opposition to bail. Rankin was released on his own recognizance pending further investigation. Few believed the case would ever come to trial.

Valentino and Harriet attended a party thrown by Rankin to celebrate his freedom, this time without costumes. Their host asked them to join him in his study, where he poured them each a glass of champagne from a stock unavailable to his other guests. The Persian rug had been removed, along with every other reminder of the tragedy that had taken place in that room.

"I won't join you," he said, pouring himself a glass of water from a pitcher. "I gave up the stuff when this mess began. You want your wits about you when you're being bled dry."

Valentino proposed a toast to liberty, but Rankin vetoed it. "To Miss Johansen." He raised his glass. "If she hadn't given me the shock of my life, my sad case might never have fallen into Valentino's hands."

As the pair stirred themselves to rejoin the others, Rankin held up a hand and slid aside a framed photograph of Garbo and Andrea Rankin, swathed in striped terry and wearing picture hats, laughing at some poolside. He worked the combination of the safe thus exposed and removed from it two flat aluminum cans nearly as big as bicycle wheels, which he extended to Valentino. "You went a roundabout way of earning it, but I'm not complaining."

The cans were labeled in Swedish. Harriet translated. "*How Not to Dress.* Congratulations, Val. It's the next best thing to a private conversation with her."

"It's better," he said. "Silence lasts longer than talk."

That night he screened Greta Garbo's first picture on the reconditioned Bell & Howell projector in The Oracle, the dilapidated movie theater he lived in and had been renovating forever, and which was still forever away from completion. Harriet, who knew him better than anyone, had not asked to share this highly personal experience. A dreary period promotional feature, the two reels were notable only for the world's first glimpse of the immortal star at sixteen, plump and awkward, yet possessing even then that Certain Something that separated the greats from the vast gray crowd. It was a valuable artifact, if undiverting for general audiences.

When it ended, he resealed it and threaded another film into the machine. It was one of two he'd signed out from UCLA that day, unaware of the boon coming his way from Rankin: *The Temptress*, one of Garbo's very best silents, and *Anna Christie*, her first talking picture. Valentino watched them back to back. Whatever she'd sacrificed in the way of mystery during the transition to sound, she'd more than made up for in raw animal allure. That unexpectedly guttural voice, heavily accented, had made an instant classic of her first spoken line: "Gimme a vhisky. Ginger ale on the side. And don't be stingy, baby."

His telephone rang just as her order was delivered. He stopped the film, turned off the projector, and answered.

"I knew you'd still be up," greeted Harriet. "You can't sleep with a new acquisition burning a hole in your pocket."

"What's your excuse?"

"Too much champagne. It puts me to sleep, then wakes me up in the middle of the night. I turned on the TV for company. You'd be surprised what they pick out to put on the late news."

After that conversation, Valentino dialed Rankin's number. The master of the house came on after just two rings. "Housekeeper's in bed," Rankin said. "I seldom turn in earlier than three A.M. after a party. This old recluse can't take the strain."

"Have you been watching television?"

"No, just sitting here in my study, combing the 'Net for an estimate of how much my employees are cheating me out of."

"Stockholm police arrested the man who stole the Garbo letters from the military archive. He's a Swedish citizen. They caught him trying to sell the letters on eBay. They've recovered them all."

"Oh."

"Harriet told me. She called downtown. The D.A. is considering swearing out another warrant for your arrest. The way he sees it, if Roger Akers didn't steal the letters he couldn't have committed the forgery. No forgery means no blackmail, and the whole chain of reasoning falls apart right down to your self-defense plea."

"That's ludicrous! What about the photocopy? What about all the other evidence?"

"Circumstantial. He thinks you faked it all."

"How could I forge the letter? Andrea burned all of Greta's."

"He says we've only your word on that."

"Did it occur to him *Roger* might have found some unburned letters and used them to make the fake?"

"You had better access." Valentino paused. "It would be different if they found some of them at Akers' place, but they made a complete search and came up empty."

"Complete, my foot. That headline-happy D.A. wanted me on a platter." Rankin was breathing heavily. "Thank you for the warning. I'll wake up my lawyer." The line went dead.

The next morning, Matthew Rankin, in the presence of his attorney, surrendered himself to the police at their headquarters in Beverly Hills. The judge presiding at the arraignment, annoyed to find the case before him a second time, denied the district attorney's request to hold the defendant without bail and released him on a $100,000 bond.

The news report was eclipsed later that day when a second search of Roger Akers' apartment recovered a bundle of letters in Greta Garbo's hand under a loose floorboard in the bedroom. All were addressed to Andrea Rankin and unsigned, as had been the star's habit.

Valentino and Harriet were present as invited guests when the D.A., a solid, square-built fifty in a battleship-gray suit, met Rankin in his study to apologize. Three local TV stations were represented with cameras and microphones; part of Rankin's terms for agreeing not to sue the city for false arrest. A Beverly Hills officer was also on hand, carrying a video camera no larger than a squab.

Rankin noted the last with a malicious smile. "A personal record, to prevent you from repeating the mistake?"

The D.A.'s face was expressionless. "He's not here to tape anything. Officer?"

Rankin stood in the center of the room. The officer stepped forward and turned the camera to show him the tiny monitor that flipped out from the side. The reporters moved in tight, their much larger cameras recording Rankin's reaction to the tape that was playing. Valentino and Harriet stood clear. They'd seen it already: a clear image of Matthew Rankin prying up a floorboard in Roger Akers' bedroom and depositing a bundle of letters in the recess beneath. Greta Garbo's distinctive handwriting was visible on the envelope on top of the bundle.

"Nanny cam," said the D.A. "Ironic, considering how much time Garbo spent on camera and how many years she spent avoiding them. We didn't know where you'd hide the letters, so we set one up in every room. We barely got them planted in time. You moved pretty fast after Mr. Valentino called you."

There was no response. The D.A. took the camera from the officer, freeing his hands to place manacles on Rankin's wrists.

"I poisoned my wife."

Matthew Rankin looked aristocratic no longer. Seated at a plain maple table across from the detective interviewing him, his well-dressed lawyer looking tragic in a corner, he was just an old man with a tired face wearing an orange Los Angeles County jumpsuit. Even his tan had begun to fade. Valentino and Harriet, whose credentials had gotten them in, watched him through two-way glass and listened to his beaten voice droning through the intercom.

"I started out as a chemist, you know," he said. "I put in so much work developing a toxin that would counterfeit the symptoms of a heart attack I thought it was a shame I couldn't market it."

"Why did you kill her?" asked the detective.

"She inherited the department-store business. I was just a glorified employee, and when the malls threatened all the downtown stores, she blamed me for poor management. She was going to replace me with some young hotshot. I'm sorry she didn't live to see me reinvest what she'd left me into the technology necessary to turn the business around. I designed the program. Compared to that, using an ordinary PC to forge that Garbo letter was kid stuff. A little public humiliation over having been married to a lesbian isn't a patch on a first-degree murder charge."

"How did Roger Akers find out you'd killed Andrea?"

"I got drunk and said something. I didn't remember it later, but he made sure to remind me. That's why I quit drinking. I couldn't take the chance of betraying myself in front of someone else and adding another blackmailer to the list."

"When did he start blackmailing you?"

"He sprang it on me just before the trip to Stockholm. I spent the whole trip worrying what a toxicologist would find if Akers reported me and the body were exhumed. I started paying right after we got back. Then when I heard some Garbo letters disappeared from the Swedish archives at the same time we were over there, I saw my way out.

"I went on paying him for months," he continued, "building up evidence to support my story. Claiming I'd finally decided to stop established a motive for him to attack me, and I doubted the law would go out of its way to convict the victim of a rotten extortionist. I even tricked Akers into putting his fingerprints on the photocopy of the fake letter by pretending I'd mixed it up with another document I wanted him to handle. He gave it right back. He'd picked up just enough Swedish to get by in Stockholm; I was pretty sure he couldn't read a word of the written language. That's why I didn't write it in English. I got a good education listening to Andrea's conversations with her mother all those years ago. A little study helped me brush it up."

"How'd you get Akers to put his prints on the murder weapon?"

Rankin smiled bitterly. "I told him his latest payment was in an envelope under the bust. He though I was being churlish. When he picked it up, I shot him."

"What made you choose Valentino as your witness?"

"It could have been anyone. I made up my mind to plant the story with him right there in my study, that night I fainted." He shuddered. "Lord, that girlfriend of his was the spitting image of Garbo in that costume. I thought I was being haunted for my sins. Anyway he was a civilian—a cop would have arrested Roger, and he'd have talked—and that 'film detective' conceit gave me a plausible reason to rope him in."

"You need to have new cards printed," Harriet whispered to Valentino. " 'Archivist' wouldn't have landed you in this mess."

He shushed her. Rankin was speaking again.

". . . overlooked a bunch of letters when she burned the rest; there were so many to begin with, I half suspected they *were* having a homosexual affair. I suppose that's what put the idea in my head after that theft took place in Sweden. I only hung on to the leftovers because I thought they might be valuable. I was right; they gave me more than I needed to create a font using Garbo's handwriting. It didn't have to hold up to scrutiny. I just had to convince people I'd been duped."

"For the record," said the detective, "here in the presence of your attorney, you, Matthew Rankin, confess to planning the murders of your wife, Andrea Rankin, and your assistant, Roger Akers, and carrying out those murders."

"Yes. If it will spare me from the executioner."

In the elevator on their way to the ground floor and out, Valentino was silent. Harriet took his hand. "You didn't betray him," she said. "He used your relationship with him to get away with murder, and you used it right back at him to put a killer behind bars. The evidence might never have surfaced if you hadn't tricked him into producing it himself."

"I know. I'd feel better about it if he hadn't given me *How Not to Dress*."

"He saw it as paying you off for services rendered."

"That's what I mean."

"It's your life's calling to rescue the past from extinction."

"Yes, and that's how I'll get over it."

She leaned against him and lowered her voice a full octave. "Do you vant to be alone?"

He pressed the stop button. As the elevator lurched to a halt, he took her in his arms. "What do *you* think?"*

The Profane Angel

Pegasus made his majestic way down the San Diego Freeway, waiting with wings partially folded through the relatively steady stop-and-go before the morning crush and the noon rush; took brief flight on Sunset Boulevard; and settled down to wait through the standard three light changes at each intersection in West Hollywood.

The sight of the mythical beast, painstakingly worked in plaster and spray-painted all the colors of the Day-Glo rainbow, drew no more than the occasional curious glance toward its perch on the open rented trailer. L.A. had seen stranger sights on an almost daily basis.

Nevertheless, Valentino was relieved when he pulled into the alley next to the Oracle Theater and found Kyle Broadhead waiting with a pair of husky undergraduates to help him unload the sculpture. He disliked attracting attention, and had chosen the one place in America to live where it was virtually impossible.

Broadhead wrinkled his nose at the garish paint job. "What a hideous way to treat a noble creature that never existed. Where'd you find him, Fire Island?"

"Close." Valentino got out of the car and stretched. "An Armenian rug dealer in the Valley stuck it in front of his shop to attract business. Some students from State have been redecorating it once or twice a week for five years. It'll take ten gallons of mineral spirits just to get down to the original workmanship."

One of the burly UCLA students snorted. "Everybody knows you can't trust a Statie with a box of Crayolas."

"Spoken by the young man who credited *Stagecoach* to Henry Ford on his midterm." Broadhead, rumpled and dusted with pipe ash, patted Pegasus on the flank. "Welcome home, Old Paint. Your brother's missed you."

Valentino untied the ropes that lashed the statue in place, the students bent their shoulders to their task, and after much grunting, mutual accusations of sloth, and two pinched fingers, the winged horse stood at last on a pedestal opposite its twin at the base of the grand staircase in the littered lobby.

"There's teamwork." Broadhead admired the tableau.

Valentino said, "What's that make you, the coach? I missed your contribution."

The professor took his pipe out of his mouth. "Do you realize how much concentration it takes to keep one of these going?"

The student who had suffered the casualty stopped sucking his fingers. "The new one's bigger."

"It won't be when we strip off all those coats of paint," Valentino said. "It isn't any newer than the other one. They were sculpted at the same time by the same artist. If I hadn't tracked this one down by way of the Internet, duplicating it would have cost me a fortune."

"As opposed to the several you've already sunk into this dump." Broadhead nursed his pipe.

"A man has to have a hobby."

"Movies are only a hobby when your work hasn't anything to do with them. You spend all week procuring and restoring old films and all weekend rebuilding a theater to show them in. Which reminds me. Someone called while you were out riding and roping." Broadhead unpocketed a foil-lined wrapper that had contained tobacco and handed it to Valentino.

"What's it say?" He couldn't read what was scribbled on it.

"An old lady in Century City says she has something to sell. Probably a home movie of her playing jacks at Valley Forge. I told you that interview you gave the *Times* would draw more pests than genuine leads."

Valentino went up to the bachelor quarters he'd established in the projection booth and dialed a number off Caller ID. He couldn't distinguish letters from numerals in Broadhead's scrawl. A young woman told him he'd reached the residence of Jane Peters. He got as far as his name when she interrupted.

"Yes, Miss Peters is expecting your call. She's resting at the moment. Are you free to come to the apartment later today? She has a property she thinks might interest you."

"May I ask what it is?"

"A movie called *A Perfect Crime*."

"The title's kind of generic. Can you give me any details?"

Paper rustled. "It's a silent, released in nineteen twenty-one. The director's name is Dwan." She spelled it.

"*Allan* Dwan?"

"Yes, that's the name."

He steadied his voice. "What's the address?"

Broadhead was alone when he returned to the lobby. "You owe me twenty apiece for the grunts," the professor said. "I offered them extra credit instead, but any dolt can pass a film class."

"Here's fifty. I'm feeling generous."

"What's the old lady got, *The Magnificent Ambersons* uncut?"

"Almost as good. Carole Lombard's first film."

He dropped off the trailer at the rental agency and day-dreamed his way across town. Carole Lombard, the slender, dazzling blond queen of screwball romantic comedy, had made an insignificant debut at age twelve, then blazed across the screen in the 1930s, reaching her peak of fame when she married Clark Gable, the King of Hollywood. Stories of her bawdy sense of humor and outrageous practical jokes were legend, and by all accounts the couple was deliriously happy. But it all ended tragically in early 1942, when the plane carrying Lombard home from a war-bond rally slammed into a mountain thirty miles from Las Vegas. She was thirty-three years old.

Valentino hadn't had cause to revisit Century City since he'd moved out of a high-rise to take up residency in the Oracle, where he awoke in the morning to the zing and chatter of the renovators' power saws and nail guns and went to bed in the evening past walls where there had been empty spaces and empty spaces where there had been walls only hours before. But in Jane Peters' building he congratulated himself on the move: A brat hit every button on his way out of the elevator, sentencing its only remaining occupant to stopping at every floor.

"Mr. Valentino? I'm Gloria Voss, Miss Peters' health-care provider. We spoke on the phone."

He shook the hand of the tall, slim brunette in a white blouse, pressed jeans, and new running shoes. The living room was clean, spacious, and decorated tastefully in shades of gray and slate blue, but smelled of many generations of cigarettes under a thin layer of air freshener.

His nose must have twitched, because she said, "She tries to fool me by flushing the butts down the toilet, but the place always smells like a smoking car. I think she bribes the nasty kid downstairs to smuggle them in. He probably shoplifts them."

"I might have met him."

"That explains why you're late. Some day he's going to try that button trick on Miss Peters and get a tongue-lashing to make him wish she'd used a paddle. She has an impressive vocabulary."

"No wonder she likes Carole Lombard. They say she had her brothers teach her every curse word they knew, to put her on level ground with every man she dealt with. They called her the Profane Angel."

"Jane told me that; and many other stories as well. I'll have to rent a Lombard film sometime. Anyone whose escapades can make a trained nurse blush is worth checking out."

"You haven't seen *A Perfect Crime?*" He had a sinking feeling he'd been lured there under false pretenses.

"No projection equipment here. But she tells me I'm not missing much. 'Child actors should be drowned, like kittens.' That's a quote."

She excused herself to knock on a door across from the entrance. "Mr. Valentino's here." After a muffled invitation she opened the door and held it for him.

As he stepped past, she lowered her voice. "Find out where she hides the cigarettes."

When the door closed behind him, he was in a large bedroom done in white and gold. There was a white four-poster bed, neatly made, a dresser and vanity table, and a sitting area made up of two reproduction Louis XIV chairs and a chaise, all upholstered in Cloth of Gold. Plastic prescription containers and over-the-counter pill bottles took up every horizontal space except one: Valentino's practiced eye went immediately to four flat aluminum film cans stacked on the vanity table.

"You look like a Valentino. Family resemblance, or plastic surgery?"

The tobacco-roughened voice came from a very old, very plump woman seated in one of the chairs. She wore a red sweater that made her look like a tomato, blue sweatpants with sharp creases, and thick socks in heelless slippers. Her hair was shorn to a white haze on her scalp. She had blue eyes.

"Neither," Valentino said. "There might be some relation way back; not enough to inherit."

"He didn't have much to leave. His career was on the skids when he died at thirty-one. 'Good career move,' someone said. It was the same with Lombard. She hadn't made a movie worth shouting about in years when that plane cracked up. She was mostly famous as Mrs. Clark Gable."

"So much for breaking the ice."

"I'm ninety-eight. I can't wait for it to melt on its own. Sit down."

As he lowered himself into the chair facing hers, she took the top off a fat pill bottle and drew out a filterless cigarette. A smaller container yielded a slim throwaway lighter. "If you tell Field Marshal von Voss about my stash, the deal's off." She blew twin jets of smoke out her nostrils.

"Trying to keep you healthy doesn't make her a Nazi."

"I gave up two breasts for the privilege years ago. Fortunately, they weren't much to begin with. It was practically out-patient surgery."

He laughed, more in response to the wicked gleam in her eye than to the black humor. His work put him in frequent contact with senior citizens, veterans of the Golden Age, and he found them more entertaining company than most of his own generation. "How did you come into possession of *A Perfect Crime?*"

"It was no feat. They hadn't invented re-releasing back then, no TV or video markets, so no one gave them any thought after the first run. But you know that. If the studios had kept better track of the inventory, we'd be up to our butts in celluloid and you'd be out of a job."

"Were you in the industry?"

"I came out here when I was eight years old. It wasn't an industry then. But it was the only factory in town, and if you wanted to work, that's where you went."

He excused himself and got up to look at the film cans. *A Perfect Crime* was stenciled on the lid of the one on top, with the year and production number. It looked genuine, but he'd been fooled before. "Silver nitrate?"

"No. I had it transferred to safety stock before you were born. I burned the original negative before it burned me. That stuff's worse than nitroglycerine."

"Were you a technician?"

"I could've joined the union if I'd wanted. I always got on with all my crews. They like to talk about their work, like everyone else."

He went back and sat down. Time had done its work on her face and figure, but essential beauty leaves a glowing memory, stubborn as embers clustered here and there. "Were you an actress?"

She laughed, coughing smoke, and deposited the smoldering stub in a water glass. It spat and died in the inch of liquid in the bottom. "The critics didn't all agree on that. I used to be Carole Lombard."

He was silent long enough for her to fish out a fresh cancer stick and set fire to it.

"Jane Peters," he said. "Lombard's real name was Jane Alice Peters. I didn't make the connection."

"I was still fooling with it until I was almost thirty, when I made it legal. I was Carol without the *e* until *Fast and Loose*; my twenty-eighth, for hell's sake, counting the Sennett shorts. Spelling mistake in the credits. That *e* made me a star."

He almost said, *It wasn't that that made you a star*, then remembered she was a fraud or delusional. "Lombard's been dead more than sixty years. Even you said so."

"I said her plane cracked up. I didn't say she was in it. I mean *I*. I've been talking about myself in the third person so long I sometimes get to thinking I'm somebody else."

"Her remains were found on the scene, along with the pilot and all the other passengers. One of them was her mother."

"I never got over that." She used the little finger of the hand holding the cigarette to sop a tear from the corner of one eye. "She was my buddy. Pa was nuts about her. Gable, I mean. We called each other Ma and Pa, not Carole and Clark. Sounds like an advertising agency." She took a long, shuddering drag and seemed to collect herself. "They found some wisps of blond hair and a mass of pulp in a section of fuselage squashed into a block ten feet long. It wasn't me. I gave up my seat to an army nurse when we landed in Albuquerque to refuel. I told Mom to stay aboard and tell Pa I'd be along later by train. I said it was my patriotic duty, but what I really wanted was to drive him so batty he'd take me right there in the station. We were always pulling pranks like that on each other."

Valentino said nothing. He'd encountered cases of Alzheimer's and senile dementia often enough to know better than to upset the afflicted party by contradicting her.

"I scrubbed off my makeup and tied a scarf around my hair before I boarded the train in Albuquerque," she said. "I was tired of signing autographs and grinning at fans. I found out about the crash when we stopped in Flagstaff, where the newsboys were shouting. 'Carole Lombard Dead,' that knocked all the tired out of me. I got out and bought a paper. I didn't make it through the first paragraph before I fainted.

"I woke up in a doctor's office. He told me I was pregnant."

"Clark Gable's child." He couldn't keep the cynicism out of his tone.

She nodded. "In the course of thirty minutes I learned I was an orphan, I was responsible for an innocent young woman's death, and that I was going to be a mother. It starts you thinking." She smiled crookedly. He wondered if she'd rehearsed the expression in front of a mirror with Lombard's picture taped to it. " 'Madcap.' 'Screwball.' Those were the words that came up most often when people talked or wrote about me. Not much of a legacy to leave your kid with. I was getting a little long in the tooth to get away with the reputation much longer before it became pathetic. The public already sensed it, and had stopped going to see my pictures. A star fades quickly under those circumstances; neither the doctor nor the people who carried me to his office nor his nurse recognized me. So what was I working so hard for?"

"You're forgetting Gable. He grieved the rest of his life."

"When I heard he'd volunteered to serve as a tailgunner in the air force, I almost came forward," she said. "It was a suicide's cry for help. But then I realized MGM would protect him if it meant bribing Hitler to send the Luftwaffe in the other direction. And later, when he remarried, he seemed happy. I kept up with him through the trades and film magazines right up until he died. I cried that day, too. But, you see, I didn't love him."

Anger flared. He tamped it down through an effort of will. "Gable and Lombard is Hollywood's greatest love story. Greater than Bogie and Betty. Greater than Pickford and Fairbanks and Garbo and Gilbert and all the rest."

"You're overlooking the fact that Garbo left Gilbert at the altar. That Pickford and Fairbanks broke up. That Bogie may have cheated on Betty and vice versa. The rest is PR. You've been around this town long enough not to judge by appearances. Russ Columbo was the love of my life."

"The bandleader. He and Lombard were seeing each other when he was killed in a hunting accident."

"For a long time after that, I expected to die any minute of a broken heart. Well, I didn't and I knew Pa wouldn't either. Deep down, under the public show of tragedy, I think he knew we couldn't have lasted. He'd been through divorce; me too, and it stinks. Drives a wedge right down through the center of your fan base. But everyone gathers around a handsome widower.

"Meanwhile," she continued, "I had someone new to love, a beautiful daughter. I raised her in Buffalo, New York, which is as far as you can get from Hollywood culture without going Amish. She died four years ago of leukemia, still thinking her father was the man I married, the owner of a fleet of Great Lakes ore carriers." She flicked away another tear, leaving a smudge of ash on her temple. "By then he was dead, too, so I moved back here, away from the Buffalo winters. The old bastard left me loaded. I never did take his name."

"Why are you telling me all this now?"

She was busy lighting a fresh cigarette from the butt of the last. She dropped the remnant among the others floating in the water glass. "I keep thinking about that poor girl, that army nurse who took my place on the plane. There's a family somewhere that doesn't know if she was murdered or ran away or if she is lying at the bottom of a well. They can identify people now by DNA. If they exhume the body interred under my name in Forest Lawn and run tests, maybe someone can be notified, even if it's a grandnephew who wasn't even born at the time of the crash. What's that word? Closure? Everyone deserves that."

"Are you telling me the film's a dummy, just to get me to listen to your story?"

"Of course not. It's the McCoy. I'll even let you take a reel with you to screen. Reel three, to guarantee you won't just run off with it. No one wants to come into a picture in the middle."

"But why now? Why not years ago, when there was a better chance some of the dead woman's immediate family was still around to hear the news?"

"Well, that's not the only reason." She blew smoke at the ceiling, tipping her head back the way actresses used to do in glamour shots to show the smooth line of a throat. Hers was festooned with loose skin. "It's part of the price for donating that turkey to UCLA. I want you to tell the world my story. You can use the campaign to promote the film as a vehicle. 'Lombard Lives!' Boffo box office."

He leaned forward, choosing his words carefully. If she wasn't just posing, his pointing out the basic inconsistency in her story could arouse paranoia and possibly violence. "I don't understand. I thought the whole point of your not coming forward was to put all that behind you."

"It was. But I miss it. I miss the fame, God help me. Gable's gone, Bogie's gone, Jimmy and Kate and Spence and Bette. At the end they were dropping like leaves, from one Oscar telecast to the next. I'm the only name-above-the-title star left from the glory days. The last dinosaur. I want to feel flashbulbs bursting in my face one more time, put my dainty foot on the red carpet, wave at whoever knows who the hell I am sitting in the bleachers on the sidewalk. Stick my hands and feet in the cement at Grauman's. I never got to do that."

"That's your price? Fifteen minutes more in the spotlight?"

She flashed that crooked smile. "Time is relative. Gloria will tell you I haven't much longer than that."

"I can't promise anything without proof. Will you submit to a DNA test?"

"Absolutely not. Even if you can find some shirttail blood relative to provide a match, I won't open my mouth for some joker to swab around inside it. How do I know they won't clone me after I'm gone? There's only one of me; that's the selling point." She extinguished another butt. "I want to be Carole Lombard again. Who wouldn't?"

He and Kyle Broadhead screened the silent reel in the projection room where the professor showed films to his students. They sat at kidney-shaped writing tables and watched the pubescent star-to-be pretending to be Monte Blue's kid sister. She was unconvincing, even in pantomime. "Howard Hawks said she couldn't act," Broadhead said. "Getting the performance he got out of her in *Twentieth Century* proves just how great a director he was."

Valentino said, "John Barrymore told her she was the best he ever worked with. She claimed she learned more from him on that shoot than she did during her previous twelve years in pictures."

"What are you going to tell the old lady?"

"I owe her a look-see into her story just for this. Do you know anyone who could check and see if any army nurses vanished around the time of the crash?"

"If I knew my way around the Net as well as the worst of my students, I could hack into the Bank of America and finance the whole preservation program. I'll ask one. Don't tell me you're buying into this fairy tale."

"Give me a break. People who are supposed to be dead are rumored to be still alive every day, and none of them has come out of hiding yet."

"If you try trotting her out like Princess Anastasia, when it blows up in your face the scandal will do more harm to the program than if this piece of tripe stayed buried."

"I know."

"The smart thing to do is to return the reel and call it off."

"I know."

Broadhead blew through his pipe. He never lit it in a room that contained film. "So how far do you think you can string her along?"

"What makes you think I won't do the smart thing and forget all about it?"

"Ten years of daily association. Every loose frame left unaccounted for is an orphan. You'd adopt them all even if it ended in disgrace for you and the institution that keeps us off food stamps."

Valentino patted his friend's knee and stood. "Put your whiz kid to work."

Star vehicles are like peanuts, and twenty minutes of *A Perfect Crime* created a hunger that demanded satisfaction. Valentino checked out *Twentieth Century*, *My Man Godfrey*, and *No Man of Her Own*—her only appearance on film with Clark Gable—from the university library and watched them back-to-back at the Oracle, using the rebuilt Bell & Howell projector and state-of-the-art composition screen that had set him back two mortgage payments. He had them all on tape and disc, but preferred to watch the classics the same way they were seen back when stars still glittered like gifts from the Milky Way and ushers prowled the aisles ready to expel any atheists who wouldn't stop talking during the feature.

There in the dark he fell in love all over again with the incendiary blonde who had won the heart of America's Rhett Butler and hundreds of thousands of moviegoers in New York and San Francisco, Terre Haute and Cincinnati. He had always found her unsympathetic in *Century*, and so had most of middle America during its first run, but now he appreciated the breezy skill with which she met every challenge from John Barrymore, the prince of players. Her ditzy debutante in *Godfrey* charmed him as it had William Powell, who despite their real-life divorce had insisted upon casting her opposite his socialite-turned-tramp-turned-butler (and netting her an Academy Award nomination), and although little of the chemistry between her and Gable showed in *No Man*, it comforted Valentino to see them together again, in a medium where no catastrophe, natural or man-made, could separate them. From her golden hair to her shimmering gowns she glowed, and there was more erotic tension in the arch of her brow and the hollow of her cheek than in the most explicit NC-17 ever shot.

Gable had known that. Valentino rejected out of hand the notion that the spark between them had been just another invention of the flacks in the MGM publicity department. What if all the legends were fake? If someone else had been at the wheel of James Dean's wrecked Porsche? If Spencer Tracy and Katharine Hepburn had secretly loathed each other? If a stunt double had hung off the high clock in Harold Lloyd's place? An industry without a healthy mythos might as well churn out bottle caps.

When the last frame flapped through the gate he rewound the final reel and retired to bed and his Deco dreams.

"Well?"

Two days had passed since their conference in the projection room. Broadhead had entered Valentino's memorabilia-cluttered office in his usual fashion, without knocking, swept a stack of French film journals off a chair, and sat scraping out the bowl of his pipe with a Tom Mix penknife he found on the desk.

"Edith Jenkins," he said.

"What about her, whoever she is?"

"Was. She enlisted as a nurse just after Pearl Harbor, to escape her abusive husband. When she'd been AWOL six weeks, the husband was arrested for questioning, but without a body or any other evidence he was released. The papers lost interest after a while, as they will when the story has no conclusion. She never turned up."

Valentino started to rise. "Then that means—"

"Don't get excited. This isn't a movie, where everything ties together just before the fade-out. She was a brunette. She wouldn't have left any blond hair in any broken airplane."

"She might've dyed it when she ran away from her husband. Lombard dyed hers."

"I'm not through."

Valentino sat.

"This kid's a freshman, but Bill Gates better watch his back. He dug up a dozen unexplained disappearances involving young women within two weeks of the accident. Two showed up alive later, three dead. No information on whether any of the others were in the army, although two were nurses, a vulnerable occupation then as now. One of them might have signed up under a nom de guerre. Point is the results are inconclusive."

"Huh."

"Eloquently put." Broadhead found high C on his stem.

"We could use that."

"*You* could. I'm a publish-or-perish academic. If I start endorsing Elvis and Bigfoot, this institution will retire me on my over-upholstered laurels and I'll wind up writing paperbacks about alien autopsies and weapons of mass destruction."

"Your liberal bias is showing."

"You're right. Scratch the alien autopsies. So what are you going to do?"

"There's always DNA."

"You said the old lady turned you down flat on that."

"She wouldn't have to take part. If we found a cousin or something of Lombard's—a 'shirttail blood relative,' as she put it—exhumed the body from

Forest Lawn, and compared samples, we could either settle the question or make her claim credible."

"Even if you could do that, say you proved the corpse is Lombard's, which of course would be the result. She might destroy the other three reels of *A Perfect Crime* out of spite."

"Not if she relinquishes possession first. We could stall for time, go ahead with the publicity arrangements as promised. No one could expect us to follow through with them once she's exposed as a pretender."

Broadhead put away the pipe. "Where'd you tell me you were from originally?"

"A little town called Fox Forage, Indiana. I saw my first movie there in a stuffy little box made of concrete."

"I think you should go back there for a vacation. You've been out here so long you're beginning to think like a grafter."

Valentino sat back, deflated. "I didn't like it when I heard myself saying it."

"Don't feel bad. I said, 'Even if you could' get Lombard's body exhumed. You can't. You'd need that theoretical cousin's permission or a court order, which you won't get because there's no probable cause for a search, and then you'd have to pay for it. Digging corpses out of mausoleums is ten times more expensive than putting them in. *Then* you have to pay to put them back. UCLA won't foot the bill; we're lucky it keeps us in paper clips. How's your cash?"

"Ask my contractor. He's seen it more recently."

"Well, there it is. You've got one reel of a film you can't exploit and a crazy old bat who thinks she's the Queen Mother of Hollywood."

"I liked her, though. If she isn't who she says she is, she oughta be."

Valentino was having a familiar dream. In it, he was standing on a thousand-foot cliff overlooking the ocean, arranging lemmings into an orderly herd to drive inland to safety. Suddenly a storm broke out. Thunder and lightning and lashing winds panicked the lemmings, who stampeded between his feet, dodging his grasping hands, and plunged over the edge of the cliff and down into the pitching waves, which swept them out to sea and out of sight.

He was grateful when the telephone woke him. The lemmings were a unique breed, black and glistening as the bits of film he gathered from both hemispheres to assemble and save from obscurity. Too often he failed just when success seemed at hand.

"I'm not getting any younger," said a cigarette-hoarse voice. "None of us is, but I'm moving faster than most. Do we have a deal or what?"

"I'm sorry, Miss Peters."

"I'm sorry, too, if 'Miss Peters' means what I think it means."

"It's just too risky without proof you're Carole Lombard. My reputation's one thing, but the preservation program's is another. A lot of important work has been destroyed in the past because someone failed to check his facts, deliberately or by accident."

"In other words, I'm a damn liar."

"There's just nothing to show the world you're telling the truth."

"What's *A Perfect Crime*, chopped liver?"

"The argument could be made that you don't have to have been in it to acquire a print. You said yourself the studios were careless in those days. You know a lot about Lombard, but she's been written about a lot. I'm sorry."

Silence crackled for what seemed a long time. "Well, people have been called phonies less politely. You know, you could have had what you wanted just by blowing smoke up my skirt until I kicked the bucket."

"I admit the idea was discussed, but I couldn't live with it. I'd have gotten a bad case of hives every time *Nothing Sacred* played on TCM."

"Bill Wellman directed that one at the top of his lungs. I waited until we wrapped, then got the crew to tie him up in a straitjacket." She exhaled, probably blowing smoke. "Toodle-oo, kiddo. Drop reel three by anytime." The line clicked and the dial tone came on.

Gloria Voss answered the door. She looked as trim and elegant as ever, but her eyes were red. "Jane passed early this morning, in her sleep."

"I'm sorry." He truly was, somewhat to his surprise. He gripped the film can he was holding so hard his fingers went numb.

The nurse excused herself and went into the bedroom. She came out carrying the rest of *A Perfect Crime* in a stack. "She asked me—told me—to give you these in case she missed you. 'Tell him to go to hell, and no hard feelings,' those were her words. It was the last thing she said before she went to sleep."

"But that wasn't the deal."

"I know. We had no secrets. She liked to come on as a tough old broad, but she had a heart as big as L.A. She ordered me not to see her films because they might corrupt me. Once, she said, she altered a contract with her agent so *he* owed *her* ten percent of everything he made instead of the other way around. He signed it without reading. She had him over a barrel, but she laughed and tore up the contract and had him draw up another."

"I've heard that story."

"I think she was testing you. Congratulations. You passed." She held out the stack of cans.

His cell phone rang. He apologized and answered. It was Kyle Broadhead. "Listen, my whiz kid found a great-grandniece of Lombard's in Fort Wayne, that's where Lombard was born. She's agreed to provide DNA samples."

"Kyle—"

"I'm not finished. I talked to Ted Turner's people. He'll finance an exhumation in return for distribution rights to *A Perfect Crime*. We've got the niece's permission, and Turner already owns everything Lombard did for MGM. He wants to put together a box set with her debut film included."

Valentino explained the situation.

"Doesn't change a thing," Broadhead said after a pause. "You can't buy publicity like this, but thank God Ted Turner can. People love a clever fake. The attention will bring in donations to the program like—like—"

"Lemmings," Valentino finished. "Tell Turner no deal."

"I heard some of that," Gloria Voss said, when he flipped shut the instrument. "It means you don't believe her, but it was a wonderful thing to do."

"I don't know what to believe. Whichever way it went, it would have spoiled a beautiful story."

"Grandma would say, 'Thanks, buster.'"

He reacted after a beat. "Grandma?"

"She's the one who talked me into becoming a nurse. She had a soft spot for them."

"So you're the granddaughter of—"

"Jane Peters and the owner of Buffalo Shipping. That's what it says on Mom's birth certificate." She thrust the cans into his arms, smiling with Carole Lombard's cheekbones and Clark Gable's mouth.

Wild Walls

C hub Garrett sat in his favorite pub in the Dublin suburb of Maynooth, drinking gin and bitters and mourning the smoky atmosphere of days gone by.

"Sure, it was poisonous, and they were quite right downtown to vote in the ban," he said. "My only complaint is it takes twice as long to kill yourself with booze. But I'm an outsider; my opinion doesn't count. I only live here because artists don't have to pay income tax. Uncle Sam glommed on to what was left after my dear parents and darling ex-wives robbed me blind."

Valentino didn't know whether to chuckle at that. Chub—right name William, before his trademark babyfat cheeks had made him the most recognizable of the Pint-Size Pirates in a series of 1930s comedy shorts—appeared to have no sense of humor. This wasn't unusual among gifted comics, who in their private lives could pose for posters for anti-depression research. Wattles spilled over his heavy turtleneck and he wore loose-fitting khakis and rubber Wellingtons. His guest, who was suffering from jet lag brought on by two long hops, from L.A. to New York and from New York to Ireland, would have chosen brighter company if Chub ("Don't call me Mr. Garrett, son; that was my father, may he rot in hell") weren't sitting on a film archivist's goldmine.

"You seem to have done all right for yourself since then," Valentino said. "Homes in Santa Fe and Ireland, royalties for your signature line of children's fashions."

"The royalties barely cover both mortgages. I could liquidate and live quite comfortably for the time I have left. Only I can't, because both properties are frozen solid until I can prove I'm not an imbecile. Bad luck for me, good luck for you. The courts overlooked the product of my art."

He used the word with irony; but "art" was what Valentino thought of those reels of safety stock Chub maintained in climate-controlled storage in Dublin: the entire existing run of Pint-Size Pirates comedies, unseen in their original state since long before Valentino was born. In the meantime the world had had to content itself with grainy prints butchered to make room for commercials during afternoon TV airings and late shows. The UCLA board of directors had been persuaded to foot his travel bill to procure the films for a reasonable price. Valentino himself had done the persuading. The loss of so valuable a collection

169

of artifacts to the history of popular entertainment would have cast in shadow all his efforts to preserve the twentieth century's past to date.

Chub drank, spilling color briefly into his sallow octogenarian features. "I wanted to will them to the Smithsonian, but my damn doctors are determined to keep me alive past a hundred, and I don't intend to spend that time in a nursing home. Eleven children from eight marriages are just as keen to declare me incompetent and divvy up my estate. I need cash to fight them in court, which is why I'm being so mule-ass stubborn about the asking price."

"It's worth it, in my opinion, but it's not my hand on the purse strings. If the university were to agree to your terms, it means passing up the next three ex-presidents speaking at commencement. They don't come cheap. The way they look at it, settling for a former secretary of state would mean accepting second-class status behind Harvard. Would you accept an honorary Ph.D. in lieu of the difference?"

"I already have two, from USC and Penn State. Not bad for a kid who bribed his tutors to give him a passing grade in math so he could play David Copperfield on radio. I think Edith took both diplomas when she cleaned out the house in Burbank. She sold them on eBay, along with my honorary Oscar. One more wouldn't get me a GED. So I guess you know my answer."

Edith was Chub's sixth wife. He'd had two more before one stuck, for fifteen years until she'd died. "That's all I can offer," Valentino said. "I might swing you an honorarium as a visiting lecturer. The film school's slim on those from the classic age."

"That's only because Jackie Coogan had the bad taste to die. I couldn't accept anything less than a hundred grand. That's the standard retainer for the legal talent I need. I can get two weeks out of it."

"The people I work with won't go that high." He felt as played out as anyone who had ever embarked upon a crusade, only to settle for less than a lousy T-shirt. He wondered if a side trip to London might yield an acceptable print of *Lassie Come Home*. Roddy McDowall, before he died, had given him hope that one still existed in the basement of an assistant director on Basil Street.

"I like you," Chub said, thumping down his glass. "If I agree to a private showing, do you think your people might reconsider?"

"I'd kill for it. But I couldn't say yes in good conscience. Chub, I'm a fan."

Chub Garrett, the brains of the Pint-Size Pirates, stewed over the question, glass in hand. Despite his bald head and age spots, he remained an icon of Valentino's youth, the mischievous savant of a band of juvenile delinquents with the best of comedic intentions. While he was considering, a plump, buxom barmaid—she ran so true to type that no pangs of liberated shame entered into the choice of terminology—came over and offered them a pint on the house, in deference to Chub's good reputation. A twinkle of old times sparked in the old man's pale blue eyes, but he asked her for the bill. Valentino covered it with a five-pound note.

"Boyo, you couldn't have settled it better with a knighthood." The former child star hoisted himself from his seat. "Let's go see just how cruel the passage of time can be to a boy from the Lower East Side."

Chub drove, at the wheel of a stubby little car with a windscreen close enough to bend Valentino's eyelashes, his fingers clutching the dash on the left side where the steering wheel belonged, oncoming traffic threatening him from the wrong lane, explosions from the exhaust pipe farting black smoke, and the driver using his horn in preference to the brake. When they rocked to a stop in front of a charming ivy-jacketed cottage straight out of *The Quiet Man*, the passenger unclamped his fingers from vinyl and remarked upon the beauty of the place.

"I'll take credit for that," Chub said. "Me and Miles, my groundskeeper. It was overgrown with thistles when I bought it and hired him from the village. He's got enough poison stored in the old smokehouse to wipe out the British Army."

The interior of the cottage was open, the stone-paved medieval kitchen flowing into a comfortably furnished living room. The rotund host manipulated hidden switches, lowering a screen from the ceiling in front of a painting of peasants at work in a field and raising a bullet-shaped projector from inside a table between two leather armchairs.

Valentino enjoyed immensely the next two hours. Chub had spliced seven Pint-Size Pirates shorts onto four reels, and his guest laughed loudly throughout: Chub, in his trademark letter sweater and shabby fedora, "Sassafrass," the group's poker-faced spokesman, Glory, a ten-year-old glamour queen, and Shadow and Moon Pie, the stereotypical black children, outsmarted Mugs, the swaggering bully, at every turn, frequently with results humiliating and messy for the slow-witted antagonist. Alonzo, the Pirates' scruffy little dog, was always on hand to lick custard pie off Mugs's face. Every member of the cast was a gifted comic and, disregarding the shuffling behavior of the two minority members, their performances would stand up against any on the modern screen. Valentino had always enjoyed the features on cable, mutilated as they had been, but seeing them as they were intended to be seen was like spending quality time with the *Mona Lisa*, only with pratfalls.

The old man switched off the projector and turned on a lamp. "I went into debt snapping up the prints when the studio went under and transferring them to safety stock, but I made it back in a hurry renting them to local TV stations across the country. I was smart enough to dupe off copies, knowing how scissor-simple those affiliates can be. I tried to get Bernie to go in with me on it, to reduce the outlay, but he was still hemming and hawing when he died."

Bernard Leibowitz was Sassafrass.

"He was killed, wasn't he?

"He got himself into a crooked pool game in Tijuana, as if there were any other kind down there. He squawked and somebody knifed him. What a waste."

The curse of child stardom had stalked most of the Pint-Size Pirates later in life. Edward Washington, Moon Pie, had overdosed on heroin, and Shadow, born Toby Goss, had died fighting in Korea. The last Valentino had heard, Gerald "Mugs" McDermott was in prison for armed robbery. He might have died inside.

"What about Glory?"

"Gloria," Chub said, smiling. "Sweet girl. She had a weakness for musicians. She married a drummer who beat her like his traps, then divorced him and took up with a saxophonist who liked to wear her underthings. That was a happy marriage, I heard. Anyway, he died. I still got Christmas cards from Gloria until a couple of years ago. Maybe she's dead, too. The reporters who write obituaries don't always keep up on faded celebrities."

"You came out all right."

No trace of a smile remained on his broad features. "I managed to give divorce a bad name, peed away several fortunes, and unleashed eleven ungrateful children on a world that wasn't in short supply to begin with. My own grand-daughter's the ringleader of the bunch that wants to stick me in a droolarium. She doesn't even want my money for herself. She's bleached her daughter's hair, put her in braces, enrolled her in charm school, and is paying a speech therapist to—get this—give her a lisp. Six years old and she's starred in six commercials on national TV. Blame that on me, too. If I hadn't been such a pre-pubescent success, Melanie would never have got that idea in her head. At least none of the others managed to screw up two generations."

"Judy Garland died of a deadly cocktail. The girl from *Different Strokes* stuck up a video store and committed suicide. Robert Blake, Little Beaver, stood trial for murder. All child stars. It's not your fault."

"You know what a wild wall is?"

"A portable wall made from canvas flats for a movie set. The grips can shift it around easily to accommodate the camera. During the famous dolly shot in *The Magnificent Ambersons*, Orson Welles had them rigged to drop into place just before they came inside range. It made the house seem several times bigger than it was."

"Yeah. The *point* is, a kid raised on soundstages is different from every other kind. When you grow up used to walls moving around, you're not exactly prepared to live a stable life after they switch off the kliegs for the last time."

Chub drove him back to his hotel, a small, elderly place maintained by a plump, red-faced couple who could have joined the cast of *How Green Was My Valley*, if that picture had been shot in Ireland instead of Wales. For all Valentino knew, they entertained IRA terrorists in the basement. He preferred John Ford's Celtic paradise to the urban twenty-first-century reality.

He opened his door and turned to shake Chub's hand. "I'll do my best with the university brass. Can I reach you at home tomorrow?"

"Come for dinner. My cook's off today, but I'll have her set out a real Irish spread."

"I don't want to impose."

"She'll be delighted. Feeding an old man's finicky appetite can't be much fun for her. If the news is good, I'll crack open a bottle of wine that's almost as old as I am."

"If I can make you happy, it'll be the happiest day of my life."

Chub Garrett shook his head. "I'm sorry to hear that. Take the advice of a disintegrating adolescent and start a family; one that won't turn on you the minute you start forgetting where you put your glasses."

That night Valentino placed a trunk call to California and smashed up against an accountant with the Film Preservation Department who talked in circles, coming around again and again to the same depressing sum. The man had obviously never enjoyed a movie in his life; he kept referring to Garrett as "Chubby" and thought he had something to do with the Andy Hardy series. To spare himself a restless night, Valentino programmed himself to dream about the Pint-Size Pirates, but they kept growing up on him and leading short, desperate lives.

Macaulay Culkin, Margaret O'Brien, Haley Joel Osment, Dickie Moore. There wasn't a story of true contentment in the batch, and no upbeat ending with a slide-whistle and a merry iris-out.

In the morning, two calls to London revealed the *Lassie* lead was bogus. He rented a car and toured the countryside. Swelling hills, thatched roofs, and men and women in Wellingtons herding sheep took some of the weight off his heart. Low stone walls everywhere, and not a wild one to be seen.

A large American car was parked next to Chub's squatty compact in front of the cottage. The front door was open and Valentino heard voices from inside.

"Hell's sake, Melanie, let the kid go out and play. The place is fenced and there are no snakes in Ireland."

"Shut up, you senile fool. I didn't spend an hour fixing her up to let her slip and fall into a pile of sheep dung."

"We can be civil." A man's voice, English-accented.

"That ship's sailed. He ran out on my mother when she was six."

"You want the girl to hang around for this?" Chub sounded weary.

After a pause the woman said, "Stay close to the house. And don't get dirty!"

A small-boned, grave-faced girl came out in a white dress and white shoes with a red sash tied about her waist. She had a red bow in her astonishingly yellow hair and rouge on her cheeks. When she saw Valentino she made a wide detour around him, clutching a shiny red pocketbook in both hands, and altered her course again to avoid a thick-built man trudging up the lane that led to a fieldstone building forty feet from the cottage.

The man looked a proper Irish tough, closely resembling James Cagney at sixty, in overalls, hobnail boots, and a cloth cap pulled low over his eyes. Valentino guessed this was Chub's groundskeeper. He tugged at his cap in greeting and continued past without speaking. At the door he removed the cap. "Would there be anythinq else, sor?"

"Did you get those potatoes to Cook?"

"Yes, sor. That's them boiling."

"Good. Thank you, Miles."

He put on his cap and turned away. Valentino watched him until he hopped over the stone fence on the far side of the farm. Over by the outbuilding—the old smokehouse, apparently—the little girl stood with her chin down, clasping her pocketbook like a shield to her chest. She seemed afraid to move.

Chub's face brightened when Valentino entered the cottage. He introduced his granddaughter, Melanie, and her solicitor, Clive Speedwell. She was a grownup version of her daughter, more conservatively dressed in a tailored tweed suit but with the same peroxided hair and too much makeup, although expertly applied. The lawyer was a sallow beanpole in Savile Row, with gold initials on his burgundy leather briefcase.

"Valentino's interviewing me for the university archives," Chub said, begging him with his eyes for affirmation. "I'm the last dodo."

Melanie said, "I wouldn't put too much faith in anything he tells you. His mind wanders."

"They're joining us for supper, a nice surprise. Speedwell's brought papers for me to sign. In return for putting everything in Melanie's name I get to live here the rest of my life instead of in a shelter for the criminally ga-ga."

"A crude distortion." The Englishman cleared his throat. "We're anxious to spare him five years of painful litigation out of the time he has left."

"Meanwhile his client sells my four acres in New Mexico to developers and I'm a prisoner here every damn wet Irish winter till pneumonia takes me. What a deal."

The cook, a rawboned woman nearly six feet tall with her black hair in a net, announced that supper was ready. Melanie went to the door and called her daughter, Laurette. Minutes later the little girl came in with stains on the knees of her stockings and a three-corner rip in her skirt.

Her mother bellowed. Laurette sobbed and covered her face with her hands, the pocketbook still clutched in one. When Melanie grasped her by the shoulders, Chub touched her arm. She wheeled on her grandfather. "Keep out of this or I'll put you in the worst home in Ireland! She has an interview with a casting director for the BBC in the morning! If she's skinned a knee, we're finished! He's cast all the street urchins he needs."

"Let's not say anything we'll regret," Speedwell said.

That set her off on a more strident plane, but the cook intervened, saying she'd help the child clean up; she had a sewing kit in her yarn bag, she said. Chub volunteered to serve the meal while she ushered the girl into another room.

It was an authentic Irish meal, as promised, with corned beef, cabbage, and boiled potatoes, each flavor distinct but harmonious with the others, not all mushed together as so often happened in American taverns on St. Patrick's Day; but Valentino enjoyed little of it. His bad news from work, combined with the scene he'd just witnessed, Chub's plight, and the unconvincing story the old man had invented to cover up the offer from UCLA, had destroyed his appetite.

He felt a little better when the cook presented Laurette, looking fresh, bright, and pretty with her dress restored to respectability. Her surprised mother hugged her and pecked her on a patch of cheek not covered by rouge. All seemed well, but Valentino declined a second helping of corned beef when the cook offered it. The girl took a tiny portion and passed the platter to Melanie. Her table manners, of course, were impeccable.

Such a mood could not be sustained in that company. When the cook served cake, Melanie scolded Laurette against crumbs. Chub told Speedwell to put down his briefcase because he wouldn't sign so much as an autograph on anything that came from him or the woman he represented. Melanie tored into a litany of neglect and abandonment, he reminded her that he'd settled a huge sum upon her grandmother and paid her mother child support for twelve years, Laurette bawled. Speedwell said he was sorry that things had come to a legal-competency action. Finally Melanie complained she wasn't feeling well and the trio took its leave.

As tires snatched at the turf outside, Chub drank from his water glass. "I thought that went well, didn't you?"

"I wish I had something better to contribute." Valentino told him about his conversation with the accountant. The cook was busy washing dishes.

"Oh, well. With any luck I'll be dead before the lawyers suck me dry. Should we open that bottle of wine?"

"Not for me. I'm driving."

"Stay here tonight. You can't go home without having a genuine Irish breakfast. Sausages and eggs."

"What makes it Irish?"

"Killians instead of coffee."

"Thanks. I'm taking the first flight out tomorrow. I'm sorry I couldn't come through."

"Funny. That's the same thing I told seven wives."

His guest thanked him for his hospitality and a lifetime of entertainment and drove back to town, where he used the telephone in the hotel lobby to reserve a 7:00 a.m. flight. Packing before bed, he heard banging downstairs; some inebriated fellow, he supposed, looking for a bed to avoid going home to an angry wife. Then someone called his name.

From the second-floor landing outside his room he looked down on the two innkeepers, hair tousled and worn robes flung on over their nightclothes, standing with Chub Garrett at the base of the staircase. The old man was dressed as Valentino had left him. The hotel guest told his hosts it was all right. They shuffled back to their quarters, muttering in Gaelic. Valentino went down.

Chub's face was crimson; he was breathing heavily, and before the other cleared the last step he lunged forward and seized him by both arms in a grip Valentino'd have considered impossible for a man his age. "I accept UCLA's offer. How soon can you put a check in my hands?"

"Are you all right? Is it your health?"

"I asked you a question."

"It's daytime there. I suppose I can have the accountant fax me a letter of credit to a bank in Dublin. Why the change of heart?"

"Criminal attorneys like their money up front."

Valentino heard the sirens then, the insolent European kind, razzing off the sufaces of buildings as they neared the hotel.

"PIRATE" PINCHED! Crowed the headline on the first tabloid to hit the street. Beneath it, a preteen Chub Garrett in costume gripping prison bars in

Jail Jitters appeared beside a color shot of a drained-looking old man being ushered in handcuffs up the steps of the local police station.

Valentino, who had caught very little sleep after Chub had been taken from the hotel, bought the paper from a stall and assembled at last a snarled course of events into a coherent, if highly sensationalized, narrative:

Shortly after returning to her hotel from her ugly encounter with Chub, Melanie, his granddaughter, fell violently ill. Within minutes of admission to St. Christopher's Hospital, she'd died of what the attending physician theorized at first was acute food poisoning, but which the results of tests conducted in the emergency room determined was strychnine. After hearing her daughter Laurette's half-hysterical account of her mother's evening, police went to Chub's cottage, where while they were talking with his cook, the master of the house went out a back door and drove away in his small car. The police pursued him to Valentino's hotel, where they arrested him for suspicion of homicide.

Further investigation found a large supply of strychnine among the herbicides and vermin-killers in jars on shelves in the smokehouse behind the cottage. Although everyone in the house, including the cook, Miles the groundskeeper, and Chub himself had access to the key to the outbuilding on its ring near the front door, the circumstances of Chub's relationship with Melanie, together with his flight when the police went to interview him, made him the chief suspect in her death. Outsiders were dismissed from consideration; the smokehouse was kept locked and the poisons were beyond arm's reach of the tiny window.

Valentino read the article in installments at stops on his way to the bank in busy Dublin, where he exchanged his letter of credit for a cashier's check. Back at the suburban jail, he was denied admittance to see the prisoner, but a sergeant gave him the name of the barrister who'd agreed to represent Chub at his arraignment. Back to Dublin Valentino went.

Weylin Fain, whose powdered wig and black robes hung on a peg in his office of glass and chrome, was too prominent in his profession to soil his hands with money. A large, dark man, built like a potato farmer, he instructed his secretary to take the check and give Valentino a receipt. Despite the man's imperious manner, the film archivist was impressed by his industry. After less than four hours on the case he seemed to know more than anyone else involved.

"Mr. Garrett seems quite taken with you," he said in his trilling Northern brogue. "He's instructed me to be as open with you as with himself. I'm sure you know how bad things look."

Valentino balanced himself on the edge of a sling chair facing the desk. "I'm a lifelong fan, but my experience with celebrities prevents me from being blinded by their public image. He's innocent. His own grandchild? No way."

"No way.' An Americanism I admire. It brooks no argument. I'm not convinced either way, but then I'm the one who must plead his case." He shuffled papers. "The groundskeeper, Miles, is promising. Were you aware that Garrett made arrangements to grant him permanent leasing rights to farm the property following Garrett's death?"

"No. Do you think he became impatient, and that Chub was the intended victim?"

"It's a splendid motive. Breaking one's back for oneself is generally preferable to breaking it for another. Two witnesses overheard Miles tell Garrett he brought the potatoes the cook served that evening."

"Make it three."

Fain wrote on the sheet before him. "He'd have had ample opportunity to inject those spuds with poison. The only thing against it is how he thought only Garrett would be affected."

"Maybe he was too obsessed to care how many died with him." But Valentino had already identified the flaw in the theory.

"No one else got sick," said the barrister, nailing it also. "He left before the meal was served, so even if he mixed up Melanie's and Garrett's plates, he had no chance to contaminate either one. Everyone I've spoken to who was at that meal sampled every dish."

"I did as well, although I didn't eat much of any. It was a distressing affair. What about the cook?"

"I interviewed her this morning. Of course she denied it, but she confirmed that she was appalled by the way Melanie behaved toward her little girl. The woman took quite as much time calming her down as helping her clean up. As a motive for murder, however, I doubt it's strong enough to take the jury's mind off Garrett's. Money and property are formidable, and the mutual animosity between grandfather and granddaughter had a lengthy history."

"That leaves only Speedwell, but he's no suspect. No client, no fee."

"Exactly. Of course, the victim herself has provided us with a first-cabin way out of this, if I can but convince Garrett to go along."

Valentino watched him moving his papers about his desk, like a magician testing his props. He was as suspicious of the barrister as he was of conjurors in general.

"Diminished capacity," Fain said. "She half laid the case for us with that complaint she filed. An old man not in full possession of his faculties cannot be held accountable for his actions. He'd never even stand trial."

"Incompetence? The court would put him in a nursing home. That's just what he was desperate to avoid."

"He said something on that order when I suggested it, although his language was more forceful." Fain shrugged and gathered his sheets into a tidy stack. A blob of ink from his fountain pen stained his left cuff. "Nothing for it, then, but to plead him not guilty, with no reasonable scenario to offer in place of the Queen's. In which case, our beloved Chub will expire in prison. Naturally, as his attorney of record I'll see you take possession of those films he sold you straight away." He raised his thatchlike brows. "Mr. Valentino?"

Hearing his name jarred him from his contemplation of the spot on the man's sleeve. "No hurry. I canceled my flight to the States. I may have a scenario to offer. I know a thing or two about those."

Near evening, Fain and Valentino greeted Chub Garrett in a room at the police station reserved for attorney-client conferences. The surroundings, although spare, were more comfortable than those Valentino had seen back home. The walls were painted a restful green and the chairs around the yellow-oak table were upholstered. The prisoner, still wearing the clothes in which he'd been arrested, appeared oblivious to such details. His eyes were sunken in their sockets and his skull seemed to have shriveled away from his features, which hung in gray folds. He sat with his hands palm-downward on the arms of his chair as if he expected a lethal electric current to flow through him at any time.

"You Yanks lead the world in everything but social science," Fain told Valentino cheerfully. "Dr. Mooney may appear less compassionate at first glance than the child psychologists you employ, but she gets to the heart of the matter without all the soft music and scented candles. Are you up to this, old fellow?"

"Just say it," Chub snapped. "If you'd asked me to sic the system on poor little Laurette, I'd have turned you down flat; but knowing the woman he married, I'm not surprised her father's weak enough to fold right away."

Valentino said, "He's a good man. I spent a few minutes with him while Laurette was in session in another room. He knows his daughter hadn't much chance at a normal childhood and seems determined to do what's best for her from now on, without her mother's ambitious influence."

The barrister dumped a pile of papers from his briefcase and arranged them. "It was all open and aboveboard. Speedwell was present. He's a good solicitor, whatever else you may think of him. He's withdrawn his late client's petition, by the way, at the widower's request. You have Valentino to thank for the inspiration that led to the interview. That, and my carelessness with my linen." Ruefully he displayed the inkstain on his cuff.

The film archivist read only betrayal in Chub's tired gaze. "She was the only other person with motive," he said quickly, "and the only one small enough to crawl through that tiny window in the smokehouse. She's only six, and can't be expected to understand the consequences of her actions, the finality of death. All she wanted was to stop her mother from making her sad. That's what she told the psychologist in private: 'I feel sad all the time when she's there.' Present tense."

Fain said, "She tore her dress and soiled her stockings climbing into that smokehouse. She knew what a skull-and-bones means on a label; every child with a proper British upbringing is well schooled on that. She found her opportunity to sneak the strychnine into her mother's corned beef when she passed her the platter. The chemists found traces of it in the leftovers. Laurette told Dr. Mooney the rest."

"I'd have gone to prison to spare her that," Chub said. "I'd have given up everything I own and died in a nursing home."

"Her father will see she gets the counseling she needs," said Valentino.

"He'd better have a firmer hand than he took with her mother."

Fain said, "A less firm hand is just the thing for her, don't you think?"

Valentino broke the silence that followed. "I won't hold you to your agreement with UCLA. I'll cover the part of the fee Fain's earned out of my own pocket. In time, Laurette may learn to put what's happened behind her. She has an excellent chance at a happy childhood and a normal life."

Chub worked his hands on the arms of his chair. The eyes in the slack face resembled those of the carefree leader of the Pint-Size Pirates. "Maybe I should've killed my parents when I had the chance."

Valentino returned to California and lost himself in the myriad mundane details of locating and preserving popular entertainment canned on celluloid. He resigned himself to the proposition that life was too depressing for the Hollywood Dream Factory to make inroads against it for more than an hour or two. For the first time in his career, he wondered if he hadn't dedicated his life to a facetious lie. Progress reports from Weylin Fain about little Laurette's progress in an ordinary school, with ordinary friends and the appearance of happiness in class and at recess, buoyed his spirits temporarily, but he kept returning to that sad old man and his empty victory brought about through circumstances diametrically opposed to the upbeat mood of his vehicles. Carefree comedy had lost its appeal.

Months passed with him in this frame of mind, and many attempts at other acquisitions had succeeded and failed, before Valentino allowed himself to spend any time thinking about the Pint-Size Pirates. In the celebrities column of the *Los Angeles Times*, he read a brief announcement of the wedding of Chub Garrett and a woman named Gloria Campbell in Dublin's Christ's Church. The photo that accompanied it showed the round, happy face of the groom beside the equally rotund features of his bride, who retained the mischievous eyes and dimpled smile of Glory, the puppy-love interest of Chub Garrett, Sassafrass, Shadow, and Moon Pie, and even the surly Mugs. The text explained that the couple had reunited when Gloria read of Chub's travails in a newspaper in Sydney, Australia—where she'd lived for twenty years since the death of her second husband—and flew to Ireland to lend moral support.

A few days later, a huge carton arrived at the office of the UCLA Film Preservation Department, addressed to Valentino and plastered all over with certificates from Irish and U.S. customs. He spent the day watching reel after reel of the anarchical antics of a gang of Depression-era schoolchildren, blissfully unaware of what lay ahead when the kliegs were switched off for the last time and walls stayed put, and laughed himself to tears.

Preminger's Gold

Northern Michigan wouldn't be mistaken for Southern California, despite the presence of a rocky shoreline that might have stood in for the Pacific Coast Highway in a student film with no travel budget.

The differences were apparent as Valentino drove his rental car along reddish main streets paved with asphalt and slag from extinct iron mines. Video stores had taken the place of boarded-up neighborhood theaters for the entertainment of locals, and chain motels had begun to push out rustic log bungalows, but the villages were refreshingly free of McDonald's and Wal-Marts, and when he got out with his bags, strangers on the street, dressed for the most part in ear-flapped caps and Mackinaws—the women as well as the men—greeted him in passing as if they were old friends.

"I may retire here in twenty or thirty years," he told Kyle Broadhead from the telephone in his room; his cell couldn't get a signal among all those pines and weathered granite.

His mentor's chuckle reached him all the way from his faculty office in Los Angeles. "Have you ever even *owned* a snow shovel?"

"I was born and raised in Indiana. I think I can handle a few flakes."

"'A few flakes' is what they call summer up there. You'll be on your way back home as soon as they finish de-icing the plane."

It was early autumn and the weather was quite pleasant; but Valentino had heard stories of winter residents tunneling through roof-high drifts to get about, so he chose not to strain the university budget in a long-distance argument. "I'm meeting Sigurson tomorrow for breakfast. He sounds friendly on the phone. I think this will be a worthwhile trip."

"Sigurson. Bet he talks like those characters in *Fargo*."

As a matter of fact, Leonard Sigurson had spoken with that lilting Scandinavian accent that the dialect coaches at all the studios claimed was vanishing from the northern regions of the U.S. and Canada.

Valentino didn't address the remark. Broadhead was always right and reacted immodestly whenever his opinion was confirmed. "Goodbye, Kyle. I'm turning in soon."

"So early? What is it there, eight o'clock in the evening?"

"Nine. Most of the state's on Eastern time. Anyway, I had layovers in Denver and Chicago, then a puddle-jumper and a long drive. The sun comes up here same time as back home."

"Just don't come back with plaid poisoning." Broadhead hung up.

The contact had suggested an hour unknown on the West Coast, but Valentino fell asleep quickly with Lake Superior pounding not far away and arose at sunrise, lagged but alert. He put himself together and walked through chill air to the diner.

"I keep telling the owner he should knock down that wall and expand the place," his waitress said. "We've got more customers than tables every day of the week."

Valentino grunted and made room on the checked cloth for a large oval plate of bacon and eggs. The crisp climate made him hungry, and not inclined to lecture on the value of popular culture. The wall was the reason this beanery in a barely accessible region of the American Midwest had so many customers.

Famished though he was, after the waitress left he paused a moment longer to contemplate the signatures on the wall of his booth: Otto Preminger, James Stewart, Lee Remick, George C. Scott, Ben Gazzara, and of course Robert Traver, whose experience and imagination had started it all.

In 1958—well before that young lady's time—Preminger, the most gifted and difficult Austrian film director since Erich von Stroheim, had led his troupe to Michigan's wild, wind-lashed Upper Peninsula to film *Anatomy of a Murder*, based on John D. Voelker's courtroom suspense novel inspired by his career as an attorney and judge, published under the Traver pseudonym. The result, daring for its era, was one of the three or four best legal dramas ever produced. Stewart had reestablished his star power as the quirky, canny country lawyer attempting to clear his client of a murder charge, and Remick and Gazzara, relative unknowns at the time of casting, had been catapulted into the ranks of the Hollywood elite.

Aware of good things coming their way, all had agreed to provide their autographs at the request of the diner's owner, whose hearty fare and friendly service had helped sustain them through the rigorous weeks of shooting. Included was the immortal Duke Ellington, who had written the score and appeared in a cameo onscreen. Destroying those artifacts might not necessarily harm tourism—that harsh and beautiful country drew hunters, boaters, anglers, and even would-be Ernest Hemingways eager to fish the waters and hike the trails their idol had known so well—but the loss to cinephiles would be as great as the destruction of Da Vinci's *Last Supper*.

The visitor's empty stomach tore him at last from his meditation. The food was as delicious as it was unhealthy. But as he swabbed up the remnants with whole-wheat toast and drenched his broken inner clock with black coffee from a thick mug, he began to wonder if he'd been stood up. Every time the street door opened, tinkling the bell mounted on the frame above it, he looked up, only to return his attention to his plate when the newcomer joined friends at a table or tramped straight to the counter and straddled a stool. They let no more than a curious glance stray toward the unfamiliar figure in the booth. They probably dismissed him as just another cinema buff who'd requested the seat.

When the waitress refilled his mug, he asked if she knew Leonard Sigurson.

"Ziggy? Who doesn't? He'll bend your ear talking about his big movie career."

"I was hoping he would, but he's late."

"I think his watch ran down years ago and he never got around to rewinding it. He rolls out of bed with the first shotgun blast in the woods and eats when his belly tells him to. Some nights he bangs on the door after closing and we have to fire the griddle back up so he doesn't go to bed hungry. Ziggy, he's a character." She carried the pot to another table.

When the last of the morning crowd had paid up and gone and Valentino was testing his bladder with more coffee, he sensed that the small staff was growing impatient to clear the tables for lunch. Sigurson came in then.

Valentino didn't recognize his contact at first. He'd spent some time studying the two scenes in *Anatomy of a Murder* in which Sigurson had appeared, but the old man in unseasonable shorts, polo shirt, and sailor's cap didn't bear much resemblance to that long-ago background extra. He glanced around, spotted the lone diner, and limped his way, hand outstretched.

"Keep your seat," he said when Valentino started to rise. "I just got my hip replaced and it hurts to look at you youngsters popping up and down like a lake perch." His hand was as strong as his features, bony and hawklike under sagging skin. "Cora! Over easy and burnt to a crisp."

"Ziggy, you don't think I know by now how you take 'em?"

The waitress sounded friendly, but she glared at Valentino, as if it was his fault the booth was unavailable for busing.

The old man peered at the card Valentino gave him. He didn't appear to need reading glasses. " 'Film detective.' I thought you said you was an archaeologist."

"Archivist. It's because people make that mistake I call myself a detective. Were you sitting here when that wall was signed?"

"No, this here was the grownups' table. I was over there." He pointed at a table in the corner. The worn oilcloth covering might have been the same one he'd sat in front of back then.

A scheduling glitch all those years ago was what had brought Valentino halfway across the country. Sigurson's two scenes were shot weeks apart instead of back-to-back, so he'd been paid throughout the company's time on location. He'd filled the idle days taking home movies of the cast and crew. UCLA's Film

Preservation Program, tagged to remaster *Anatomy* for a special DVD release, had sent its crack archivist to upper Michigan to secure that amateur footage for a reasonable price to include on a second disc.

"I'd of went nuts without that little Bell and Howell," the old man said. "That guy Preminger spent half a day setting up and the other half putting the same ten lines on film over and over. Inefficient. Kid here in town made a whole science-fiction picture in a week last summer."

"Preminger was a perfectionist."

"A nasty feller's what he was. When he wasn't trying to shove that pretty little thing Lee Remick into the sack he was cussing at her and everybody else. The colonel was the only one he couldn't bully."

"The colonel?"

"Jimmy Stewart. He was in the Air Force, you know, flew twenty missions over Germany. I guess the Kraut figured he'd bomb him if he didn't back off, slobbered all over him when he found out he didn't scare. He even laid off of Lee when the colonel was around. Sweet little thing, Lee. I bawled like a baby when I heard she'd died. Only fifty-five she was."

"What was Ben Gazzara like?"

"Okay. Sort of standoffish. He was one of them Method actors. You couldn't talk about the weather and such with him—you know, carry on a normal conversation. He was playing his part all the time, on and off the set."

That checked with the Gazzara Valentino had interviewed; a polite man, serious about his craft. The subject had been the forthcoming debut on video of *Run for Your Life*, the series that had made the actor a TV star, but as the only surviving member of *Anatomy*'s principal cast he could not escape probing questions about the production. He'd mentioned the home movie in passing. A great deal of research on Valentino's part had gone into identifying Sigurson as the man behind the camera and locating him, but elderly people often exaggerated their past exploits for the entertainment of a young audience. It was possible he'd come all this way over a couple of hundred frames of anonymous figures shot at a distance.

"You were a bold young man," he said. "Most amateurs would be too timid to approach a credited player with a camera."

Sigurson's eggs arrived, charred and smoking. He chewed and grinned, blackened bits showing between teeth that showed far less wear than his baggy, humorous face. "I knew you'd think I was some old crank with a tall tale to sell. That's why I brung these."

Valentino watched him take a plastic photo wallet from the cargo pocket of his shorts and spread its contents like playing cards on the table between them. They were digital stills in full color of Stewart, Remick, Gazzara, and Arthur O'Connell, the character specialist who'd nailed the role of Stewart's boozy associate, in costume and looking relaxed and casual—except Gazzara, who looked just like the simmering young man on trial for his life he'd played in the film. Surreptitious-looking shots caught the shaven-headed Otto Preminger with his mouth open, shouting at some hapless member of the talent or crew.

"After you called I had my son drive me to Marquette and paid a photo place to put the film on disc. Did you know they can print stuff on paper easier that way? I sure didn't. You got an honest face, mister, but I'll just hang on to the film and the disc till we have us a deal. Keep the prints; I got a second set for free."

Valentino thanked him, shuffled the stills into a stack, and slid them back into the wallet. His hand shook slightly. From the evidence, Sigurson had been a gifted amateur, framing his shots with skill and maintaining focus. Snaring previously unknown footage intimately connected with a classic film was as exciting to an archivist as discovering a third part to *Henry IV* would be to a Shakespearean scholar.

He willed himself to appear calm. The department budget was tight, and he lived in fear of exhausting it on something tempting only to be approached soon after by someone in possession of the entire work of Theda Bara, or some other grail as holy. He couldn't seem eager if he wanted a bargain.

"These are impressive, but I'll have to screen the original before I make an offer, if I decide to. What are you asking?"

"Not a penny."

"I'm sorry?" Obviously his ears hadn't popped yet.

Sigurson swallowed egg. "Too steep?"

Cora, the waitress, was taking an inordinate amount of time clearing and wiping down the table nearest the booth. Valentino lowered his voice. "Is there someplace we can talk in private?"

"Son, this here's the Upper Peninsula. Ain't no place you can't."

They paid for their meals and went out, strolling an empty sidewalk where the parking meters were placed against buildings so as not to obstruct snow plows in winter. The nip in the air had lost some of its edge, but the visitor was grateful for the flannel lining of his windbreaker. He couldn't understand why his companion's exposed arms and legs weren't turning blue.

"Ever hear of Little Bohemia?" Sigurson asked.

"No."

"How about John Dillinger, ever hear of him?"

"Oh, yes!" He wondered if the old man's mind was wandering.

"Back in 'thirty-four—before my time, by the way—he and his gang slipped right out from under the FBI's nose when agents had them surrounded in the Little Bohemia lodge, across the line in Wisconsin. Dillinger split off from the rest, worked his way down to Detroit, then back west. Lots of people know that. What they don't know, most of 'em, is when he left that lodge he brung along a sack of gold bullion he stole from a bank in Indiana.

"Well, bullion's heavy, so he did it to keep it from slowing him down, meaning to come back for it later. Only he didn't get around to it, because a couple of months later the FBI got lucky finally and gunned him down outside a picture show in Chicago."

"Who told you about the gold?" Valentino was humoring him. Sooner or later even the most determined babblers returned to the subject.

"Everybody around here back then knew the story, even if most of 'em thought it was hooey. There's always talk of buried treasure wherever a bandit's been. That man Preminger bought into it. What's more, he got the gold. Excuse me, son. I'm still breaking in this new hip."

They'd come to a little patch of park, where Sigurson lowered himself onto a painted bench. Valentino joined him. He was eager to hear the rest, now; implausible tales were meat and mead to a movie buff.

"We had an old town character in them days, called Shorty. I think Short was his real name. Had a face looked like the map of the Upper Peninsula. I think that's why Preminger hired him as an extra, to make his picture look authentic. You can see him in a crowd scene outside the courthouse.

"Shorty was an old-time bootlegger, had a reputation for helping folks hide out who was on the run from the law, places where he used to stash liquor. He got drunk one day and told me he ought to give up the stuff because it made him talk too much. He said he'd talked himself out of a fortune when he told Preminger he'd harbored Dillinger for a few days after Little Bohemia and Dillinger trusted him to hold his gold till he came back. The Kraut egged him on by pretending he was interested in buying the story from him for a picture."

"Don't tell me he told him where he hid it."

Sigurson nodded. "In the shaft of an iron mine that shut down in 'twenty-eight when the ore run out. He kept a still there from 'thirty to 'thirty-three."

"It had to have been there, what, twenty-four years. What kept him from spending it?"

"Franklin Delano Roosevelt. When FDR took the country off the gold standard he made it illegal for American citizens to own it or spend it. Shorty said he'd done his share of jail time for breaking the Prohibition laws and hadn't took to it. He was waiting for the government to change its mind, like it done when it said it was all right to go back to drinking."

"So Otto Preminger wound up with the gold."

"No, sir, he didn't. I busted into the Kraut's hotel room the night before he flew back to Hollywood and searched it top to bottom. I didn't find so much as a gold filling."

This evil old man shocked Valentino. "He sent it ahead."

"I asked the postmaster point-blank if anyone with the picture company had sent any large packages. He wasn't supposed to answer me, but he knew me since I was a kid, or thought he did. Couple of letters and some postcards was all. There wasn't no FedEx or UPS then, and the next post office was a forty-minute drive. Preminger never broke more than a half-hour for lunch; just long enough to get that gold and stash it someplace else. If you think he trusted a flunky to ship it out for him, you haven't listened to a word I've said about that bald bastard."

"Maybe he had better luck than Dillinger and came back."

"Mister, until that company came to town we hadn't seen a celebrity since Paul Bunyan. You think he could sneak back in? He figured it was safe where he put it till it was legal to flash it around, just like Shorty. He was still waiting when he died. Shorty's dead, too, of course. I can hold my liquor and keep a secret. You and I are the only ones know about that gold."

"Why tell me?"

The baggy face under the Gilligan cap leaned close enough for Valentino to smell the egg on his breath. "You're going to help me get it. That's my price for letting you have that home movie."

Although the air was warming, his years in the desert climate hadn't prepared Valentino for a crisp autumn in the upper Midwest. Sitting on the bench slowed his circulation and his thinking; he could swear the old man was recruiting him to hunt for hidden treasure. He asked for another change of scene.

"If you can stand an old widower's shack." Sigurson rose.

The little house set back from the state highway wasn't the hermit's hovel the visitor had expected. It wore a coat of whitewash and the functional shutters on the windows were painted a festive red. The open floor plan included a pair of worn but cozy-looking armchairs, a narrow bed neatly made on an iron frame, a white enamel sink, and a small wood-burning stove that kept the temperature pleasantly in the sixties. It wasn't a cookstove. His host appeared to depend on the diner for his sustenance.

"Privy's out back," he said when his guest looked around for what was missing. "Town ordered 'em all torn down forty years ago, but I'm a beloved local character, so the council don't see it on purpose."

Valentino wondered if the members would be so indulgent if they knew the truth about the character. "Actually, I was thinking about your projector."

"That's at my son's place on the lake, the films and the camera, too. I didn't have the space and I put away the hobby when I blew out my hip. He's been after me to come live with him, but the plain fact is I can't stand his wife and she hates my guts. Peppermint schnapps?" He took a flat bottle from the wood-box near the stove.

Valentino shook his head. It wasn't anywhere near noon. "Won't mess with glasses, then." Sigurson tipped up the bottle. It gurgled and he recapped it and put it back. He waved his guest into one of the shabby armchairs and took one for himself. "Sometimes I think I'd still have all the parts the good Lord gave me if I hadn't spent so much time ducking in and out of mineshafts and climbing down cisterns and digging holes poking around for that gold. I was never much for manual labor. I was an engineer. I helped design Big Mac."

Valentino had done some research on the area before coming there and knew that Big Mac was not a McDonald's specialty but the great Mackinac Bridge that had linked the Upper and Lower peninsulas for fifty years, eliminating the need for ferries to carry cars and passengers between them.

Sigurson continued. "Turning point come when I was sweating through a break telling myself I wasn't cut out for that type of work. Engineers work with numbers, not their backs. So do movie directors, always thinking about how many takes they need to get a scene right and staying under budget and how many pages they can shoot before the labor unions give 'em grief. Preminger'd no more swing a pick or climb a ladder than he'd paint a set.

"Well, sir, that was a revelation. A man with a head for figures, a stranger in these parts, he'd rig a hiding place the easy way, someplace where what he hid couldn't be found except by him, and he'd draw up a plan to jog his memory. But words and drawings take time, and they get lost or stolen. A puffed-up, proud-of-hisself jerk like him thought everything he shot was cut in stone. *Anatomy of a Murder*, my eye. It was a treasure map."

Valentino sat forward.

The old man twinkled at the reaction. "I got excited, too, but it didn't last. At the time I had that brainstorm, the only way you got to see a picture that had had its day was in a revival theater or on late-night TV. I can't tell you how many miles I drove to see it when it showed up in a listing anywhere around here, or how many times I set my alarm to get up and squint at it on my old Admiral when even the coyotes had went to bed. Mister, I can recite every line from memory. My son thought I couldn't get enough of it because I was in it. I let him."

"You don't trust anyone, do you?"

"Not unless there's something in it for them when I do, like you."

"There must've been a flaw in your theory, or you'd have the gold by now."

"Theory's sound, I know that now. See, back then them reels had been through so many hands there was breaks and splices every place they played, and on TV the station managers butchered 'em to make room for commercials. One time the whole panty scene was missing."

"Censorship, probably. That scene almost kept the film out of theaters in 'fifty-nine."

Sigurson looked annoyed. "What I'm saying is a map's no good when it's full of holes."

"You waited twenty years for the video revolution."

"Longer, as it turned out. Once them VCRs caught on they sold like smoked salmon, and the studios just dumped their stuff onto tape to fill the orders. No extra stuff except sometimes the original preview, and the quality wasn't always much better than in theaters and on TV. It helped a little, but there was blanks still."

"Then came DVD."

Valentino nodded. The advent of disc players had opened the floodgates. Demand for more and more material had inspired copyright holders to forage deeper and deeper into the inventory, and the initial release of *Anatomy* and hundreds of other classics to disc had helped turn nearly every American household into a screening room. From there it was only a short jump to special edition re-releases with restored scenes and hours of documentaries, expert commentary, and interviews with surviving production personnel. It all seemed like some kind of conspiracy orchestrated by this wicked old rustic to lure him to this rocky outcrop on the edge of now here.

"I put my paws on that disc the day it showed up here," Sigurson said. "I hate to say it, but seeing it the way it was supposed to be seen, the way I hadn't since it premiered, before I knew what good it could do me, I near got lost in it. The Kraut had a gift. I had to sit through it twice more with a notepad on my knee to get what I needed."

"If you got what you needed, what do you need me for?"

Sigurson showed his prosthetic teeth in that baggy evil grin. "You ever been snorkeling?"

The friendly clerk at the desk asked the guest if he was going for a walk. "Not much nightlife here, I'm afraid. We roll up the sidewalks at dusk."

"You're right about the walk." Valentino, who had packed for the latitude, pulled on a pair of jersey gloves from the pocket of his windbreaker. A knitted cap covered the tops of his ears. "It'll be nice to smell something other than auto exhaust for a change."

"The one thing we have in surplus is fresh air."

There was frost, and a stiff breeze from the lake that tightened his face and made him grateful once again for the shelter of Leonard Sigurson's tiny house. The atmosphere, however, was gloomy, with all the shades drawn and only a low-wattage lamp burning on a narrow table.

"Can't have the neighbors guessing what we're about," he said, handing his guest a bundle. "You and my son are about the same size. He won't miss it; he ain't dove in years."

Valentino groped the spongy material of the heavy-duty wet suit. "It's been awhile for me, too. I was pretty good at it, but I've only been down once or twice in the dark."

"Well, this ain't daylight work."

"Is anything about this legal?"

"I ain't Dillinger just because I busted into a hotel room one time. Statute of limitations on the bank robbery run out years and years ago, and back in 'thirty-four the accounts weren't federally insured. It's okay to own gold again. Whoever claims it, it's his, provided he makes out all the paperwork and pays taxes on it."

There was no place for privacy, but the old man had some discretion in his black heart, turning his back to feed the stove while Valentino stripped and put on the suit. He slipped back into his shoes and socks for warmth and tucked the flippers and snorkel under one arm. "How much money are we talking about?"

"Mister, that's none of your business. A deal's a deal. The film's all you get."

"I don't want any part of your gold. I don't believe it's as aboveboard as you say. If I cared to be rich there are better ways to do it in L.A. than working for a university."

"You and my son got more in common than just size. He's a marine biologist." Sigurson shook his head. "Old Shorty said that bullion was worth fifty grand in nineteen fifty-eight. Figuring in exaggeration on his part, it's right around a million now. I always wanted to see the world. Now I can do it from a first-class cabin and five-star hotels from here to China. I'll soak these old bones at Lourdes."

"What about your son?"

"Oh, I'll see Roger gets a taste once I'm gone. I don't intend to leave enough behind to put a smile on that sour puss of his wife's."

The native's only concession to the cold had been to pull on a pair of lined jogging pants and a gray hooded sweatshirt. Outside, he tugged the hood up over his sailor's cap. He looked like an impious old monk. He carried a battery-operated lantern, but left it off as he led the way over hard, uneven ground toward the lake. Obviously he knew the way in the dark. Valentino stumbled along behind.

"Math, I made my living on it a long time," said the old man in a voice so low his companion had to strain to hear it against the surging of the inland sea. "*Anatomy*'s one hundred and sixty minutes long. Divide that by forty-nine scenes—chapters, they call 'em on DVD—multiply it by the number of actors credited in the cast, and you get the number of paces Preminger took from the mineshaft he took the gold from to the shore. Shorty pointed out the shaft for me; no need to keep it a secret once it was empty.

"Just *where* on the shore stumped me for many months. Give me a hand with this, will you?"

The sky was clear, and although there was no moon, the stars hung low and huge and reflected off the choppy surface like glittering scales. As Valentino's eyes adjusted, he saw that they'd stopped at a tiny pier glistening with fish slime, and at the point where it jutted out into the water lay an oblong object covered by a canvas tarpaulin. He stooped to help untie the cotton clothesline that secured the canvas and dragged it away from a nine-foot boat of painted aluminum with a small outboard motor attached to the stern.

Sigurson returned to the subject. "I spent a year and plenty of shoe leather working out what was division and what was multiplication and whether addition and subtraction had anything to do with it, but which direction he paced had me stalled till I remembered that there."

The archivist peered in the direction he was pointing, but saw nothing beyond what appeared to be a pile of rocks a little more regular than the others that had been washed up on shore.

"Ernest and Henrietta Hubbard ran a bait-and-tackle shop on that foundation till it burned down in 'sixty-four. After that they moved back downstate and died there, I reckon. They bought a Dubbaya-Dubbaya-Two landing craft from a feller that got it from surplus to turn into a fishing boat and never got around to it, chained it up to the building, and painted it red to attract business. Hobby, I called it; they closed the shop three days of the week to comb the beach for Petoskey stones. One day they came back and the boat was gone. The sheriff never did find it, figured some punks from out of town smashed the lock, punched the deck full of holes, and shoved it off to sink out in the lake. Right in the middle of filming, that was."

"You think Preminger loaded the gold aboard and scuttled it?"

"I know it. He paced out the distance from the mineshaft in a regular goose-step. All them Kraut directors left the Old Country to get away from Hitler and set up their own little Nazi state in Hollywood. Once I figured out this was where he was headed, all I had to do was stick out my legs that same way and this is where I wound up, square on his count."

It made sense, in a lunatic sort of way. The likelihood of anyone bothering to recover a rusty old piece of war materiel was slight, even if it were ever found. It would wait for Preminger's return. "But how could he know just where it went down? How could you, for that matter?"

"For him it was easy. All he had to do was stand here and watch. It wouldn't take long, heavy old barge like that with enough holes in the decking. It was harder for me, but I had global warming on my side. Lake level's not near what it once was. I spent just a week putting about in my little luxury yacht till I spotted it, anchored on a sandbar just twelve feet down. Water's clear as glass on a sunny day."

"Too bad we don't have the sun to help out."

"Don't need it. I know how to take a sighting day and night. Bridge-building ain't exactly steady work. I put fish on the table between jobs. Took Roger out with me sometimes, that was a mistake. The life aquatic agreed with him. Marine biology pays even worse than part-time engineering."

As he spoke, Sigurson signaled to Valentino to help him push the boat into the water. They climbed aboard, and the old man tipped down the outboard's propellers and pulled the cord three times until the motor caught with a cough and a sputter.

The roll of the lake, and the maneuvers its pilot made to roll with it and avoid capsizing, reminded the passenger why he'd lost interest in diving. He was glad he'd skipped supper at the diner to prepare himself to take it back up.

Twice Sigurson snapped his lantern on briefly to read a compass. Apart from that he seemed to be steering by the stars. After what seemed an hour but was probably less than a third of that, he cut back on the motor, then switched it off. For a few minutes they drifted with the swells, then: "Hand me that anchor. The paint bucket," he added impatiently, when Valentino hesitated. The archivist complied. It was filled with concrete, with an iron ring sunk into it and a stiff coarse rope knotted to the ring. It entered the water with a splash and the rope uncoiled rapidly, singing against the metal hull. "Suit up."

While Valentino changed into the flippers and adjusted the mask and snorkel, Sigurson switched on the lantern, a powerful item in a rubberized waterproof case, and trained it over the side, where the shaft cut through the murk beneath the surface. After a minute of searching he grunted and directed his companion's gaze to a squarish bulk perched at a steep angle perhaps four yards below. The man in the wetsuit shivered involuntarily at the sight.

Sigurson handed him the lantern and slid something from under the seat that separated them. It looked like an ordinary nylon gym bag with a rigid frame. "This ought to save you a few trips. The original bank sacks would've rotted long before Preminger's time, and whatever he put the gold in won't be in any better shape after forty years."

The diver lifted it by its strap handle. It was almost weightless. The frame was hollow aluminum. "What about sharks?"

"It's fresh water, and too cold. I'd watch out for lampreys, though. Nasty critters."

Forcing himself to think about the film, Valentino motioned the old man to the other side of the boat for balance and sat on the edge, the bag in one hand and the lantern in the other. He took a deep breath and tipped over backward.

On the floor of the little house, the pile of bright beveled bricks reflected the glow from the low-watt lamp, seeming to give off their own heat. Valentino was grateful for it, wrapped as he was in a coarse blanket waiting for the chill to recede before dressing. The wetsuit was a sodden heap on the floor beside the open gym bag, the other diving gear on top.

Sigurson, humming to himself at the narrow table that supported the lamp, scribbled on a piece of paper with a stump of yellow pencil. "What you figure Preminger had in mind for it?" he asked. "He must've been a millionaire already, all them pictures."

"You don't know Hollywood. Either he wanted a nest egg or he planned to produce as well as direct. That requires an investment."

"Sounds like he was a sucker for his own racket." The old man sealed the sheet in an envelope and wrote on the outside. "This here's the address and directions. I wrote inside what I want him to do. Roger's a good boy, does what he's told."

"What about his wife?"

"Oh, Denise'll be happy enough to part with it. I can't spend ten minutes with her she ain't after me to get my stuff out of her house. Don't tell neither of 'em about the gold, or nobody else till I lay claim to it. Otherwise no film, and I can afford a lawyer to get it back."

"I hope being rich makes you happy. A friend once told me the longer you spend lusting after something, the more you wish you had that time back when you get it."

"What's he do?"

"He works for UCLA, like me."

"What I thought. If he knew what it's like to get what you want, he wouldn't be poor."

Valentino found Roger Sigurson a pleasant young man, and his wife the polar opposite of the harridan her father-in-law had described. They owned one of the more modest homes on the lake; the den where Roger screened the film for their guest was barely large enough for the purpose.

"I hope Dad didn't gouge you." He rewound the spool. "I know what it's like to work under budgetary constraints."

The visitor shook himself into the present. The film was worth the nasty old man's company, the icy dive, the severe cold he felt coming on. It offered a solid twenty minutes after editing, and the prospect of a fascinating voiceover; thanks to the circumstances under which it had been obtained, the department could afford to hire Ben Gazzara to narrate. "I'm not at liberty do discuss the terms." He sneezed violently.

"Bless you." Denise Sigurson had entered the room. "Won't you stay for dinner? A hot meal may not cure the sniffles, but it makes them easier to bear."

"Thank you, but I have an early flight. Tomorrow."

The next morning, groggy from the hour and stuffed up tight, he pushed away his tasteless ham and eggs and held up his mug for Cora to refill.

"This stuff's no good for a cold," said the waitress, pouring. "Why don't I fetch you some orange juice?"

"I'll survive. Has Leonard Sigurson been in yet?"

"Poor old Ziggy. He died."

Valentino froze with the mug half raised to his lips. "I just saw him last n—yesterday. What happened?"

"Asa Getz—that's his next-door neighbor—found him lying in his front yard just after dawn. I guess he was on his way here when his heart gave out. I told him he should order oatmeal once in a while, clean out his pipes. Anything else?"

"Just the check." He was still stunned. The excitement of the previous evening had put his own heart to the test.

"Poor old Ziggy." She wrote on her pad. "Some folks won't miss him, I guess. He wasn't what you'd call the sociable type, and he didn't tip for sour apples. I was used to him coming around, though."

"What a sad waste."

"I wouldn't say that. His son turned out all right, and the daughter-in-law's nice. This'll be tough on them. I don't imagine Ziggy had life insurance. Funerals cost money, and they're just squeaking by."

"What's the law in this state regarding the property of someone who dies intestate?"

"I know that word: means no will." She tore off the sheet and laid it on the table. "Unless it's changed since my ma died, everything goes to next of kin. Not that I wound up with anything but a bunch of old clothes that didn't fit me. Ziggy didn't even own that little-bitty house he was living in. Spent most of his Social Security on rent. Roger and Denise are in for a rough surprise."

"A surprise, anyway." Valentino paid his bill, left a generous tip, and drove his rental to the airport with the film in his carry-on, blowing his nose frequently.

The List

The shop was one of dozens like it in Tijuana, with Louis Vuitton knockoffs hanging like Chinese lanterns from the ceiling, shelves of ceramic skulls wearing Nazi biker helmets, and cases of vanilla extract in quart bottles, the kind the Customs people seized at the border to prevent parasites from entering the U.S. A muumuu covered the female shopkeeper's tub-shaped body in strips of crinkly bright-colored cloth, and until she moved to swat a *cucaracha* the size of a field-mouse on the counter, Valentino thought she was a giant piñata.

"*Buenos días, señora,*" he said.

"*Buenas noches, señor,*" she corrected, scraping off the remains on the edge of a large can of refried beans.

It was, indeed, evening. He'd started out from L.A. early enough to get there by nightfall, but the rickety heap he was driving these days had blown a radiator hose in San Diego and it had taken the mechanic two hours to fashion a replacement because that model hadn't been made since Nixon.

"*Buenas noches. Yo busto un hombre Americano se gusta—*"

"I beg your pardon, sir, but are you trying to say you are looking for someone?"

"You speak English?"

"Everyone in Tijuana speaks English, but no one understands whatever language you were speaking. Whom do you seek?"

"An elderly gentleman named Ralph Stemp."

She smacked the swatter again, but this time there appeared to be nothing under it but the counter. "I do no favors for friends of Stemp. You must buy something or leave my store."

He decided not to argue with her scowl. He took a box of strike-anywhere matches off a stack and placed it before her. She took his money and made change from a computer register; the bronze baroque antique on the other end of the counter was just for show. He said, "I don't know Mr. Stemp. I'm here to do business with him."

"If it is money business, pay me. He died owing me rent."

He had the same sudden sinking sensation he'd felt when the radiator hose blew. "I spoke to him on the phone day before yesterday. He was expecting me."

"Yesterday, in his sleep. He's buried already. He made all the arrangements beforehand, but he forgot about me."

Remote grief mingled with sharp frustration. Ralph Stemp was one of the last of the Warner Brothers lineup of supporting players who appeared in as many as ten films a year in the 1940s, more than double the number the stars made. He was always some guy named Muggs or Lefty and usually got shot in the last reel. Whatever insider stories he had had gone with him to his grave.

That was the grief part. The frustration part involved the unsigned contract in Valentino's pocket. A cable TV network that specialized in showing B movies was interested in a series of cheap heist pictures the ninety-year-old retired actor had directed in Mexico a generation ago, and Stemp had agreed to cut the UCLA Film Preservation Department in on the sale price if Valentino represented him in the negotiations. The films were trash, but they were in the university archives, and the department needed the money to secure more worthwhile properties. Without the old man's signature, the whole thing was off.

He excused himself to step out into the street and use his cell. Under a corner lamp a tipsy *norteamericano* couple in gaudy sombreros posed for a picture with a striped burro belonging to a native who charged for the photo op.

"Smith Oldfield here." There was always a whiff of riding leather and vintage port in that clipped British accent. The man who for all Valentino knew ate and slept in the offices of the UCLA Legal Department listened to the bad news, then said, "You should have faxed him the contract instead of going down there."

"He didn't trust facsimile signatures. It was his suspicion and resentment that swung the deal. He never forgave the country for branding him a Communist, or the industry for turning its back on him. He agreed to the split so he wouldn't have to deal directly with anyone in the entertainment business."

"I'm surprised he trusted you."

He took no offense at that. "I ran up a monstrous long-distance bill convincing him. I suppose now we'll have to start all over again with his estate."

"A U.S. citizen residing in Mexico? With two governments involved, you'd be quicker making peace in the Middle East. And the heirs might not share his distaste for Hollywood. In that likelihood they'd cut you out and make the deal themselves."

"He outlived all his relatives, and judging by his crankiness in general I doubt he had any close friends."

"Have you any idea what happened to his personal effects?"

"I can ask his landlady. Why?"

"It's a longshot, but if he left anything in writing that referred to the terms of your agreement, even a doodle, it might accelerate the process. The probate attorneys could take their fees out of his share in the sale."

Valentino thanked him and went back inside to talk to the human piñata. She said, "The room was furnished. Everything he owned fit in a suitcase. No cash, and not even a watch worth trying to sell. Some rags and papers. You can have it all for what he owed me. One hundred sixty dollars American."

"What kind of papers?"

She smirked. "A map to a gold mine in Guadalajara. Go down and dig up a fortune."

"Can I take a look?"

"This is a retail shop. The peep show's across the street."

He exhaled, signed three traveler's checks, and slid them across the counter. The woman held each up to the light, then locked them in the register and moved with the stately grace of a tramp steamer through a beaded curtain in back. She returned carrying an old-fashioned two-suiter and heaved it up onto the counter.

He frowned at the shabby piece of luggage, held together by a pair of thread-bare straps. He'd be months wheedling reimbursement out of the department budget, if the bean-counters even signed off on it. He'd given up on disposable income the day he undertook the mortgage on a crumbling movie theater that resisted each step in the renovation the way a senile old man fought change. It was his home and his hobby and his curse.

"I'm closing," she said when he started to unbuckle one of the straps. "Open it someplace else."

Tijuana reminded him too much of *Touch of Evil* to stay there any longer than he had to, but he didn't want to risk taking the suitcase to the American side without knowing what it contained; an undeclared bottle of tequila, or perhaps an old movie man's taste for the local cannabis, would look bad on a job application under "Have you ever been convicted of a felony?" after UCLA let him go. He drove around until he spotted a motel belonging to an American chain and booked a room. He was free of anti-Mexican prejudice but border towns were affiliated with no country but Hell. Alone in a room with all the personality of a Styrofoam cup, he hoisted the suitcase onto the piece of furniture motel clerks regard as a queen-size bed and spread it open.

He sorted the contents into separate piles: a half-dozen white shirts with frayed collars and yellowed buttons, three pairs of elastically challenged sweat-pants, a gray pinstripe suit with a Mexican label, fused at the seams rather than sewn, filthy sneakers, a pair of down-at-heels wingtips, socks and underwear in deplorable condition, an expired Diners Club card in a dilapidated wallet empty but for a picture of Deanna Durbin (just how long *had* it been since wallets came with pictures of movie stars?), a Boy Scout knife, two tablets of Tums in foil wrap—pocket stuff—a three-dollar digital watch, still keeping time after its owner had ceased to concern himself with such information, restaurant receipts

(Stemp seemed to have gone out of his way to avoid Mexican cuisine, but his tastes and more likely his budget had run toward American fast food), dozens of folded scraps of paper that excited Valentino until they delivered only grocery lists of items that could be prepared on a hot plate or microwave; receipts for prescription drugs, which if he'd left any behind, his landlady had appropriated for sale on the black market. Other ordinarily useful things, pens and pencils and Band-Aids, had probably been seized by default for the service they offered.

A sad legacy, this; that nine decades of living should yield so little of material value made a bachelor in his thirties wonder about his own place in the Grand Scheme. Well, he had hardly anticipated a complete print of *Metropolis*, but even the gossamer hope he'd been handed by Smith Oldfield, of some evidence to support the agreement he'd spent so many user minutes hammering out with the old man, had come to nothing.

Valentino lingered over the heaviest object in the case, a nine-by-twelve loose-leaf notebook bound in green cloth, faded, grubby, and worn shiny in patches by what appeared to have been many hands. The yellowed ruled sheets inside, dog-eared and thumb-blurred, reminded him of a dozen last days of school, when the detritus at the bottom of his locker served up the remains of the crisp stationery of the back-to-school sales of September. It seemed to contain a list, neatly type-written in varying fonts as if it had been added to on different machines over time, and totally indecipherable. It appeared to be made up of random letters, suggesting no language he'd ever seen.

A code. Wonderful. From crossword puzzles to Rubik's Cube to Sudoku, there wasn't a conundrum or a cryptogram in existence that couldn't leave Valentino in the dust. He could track down a hundred feet of *London After Midnight* in a junk shop in Istanbul, but *Where's Waldo?* stumped him every time. If there wasn't an obvious motion-picture connection, he was useless.

There were a hundred pages at least, many of them torn loose of the rings and as yellow and tattered as ancient parchment, scattering crumbs like old bread when he turned them. He was a paleontologist of a very special sort, brushing the dust off the bones of obsolete civilizations, dead-end species (early 3-D, Sensurround, scenes hand-tinted frame by frame), but this was an artifact outside his area of expertise.

A prop, possibly, from one of Stemp's Mexican-movie atrocities; although from prima facie evidence the old man had saved nothing from his long career in movies, probably because of bitter memories.

He laid the notebook aside, exhaled again. Success and fame had always been a crapshoot, but a man's life ought to boil down to more than the contents of a suitcase in Tijuana.

"You might have thought to bring me a bottle of mescal, with a real worm in the bottom," Kyle Broadhead said. "All you can get up here is a piece of licorice. Fine protégé you turned out to be."

They were sitting in the professor's Spartan office in the power center, unchanged since the campus had ceased to draw all its utilities from a single source. Only a smiling picture of the shaggy-haired academic's young love interest on the desk relieved the palette of gray cinder block and steel. Valentino smiled, opened his bulky briefcase, and set a bottle on the desk. "I had just enough cash left to pay the duty. Señora Butterworth took all my traveler's checks."

Broadhead beamed and stood the bottle in his file drawer, which rattled and clinked when he pushed it shut. "I talked to Smith Oldfield this morning. Any luck with Stemp's things?"

"I don't know how a man can live so long and leave so little behind. I'm one-third his age and I needed a tractor-trailer to move half a mile from my old apartment into the Oracle."

"That's because you're a pack rat. Your office looks like the Paramount prop department. You have to travel light in this life or your heirs will pick apart your carcass. What else is in the case? You didn't need it to run liquor across the hall."

"I was hoping you could tell me." He took out the heavy loose-leaf notebook and laid it on the desk.

The professor's expression alarmed him, as blank and gray as the walls of the office, his eyes fixed on the object as if it were a dangerous animal. Valentino thought he was having a seizure "Kyle, what's wrong?"

"Where did you get that?"

"Stemp's suitcase. Do you know what it is?"

"Do *you* know what it is?"

Under other circumstances he'd have suspected his mentor of teasing, but the dead grimness on his face was something new in their long association. "I can't make head or tail of it. It seems to be written in code. I'm pretty sure it's a list of some kind."

"A list of some kind. You young fool. You carried that across the border? You should've thrown in into a volcano in Mexico."

"What is it, the formula for the atomic bomb?"

"As bad as. Sixty years ago it blew Hollywood to smithereens."

Valentino kept the lid clamped on his curiosity while Broadhead fired up his ancient computer, a great steel-cased anachronism that was all one piece, monitor, keyboard, and tower; he practically expected the professor to start it by pulling a rope. It made various octogenarian noises under the whoosh of a built-in cooling fan while he worked the keys in a blur of index fingers.

"I'm looking up Stemp's biography," he said, his face bathed in the greenish glow from the screen. He looked like a mad scientist in a Hammer film. "There has to be some explanation for how he came by that thing."

"Right now I'd settle for an explanation of how you know what it is."

"The one and only time I saw it was in Darryl Zanuck's office at Fox. It isn't likely I'd forget it. He was in a power struggle with his son at the time, and pre-occupied; he left the thing out while he went to see what became of his secretary. I was interviewing him for my book, and I wasn't about to give up the oppor-tunity to snoop. I wish I had. It'd be easier to convince myself it was a myth."

"What *is* it?"

"You haven't guessed? I did, and I'd never even heard it described. Ah!" He sat back, still staring at the screen.

Valentino got up and went behind the desk to watch over his shoulder. A postcard-size photo of a young Ralph Stemp in padded shoulders and a snapbrim hat accompanied a lengthy text and a sidebar listing his screen cred-its, beginning with a nonspeaking bit in *Hot Town* in 1937 and ending with an unbilled cameo in *Clash of the Gladiators*, shot in three weeks in Mexico in 1962 on a shoestring budget. When the House Un-American Activities Committee interrogated him in 1950 about the presence of his name on a list of subscribers to *The Daily Worker*, he refused to answer, spent a month in jail for contempt of Congress, then went south to form an independent production company after U.S. studios turned their backs on him. He never returned to his native soil.

"No help," Broadhead said. "The rest is personal. Married, divorced, prede-ceased by a son. I saw the notebook in Zanuck's possession twenty years after Stemp expatriated."

" 'Son' is highlighted. Try clicking on it."

He did so, and stuffed his pipe while waiting for the computer to respond. It wasn't geared to take advantage of the university's high-speed connection.

When at last the son's entry appeared, they looked at a grainy résumé shot of a pasty-faced young man who bore scant resemblance to his father and two brief paragraphs on his life.

Broadhead laid aside the pipe. "Ralph Stemp, Junior. Had his name legally changed to Richard Stern, for obvious reasons, not that it did much for his career."

Valentino's eyes moved faster. "Keep reading."

"Huh."

Stern had been arrested for questioning after Darryl Zanuck's office at Twentieth Century Fox was broken into and vandalized in 1970. He'd been overheard making threats against the studio for dropping his contract after small parts in drive-in features, but the police released him when Zanuck declined to press charges. A month later, accidentally or on purpose, Stern died of an overdose of sleeping pills.

"Not before doing his old man a favor," Broadhead said. "I wonder if he sent him the notebook or delivered it in person."

"It doesn't say anything was reported missing."

"That would make it hard to deny it ever existed. A trial would have brought it out into the open, and the lawsuits would've bankrupted every studio in town. Zanuck was losing his grip or he'd have burned it. The witch hunts were over."

Valentino saw the dawn then, shining merciless light on the darkest chapter in Hollywood history. "You mean this list—"

Broadhead picked up his pipe and tamped the tobacco with his thumb, watching him over the bowl. "You didn't really think it was black, did you?"

The film archivist returned to his seat. His legs felt rubbery. All his life he'd heard about the Hollywood Blacklist, compiled early in the Cold War when Washington had shifted its attention from Axis saboteurs to Communist infiltration of American society. Investigations into the alleged subversive influence of films had panicked the industry into expunging from its midst everyone who came under suspicion of harboring sentiments Congress considered unpatriotic. If your name appeared on the list, you were through in pictures.

"I always thought the list was symbolic," he said. "I thought it was just word-of-mouth."

"It was the only thing those old moguls ever shared with one another." Broadhead lit his pipe, violating university regulations and California law; he wasn't likely to be turned in by anyone who valued him as a pillar of the institution. "They were scared, sure, but it gave them a honey of an excuse to trim personnel and the budget with the Supreme Court pressuring them to sell off their theaters. A lot of innocent names wound up in that notebook."

"They were *all* innocent, Kyle. The Constitution protects every citizen's right to his beliefs, whatever his politics."

"You know nothing about that time. Your parents weren't even born when the Hollywood Ten stood trial."

Valentino was shocked by his friend's vehemence. He'd never seen him so worked up over events, current or otherwise. He said himself he hadn't voted in the last six presidential elections. A little levity seemed indicated. "I thought all you college professors were flaming liberals."

"Not quite all. Our employers are government-funded, so it's no surprise so many of my colleagues don't support conservatism and tax breaks. An old widower like me doesn't need much to live on, and I have an income from outside these hallowed halls." Which was no less than fact. *The Persistence of Vision*, his seminal work on the history and theory of film, had been in print for thirty years. Broadhead was the only film instructor in the country who hadn't made it a required text in his classes.

In any case, his feathers appeared to be smoothing out. He cut the power to his computer (he never bothered to shut down programs, and never complained about losing anything as a result); it made a whistling noise like a bomb falling in a war movie and went silent. "Do you know how the list got started?"

"It was based on names provided by witnesses friendly to the Congressional investigation."

"No. Those came later. The first forty or so were taken from a statement signed by a hundred and fifty American intellectuals in support of Stalin's purge of his political enemies in nineteen thirty-eight. Bud Schulberg and Dorothy Parker were among them, and they recruited as many of their show-business friends as possible. Bear in mind, the next time some neo-pinko squirt starts sniveling about all those poor souls who lost their jobs, that it all began with a petition that condoned mass murder by a man responsible for slaughtering twenty million of his own people."

"I didn't know that."

"To be fair, neither did they at the start. But I never heard of any of them coming forward later to set the record straight. Take the *c* out of 'activist' and what do you have?"

Valentino smiled. " 'Atavist'; but only if you can't spell."

"That's why God made copyeditors." Broadhead puffed smoke at the nicotine stain on the ceiling. "At least the studio chiefs suspected on some level that what they were doing was wrong, and that they might have to pay for it someday. That's the reason they put the list in code and kept the key."

"What *is* the key?"

"Who cares now? The men who shared the list are dead and so are most of the people on it. The damage to the rest can't be undone. Cracking it would be a waste of time."

"Kyle, you're the least curious academic I ever met."

"At my age I haven't time to be generous with my curiosity."

"Do you think Richard Stern's death is suspicious?"

"If it was arranged, it flopped, or they'd have gotten the list back. I never buy a suicide cocktail as a murder weapon. It's a Hollywood cliché. I'm more interested in what Stern's father had to gain by hanging on to the list."

"Blackmail?"

"Ransom, at first. But the men who built the movies would have been stubborn enough to tell him where to stick it, and try to reconstruct it from memory. Later, when the studio system tottered, he might've squeezed an income from them in return for not going public. By then, his Mexican film venture had failed. Then, when the last of the moguls died, he'd have been on his own again, living hand to mouth. That's why he died owing rent."

"Leaving the Film Preservation Department in the lurch."

"Wake up. What are a bunch of badly dubbed crime movies worth to a station broadcasting to insomniacs at four A.M.?"

"Hundred thousand, give or take; too much to sniff at, the state our treasury's in. And my ten-percent finder's fee would put me a step closer to finishing the Oracle before I'm too old to attend the grand opening."

The professor grimaced and knocked the smoldering plug out of his pipe into his empty wastebasket. He kept a paperless office, with his vast store of motion-picture history locked in his head. "Last year an advance poster for the original nineteen thirty-one *Frankenstein* went on the block at Christie's. It was the only one known to exist that advertised Bela Lugosi as the monster, before he dropped out of the production and Boris Karloff took his place. Do you remember what it went for?"

"I was in England at the time, chasing down *Charlie Chan Carries On*. It was predicted to go for a million."

"Seven hundred thousand. The second-highest bidder dropped out, believing that a duplicate poster might surface sometime and slash its value in half. There was no guarantee that only one was printed."

"I see where you're going."

"If you didn't, I'd resign as your mentor." Broadhead pointed at the notebook but refrained from touching it; it was as if he thought it might spit venom. "This is a one-of-a-kind item, no warranties necessary. There are no copies, because that would have multiplied the risk of the studios' biggest secret falling into the wrong hands. It's more famous than *Citizen Kane*, *Gone With the Wind*, and the Jerry Lewis canon combined."

"Jerry Lewis?"

"He cracks me up; sue me. And don't get me wrong just because I played devil's advocate a minute ago: It's a symbol of tyranny. A screenwriter took his life because he happened to have the same name as a writer on the list and could no longer make a living. That's evil. Don't ask me why Hitler's autograph is worth ten times as much as Churchill's. There's no arguing with the market. Evil sells. The moment the word gets out that the Hollywood Blacklist—*the* Blacklist—is available, the offers will stream in from all over the world. UCLA will have the monopoly on every elusive foot of silver-nitrate stock in both hemispheres, and you'll be able to rebuild five theaters like the Oracle from your end."

He took a cab to the Commerce Bank of Beverly Hills, holding the briefcase in his lap with both hands. His car was in the university parking garage, but he was afraid it would break down again, leaving him stranded with an armload of dynamite. The bank was the closest one to campus and he wasted no time in arranging for a safety deposit box and locking away the notebook. He hoped there wouldn't be an earthquake.

Work on The Oracle was progressing slowly. The man Valentino's contractor had engaged to apply the gold leaf to the auditorium ceiling, a Tuscan, moved like a snail, but left behind a trail that glittered, and the peacocks on the new Oriental carpet slumbered beneath a dropcloth. When the film archivist had gone house-hunting, he'd had no intention of rescuing a historic picture palace from destruction, but when the opportunity had presented itself he'd lacked the fortitude to ignore it. Now he was taking peanut butter sandwiches to work, sleeping on a sofa bed in the projection booth, and spending his weekends browsing for doorknobs in shops that sold fixtures reclaimed from demolished buildings.

Of which there were more in Los Angeles than Thai restaurants and Starbucks. Sometimes he felt he was the only resident who was building up instead of tearing down.

Whenever he had the energy, Valentino liked to recreate the moviegoing experience of the first half of the twentieth century. He fired up the Bell & Howell projector he was still paying for, selected a film from his small personal library of classics on safety stock, and projected them onto the new polyester screen through the aperture in the booth. But tonight he was exhausted. Rather than spend a night in the cheap motel in Tijuana, he'd driven all the way back home, arriving in the gray light of day, and had caught only two hours' sleep before reporting to work. He poked a disc into the DVR and settle himself in front of his forty-two-inch flat-panel TV.

He watched *The Front*, Woody Allen's tribute to the victims and survivors of the Hollywood witch hunt. He laughed during the funny parts and sat riveted when Zero Mostel's desperate funnyman was forced to suicide for the indiscretion of having attended a Communist Party rally to impress a girl ("I was just trying to get laid!"). At the end he read the long list of contributors to the movie who had spent time on the Blacklist, a virtual Memorial Wall of casualties of intolerance. He'd seen it before, of course, but until he'd actually held the list in his hand it had never seemed quite real.

Paranoia had done as much as anything else to destroy the Dream Factory. The old system of feudal bosses and contract players might have survived competition from television; when Anti-Trust forced the studios to break up the theater chains that had secured their monopoly for decades, they might have muddled through. But in the end it was the industry pioneers who shot themselves in the foot. The resentment they created led to the rise of the Screen Actors Guild. From that had come power to the proletariat: The on-screen talent seized the ability to choose the roles it wanted, reject the ones it didn't, and place the future of film in dozens of hands instead of only a few.

It had been a blow for individual freedom. But it had come at a cost.

As a movie buff, Valentino remembered that some of the greatest motion pictures of all time had been made in spite of the casts' unwillingness to appear in them (*Casablanca*, for one), and that some of the worst flops had stemmed from the vanity of actors and directors overcoming doubts about whether the vehicles were appropriate (*Ishtar; Robin Hood, Prince of Thieves; Heaven's Gate,* to name a few.) An L.B. Mayer or a Sam Goldwyn would have had the gut instinct to reject such projects or reassign them to someone more appropriate. The after-match had made the case for autocracy, even as the event that had preceded it had made the case against.

That was the clinical view. Humanity said that the life of one disillusioned screenwriter was worth more than a couple of hours spent squirming through a bad movie.

When the banging came to the front door, Valentino shot bolt upright in the sofa bed, heart pounding like *The Guns of Navarone.* He'd dreamt he was a victim of the American version of Stalin's purge, and was certain they'd come for him.

He went downstairs in his robe and opened the door on Kyle Broadhead, wearing the corduroy coat and flat tweed cap that made him look like a refugee from the Iron Curtain. "Fanta says I should apologize for the hour, but I'm not responsible for the clock. Am I too late for the last show?"

"How *is* that child you kidnapped?" Valentino let him in.

"Past the age of consent." He followed his host up the steep unfinished stairs to the projection booth and looked at the DVD case Valentino had left open. "Research, I see. Watch *High Noon* again. Allegories make better box office than polemics."

"You're unpredictable. I expected you to make some comment about Woody Allen losing his sense of humor, followed by a paragraph on Chaplin."

"*The English Patient* was funnier than both of them put together. Here." Broadhead drew a stiff sheet of pasteboard out of a saddle pocket and held it out.

Valentino took it. It was soiled and tattered at the edges, and punched full of square holes in what appeared to be a random pattern. "It looks like an old-fashioned computer punchcard."

"Yours is the last generation to make that comparison. Welcome to Old Fogeyhood. Mine would say it belongs in a player piano." Broadhead unbuttoned his coat and sat in a canvas director's chair with Anne Hathaway's name stenciled on the back. "I couldn't sleep. That exasperating young woman wrung a confession out of me and sent me over. I don't suppose you'd care to offer an old man a drink on a chilly November evening."

The thermometer had read seventy when Valentino went to bed, but he rummaged out a fifth of Jack Daniel's the professor had given him for his birthday. "I don't have any Coke."

"Really. A non sequitur, I hope. Anyone who would defile premium bourbon with sugar and syrup would slap a coat of Sherwin-Williams on top of the Sistine ceiling." He poured two fat fingers into the Old Fashioned glass Valentino put before him and set down the bottle. "I attended Darryl Zanuck's estate sale in 1980, purely out of scholarly curiosity. I didn't expect to buy anything. I'm not a hoarder, as you know."

"You make Gandhi look like a compulsive collector."

"Zanuck was a big reader; most people don't know that, but he started out as a screenwriter, and you need to be literate to commit plagiarism. His complete set of Shakespeare got no takers, generic thing that it was, so in the spirit of sportsmanship I bid fifty bucks, and damn if no one took up the challenge. That slip fell out of *Richard III* when I took it home." He pointed at the item in Valentino's hand. "I like to think he chose the hiding place out of guilt, but his bumps of greed and lechery were too big to leave room for any other human emotion."

"I'm not sure I know what you're getting at."

"I'm sure you do."

Valentino nodded. "It's the key, isn't it?"

"The simplest in the world, but without it, the code might slow down even Stephen Hawking. I'd never have guessed what it was if you hadn't plunked that notebook down on my desk. You have to understand it was ten years between the few minutes I had at Zanuck's and the moment that thing slid into my lap."

"I'm surprised you kept it."

"I was still curious then. I never made the connection until now. I might still be wrong." His eyes pleaded for a conclusion he seemed reluctant to suggest.

Valentino spoke carefully. "Fortunately, I can't do anything tonight because the notebook's in the bank and it's closed. Otherwise we'd be up all night. We'll go over it together in the morning when we're fresh."

"Sounds fair." Broadhead finished his drink and stood. "Don't expect any big names. Edward G Robinson was washed up already, and if you think Larry Parks was any loss, go back and watch *The Jolson Story* again. Congress took a swipe at Lucille Ball and went down hard. It gave up on Hollywood because it couldn't win votes by ruining people no one had ever heard of."

"I won't peek, Kyle."

"Of course you will. I recommended you for your job because you're a bloodhound."

The next morning, the professor lifted a stack of *Photoplay* magazines off the chair in Valentino's office, saw no place to put it down, and sat with it on his lap. "You look like you've been up all night with Harry Potter," he said.

"Just since the bank opened." Valentino planted an elbow on either side of the notebook on his desk and rested his chin on his fists. "That piece of cardboard fit right over the sheets. The names read diagonally, the letters showing through the holes. Some surprised me, especially on the last pages. The studio bosses got carried away near the end."

"Would you have recognized any if you weren't a film geek?"

"Never having been anything else, I can't be sure. Why didn't you tell me you were on it?"

"How could I know? I only had a minute with it and I didn't have the key then. I guessed what it was, because that's what I always thought it would look like."

"You don't seem surprised."

Broadhead chuckled. "You can label anyone you don't like a subversive. I worked on *The Persistence of Vision* for twenty years, reading excerpts to book clubs and film societies. I revealed that Jack Warner shut down the Warner Brothers animation studio when he found out he didn't own Mickey Mouse. I was the first to call Howard Hughes a nut publicly. I'd be disappointed if I *weren't* on the list."

"Why did they bother? It was discredited by then."

"They'd tinkered with it too long to quit. They'd lost most of their power; the Film School Generation was forcing them out. That notebook was the one thing they still had control over. Nowadays I suppose it would be called therapeutic. They say Nixon was still adding to his Enemies List in San Clemente." He took out his pipe, but to play with, not to smoke. "Have you decided how you're going to sell it?"

"Kyle, I can't. Some of these people are still around. Even if I withheld the key, someone would be bound to crack the code, causing a lot of embarrassment. Not for you, but I see nothing but legal action against the studios for ten years. They'd go bankrupt, which would affect the entire entertainment industry.

What's it matter how many old films we can buy if no one will distribute them? They cost money to restore and preserve."

"You'd still profit personally."

Valentino smiled—ironically, he hoped. "I didn't apply for this job to get rich. If they stopped making movies, what would I spend it on?"

"You can always do what Zanuck should've done."

"I can't burn it either. Knowing I'd destroyed so large a part of Hollywood history would haunt me forever."

Broadhead got up, returned the magazines to the chair, and held out a hand.

Valentino didn't move. "It would be the same if I let you burn it."

"I won't burn it. I'll slip it onto a shelf at Universal, where anyone who finds it will just think it's a prop from a spy picture. Even if he suspects what it is, he couldn't prove it without your testimony or mine, and why would he even ask us? Can you think of a better place to hide an important historical artifact than in the land of make-believe?"

"Why do I keep thinking about the government warehouse scene in *Raiders of the Lost Ark?*"

"I knew you'd appreciate it. Just as I knew you would never sell the list."

Valentino picked up the notebook and held it out. Broadhead took it, touching it for the first time. He slid the riddled sheet of cardboard from between the pages where the other had left it and put it on the desk. "No sense making it easy."

The film archivist picked up the key to the code, opened a drawer, and took out the box of strike-anywhere matches he'd bought from the woman in Tijuana. "I knew these would come in handy sometime." He struck one.

Valentino: Film Detective

Valentino: Film Detective by Loren D. Estleman, is set in Times New Roman (the text) and printed on sixty-pound Natures acid-free recycled paper. The cover painting is by Carol Heyer and the design is by Deborah Miller. The first edition was printed in two forms: trade softcover, notchbound; and two hundred copies sewn in cloth, signed and numbered by the author. Each of the clothbound copies includes a separate pamphlet, *Who's Afraid of Nero Wolfe* by Loren D. Estleman.

Valentino: Film Detective was printed and bound by Thomson-Shore, Inc., Dexter, Michigan and typeset by White Lotus Infotech Pvt. Ltd., Puducherry, India and published in February 2011 by Crippen & Landru Publishers, Inc., Norfolk, Virginia.

CRIPPEN & LANDRU, PUBLISHERS

P. O. Box 9315
Norfolk, VA 23505
info@crippenlandru.com; toll-free 877 622-6656
www.crippenlandru.com

Crippen & Landru publishes first edition short-story collections by important detective and mystery writers. The following books are currently (February 2011) in print; see our website for full details:

REGULAR SERIES

Speak of the Devil by John Dickson Carr. 1994. Trade softcover. $15.00.

The McCone Files by Marcia Muller. 1995. Trade softcover, $19.00.

Diagnosis: Impossible, The Problems of Dr. Sam Hawthorne by Edward D. Hoch. 1996. Trade softcover, $19.00.

In Kensington Gardens Once by H.R.F. Keating. 1997. Trade softcover, $12.00.

Shoveling Smoke by Margaret Maron. 1997. Trade softcover, $19.00.

The Ripper of Storyville and Other Tales of Ben Snow by Edward D. Hoch. 1997. Trade softcover. $19.00.

Renowned Be Thy Grave by P.M. Carlson. 1998. Trade softcover, $16.00.

Carpenter and Quincannon by Bill Pronzini. 1998. Trade softcover, $16.00.

Famous Blue Raincoat by Ed Gorman. 1999. Signed, unnumbered cloth overrun copies, $30.00. Trade softcover, $17.00.

The Tragedy of Errors and Others by Ellery Queen. 1999. Trade softcover, $20.00.

McCone and Friends by Marcia Muller. 2000. Trade softcover, $19.00.

Challenge the Widow Maker by Clark Howard. 2000. Trade softcover, $16.00.

Fortune's World by Michael Collins. 2000. Trade softcover, $16.00.

The Velvet Touch: Nick Velvet Stories by Edward D. Hoch. 2000. Trade softcover, $19.00.

Long Live the Dead: Tales from Black Mask by Hugh B. Cave. 2000. Trade softcover, $16.00.

Tales Out of School by Carolyn Wheat. 2000. Trade softcover, $16.00.

Stakeout on Page Street and Other DKA Files by Joe Gores. 2000. Trade softcover, $16.00.

The Celestial Buffet by Susan Dunlap. 2001. Trade softcover, $16.00.

The Old Spies Club and Other Intrigues of Rand by Edward D. Hoch. 2001. Signed, unnumbered cloth overrun copies, $32.00. Trade softcover, $17.00.

Adam and Eve on a Raft by Ron Goulart. 2001. Signed, unnumbered cloth overrun copies, $32.00. Trade softcover, $17.00.

The Reluctant Detective by Michael Z. Lewin. 2001. Signed, numbered clothbound, $42.00. Trade softcover, $17.00.

Nine Sons by Wendy Hornsby. 2002. Trade softcover, $16.00.

The 13 Culprits by Georges Simenon, translated by Peter Schulman. 2002. Trade softcover, $16.00.

The Dark Snow by Brendan DuBois. 2002. Signed, unnumbered cloth overrun copies, $32.00.

Come Into My Parlor: Tales from Detective Fiction Weekly by Hugh B. Cave. 2002. Trade softcover, $17.00.

The Iron Angel and Other Tales of the Gypsy Sleuth by Edward D. Hoch. 2003. Signed, numbered clothbound, $42.00. Trade softcover, $17.00.

Cuddy – Plus One by Jeremiah Healy. 2003. Trade softcover, $18.00.

Problems Solved by Bill Pronzini and Barry N. Malzberg. 2003. Signed, numbered clothbound, $42.00. Trade softcover, $16.00.

A Killing Climate by Eric Wright. 2003. Trade softcover, $17.00.

Lucky Dip by Liza Cody. 2003. Signed, numbered clothbound, $42.00. Trade softcover, $17.00.

Kill the Umpire: The Calls of Ed Gorgon by Jon L. Breen. 2003. Trade softcover, $17.00.

Suitable for Hanging by Margaret Maron. 2004. Trade softcover, $19.00.

Murders and Others Confusions by Kathy Lynn Emerson. 2004. Signed, numbered clothbound, $42.00. Trade softcover, $19.00.

Byline: Mickey Spillane by Mickey Spillane, edited by Lynn Myers and Max Allan Collins. 2004. Trade softcover, $20.00.

The Confessions of Owen Keane by Terence Faherty. 2005. Signed, numbered clothbound, $42.00. Trade softcover, $17.00.

The Adventure of the Murdered Moths and Other Radio Mysteries by Ellery Queen. 2005. Trade softcover, $20.00.

Murder, Ancient and Modern by Edward Marston. 2005. Signed, numbered clothbound, $43.00. Trade softcover, $18.00.

More Things Impossible: The Second Casebook of Dr. Sam Hawthorne by Edward D. Hoch. 2006. Signed, numbered clothbound, $43.00. Trade softcover, $18.00.

Murder, 'Orrible Murder! by Amy Myers. 2006. Signed, numbered clothbound, $43.00. Trade softcover, $18.00.

The Verdict of Us All: Stories by the Detection Club for H.R.F. Keating, edited by Peter Lovesey. 2006. Numbered clothbound, $43.00. Trade softcover, $20.00.

The Archer Files: The Complete Short Stories of Lew Archer, Private Investigator, Including Newly-Discovered Case-Notes by Ross Macdonald, edited by Tom Nolan. 2007. Numbered clothbound, $45.00. Trade softcover, $25.00.

The Mankiller of Poojeegai and Other Mysteries by Walter Satterthwait. 2007. Signed, numbered clothbound, $43.00. Trade softcover, $17.00.

Quintet: The Cases of Chase and Delacroix by Richard A. Lupoff. 2008. Signed, numbered clothbound, $43.00. Trade softcover, $17.00.

Murder on the Short List by Peter Lovesey. 2008. Signed, numbered clothbound, $43.00. Trade softcover, $17.00.

Thirteen to the Gallows by John Dickson Carr and Val Gielgud. 2008. Numbered clothbound, $43.00. Trade softcover, $20.00.

A Little Intelligence by Robert Silverberg and Randall Garrett. 2008. Signed, numbered clothbound, $42.00. Trade softcover, $16.00.

A Pocketful of Noses: Stories of One Ganelon or Another by James Powell 2009. Signed, numbered clothbound, $42.00. Trade softcover, $17.00.

A Tale About a Tiger by S. J. Rozan. 2009. Signed, numbered clothbound, $43.00. Trade softcover, $17.00.

The Columbo Collection by William Link. 2010. Trade softcover, $18.00.

Valentino: Film Detective, by Loren D. Estleman. 2011. Signed, numbered clothbound, $43.00. Trade softcover $17.00.

CRIPPEN & LANDRU LOST CLASSICS

Crippen & Landru is proud to publish a series of *new* short-story collections by great authors who specialized in traditional mysteries. Each book collects stories from crumbling pages of old pulp, digest, and slick magazines, and most of the stories have been "lost" since their first publication. The following books are in print:

The Newtonian Egg and Others Cases of Rolf le Roux by Peter Godfrey, introduction by Ronald Godfrey. 2002. Trade softcover, $15.00.

Murder, Mystery and Malone by Craig Rice, edited by Jeffrey A. Marks. 2002. Trade softcover, $19.00.

The Sleuth of Baghdad: The Inspector Chafik Stories, by Charles B. Child. Cloth, $27.00. 2002. Trade softcover, $17.00.

Hildegarde Withers: Uncollected Riddles by Stuart Palmer, introduction by Mrs. Stuart Palmer. 2002. Trade softcover, $19.00.

The Spotted Cat and Other Mysteries from the Casebook of Inspector Cockrill by Christianna Brand, edited by Tony Medawar. 2002. Cloth, $29.00. Trade softcover, $19.00.

Marksman and Other Stories by William Campbell Gault, edited by Bill Pronzini; afterword by Shelley Gault. 2003. Trade softcover, $19.00.

Karmesin: The World's Greatest Criminal – Or Most Outrageous Liar by Gerald Kersh, edited by Paul Duncan. 2003. Cloth, $27.00. Trade softcover, $17.00.

The Complete Curious Mr. Tarrant by C. Daly King, introduction by Edward D. Hoch. 2003. Cloth, $29.00. Trade softcover, $19.00.

The Pleasant Assassin and Other Cases of Dr. Basil Willing by Helen McCloy, introduction by B.A. Pike. 2003. Cloth, $27.00. Trade softcover, $18.00.

Murder – All Kinds by William L. DeAndrea, introduction by Jane Haddam. 2003. Cloth $29.00. Trade softcover, $19.00.

The Avenging Chance and Other Mysteries from Roger Sheringham's Casebook by Anthony Berkeley, edited by Tony Medawar and Arthur Robinson. 2004. Cloth, $29.00. Trade softcover, $19.00.

Banner Deadlines: The Impossible Files of Senator Brooks U. Banner by Joseph Commings, edited by Robert Adey; memoir by Edward D. Hoch. 2004. Cloth, $29.00. Trade softcover, $19.00.

The Danger Zone and Other Stories by Erle Stanley Gardner, edited by Bill Pronzini. 2004. Trade softcover, $19.00.

Dr. Poggioli: Criminologist by T. S. Stribling, edited by Arthur Vidro. Cloth, $29.00. 2004. Cloth, $29.00. Trade softcover, $19.00.

The Couple Next Door: Collected Short Mysteries by Margaret Millar, edited by Tom Nolan. 2004. Trade softcover, $19.00.

Sleuth's Alchemy: Cases of Mrs. Bradley and Others by Gladys Mitchell, edited by Nicholas Fuller. 2005. Trade softcover, $19.00.

Who Was Guilty? Two Dime Novels by Philip S. Warne/Howard W. Macy, edited by Marlena E. Bremseth. 2005. Cloth, $29.00.

Slot-Machine Kelly by Michael Collins, introduction by Robert J. Randisi. Cloth, $29.00. 2005. Trade softcover, $19.00.

The Evidence of the Sword by Rafael Sabatini, edited by Jesse F. Knight. 2006. Cloth, $29.00. Trade softcover, $19.00.

The Casebook of Sidney Zoom by Erle Stanley Gardner, edited by Bill Pronzini. 2006. Cloth, $29.00. Trade softcover, $19.00.

The Detections of Francis Quarles by Julian Symons, edited by John Cooper; afterword by Kathleen Symons. 2006. Cloth, $29.00. Trade softcover, $19.00.

The Trinity Cat and Other Mysteries by Ellis Peters (Edith Pargeter), edited by Martin Edwards and Sue Feder. 2006. Trade softcover, $19.00.

The Grandfather Rastin Mysteries by Lloyd Biggle, Jr., edited by Kenneth Lloyd Biggle and Donna Biggle Emerson. 2007. Cloth, $29.00. Trade softcover, $19.00.

Masquerade: Ten Crime Stories by Max Brand, edited by William F. Nolan. 2007. Cloth, $29.00. Trade softcover, $19.00.

Dead Yesterday and Other Mysteries by Mignon G. Eberhart, edited by Rick Cypert and Kirby McCauley. 2007. Cloth, $30.00. Trade softcover, $20.00.

The Battles of Jericho by Hugh Pentecost, introduction by S.T. Karnick. 2008. Cloth, $29.00. Trade softcover, $19.00.

The Minerva Club, The Department of Patterns and Other Stories by Victor Canning, edited by John Higgins. 2009. Cloth, $29.00. Trade softcover, $19.00.

The Casebook of Gregory Hood by Anthony Boucher and Denis Green, edited by Joe R. Christopher. 2009. Cloth, $29.00. Trade softcover, $19.00.

The Murder at the Stork Club and Other Stories by Vera Caspary, edited by Barbara Emrys. 2009. Cloth, $29.00. Trade softcover, $19.00.

Appleby Talks About Crime by Michael Innes, edited by John Cooper. 2010. Cloth, $29.00. Trade softcover, $19.00.

Ten Thousand Blunt Instruments by Philip Wylie, edited by Bill Pronzini. 2010. Cloth, $29.00.Trade softcover, $19.00.

The Exploits of the Patent Leather Kid by Erle Stanley Gardner, edited by Bill Pronzini. 2010. Cloth, $29.00. Trade softcover, $19.00.

SUBSCRIPTIONS

Subscribers agree to purchase each forthcoming publication, either the Regular Series or the Lost Classics or (preferably) both. Collectors can thereby guarantee receiving limited editions, and readers won't miss any favorite stories. Subscribers receive a discount of 20% off the list price (and the same discount on our backlist) and a specially commissioned short story by a major writer in a deluxe edition as a gift at the end of the year.

The point for us is that, since customers don't pick and choose which books they want, we have a guaranteed sale even before the book is published, and that allows us to be more imaginative in choosing short story collections to issue. That's worth the 20% discount for us.